L...dy

Spring Comedies

Lady Barker

Spring Comedies

Reprint of the original, first published in 1871.

1st Edition 2022 | ISBN: 978-3-36812-618-6

Verlag (Publisher): Outlook Verlag GmbH, Zeilweg 44, 60439 Frankfurt, Deutschland
Vertretungsberechtigt (Authorized to represent): E. Roepke, Zeilweg 44, 60439 Frankfurt, Deutschland
Druck (Print): Books on Demand GmbH, In de Tarpen 42, 22848 Norderstedt, Deutschland

SPRING COMEDIES.

BY

LADY BARKER,

AUTHOR OF "STATION LIFE IN NEW ZEALAND,"
AND "STORIES ABOUT:—"

" All Comedies are ended by a Marriage."—BYRON.

London and New York:

MACMILLAN AND CO.

1871.

LONDON :
R. CLAY, SONS, AND TAYLOR, PRINTERS,
BREAD STREET HILL.

CONTENTS.

I.

A WEDDING STORY.

CHAPTER I.

II.

A STUPID STORY.

III.

A SCOTCH STORY.

CHAPTER I.

CHAPTER II.

CHAPTER III.

CHAPTER IV.

CHAPTER V.

IV.

A MAN'S STORY.

I.

A WEDDING STORY.

IV.

A MAN'S STORY.

CHAPTER I.

CHAPTER II.

CHAPTER III.

CHAPTER IV.

CHAPTER V.

CHAPTER VI.

I.

A WEDDING STORY.

SPRING COMEDIES.

I.

A WEDDING STORY.

CHAPTER I.

INTRODUCTORY.

I SUPPOSE people who are going to be married think that all seasons and places are convenient and appropriate. I have heard arguments advanced in favour of a Christmas wedding, and have been often told that spring is a delightful time for choosing new bonnets and new furniture. As for the east wind—perhaps it won't blow for more than three consecutive months this year; and, after all, what does it matter?

But in spite of this sophistry my convictions remain unaltered, and I hereby give notice that I

refuse my consent to the marriage of all my
female friends and relations unless the ceremony
is arranged for Midsummer. And it must also
take place in the country. A London wedding
is too profoundly dispiriting. Everything and everybody looks so cold and hard and business-like.
It seems a mere question of getting the whole
affair over with as much speed and as little
sentiment as possible. The officials have not a
thought beyond their backsheesh, and argue in
favour of the bride's chances of happiness in proportion to the amount of the bridegroom's fee.
Poor man! I suspect even the bridesmaids judge
of his character and disposition according to the
value of their lockets.

I once saw some flowers strewn before a bride at
a London wedding, but the camellias and azalias
had a palpable florist-look about them, not in the
least like those grown in a country greenhouse.
They were cut with an economy of stalk and leaf
which spoke plainly of a professional knife; and
the prim, smartly-dressed maidens, who allowed
them to slip through their well-gloved fingers over
the sooty pavement, did it with an air which said
as plainly as words, "There goes eighteenpence,—
this one cost half-a-crown." Even the bride

could not find it in her feet to tread on them,
and after we had all passed on I saw ragged,
sharp-eyed children scrambling for their possession,
fighting and quarrelling over the frail treasures.

No! my grandchildren and nieces, and even
my goddaughters, must all be married on a fine
summer's day quietly in the country, if they
want to see me and my gold-headed cane at the
ceremony.

Yet if any one in the world ought to have had
their faith shaken in weddings, even when the
June roses are in fullest beauty, I am that person,
for I was once engaged to be bridesmaid at a
Midsummer marriage which never came off; and
it is about this failure I am going to tell you.

It all happened so very, very long ago that
I have no fear of reviving painful memories in the
thoughts of the principal actors; most of them
have passed away to the happy land where hearts
are open and partings are over. Those who still
remain behind on earth do not dislike to think or
speak of that time, though it was certainly one
of great family embarrassment.

School-girl friendships are proverbial. Helen
Ramsay's and mine was no exception to the rule.
Of course our appearance contrasted as strongly

as our characters; for I was a little pale, quiet thing, with a very decided will hidden under a meek exterior, and I ruled Helen with a firm hand. She was one of those people who like to be ruled, and that made her sudden development of an invincible determination all the more remarkable.

It was I who used to spirit up Helen to achieve wonders for her music-master, and who insisted on her trying for the prize in English composition.

"Dear me," said Helen, when the idea was first suggested to her, "I'm quite sure I can't compose English or anything else." But her little friend marched up and down the long dingy school-room, declaiming with so much eloquence on the excitement of the coming strife, and the glories awaiting the Minerva Victrix of Miss Pringle's establishment, that at, last poor, worried Helen gave way, and consented to try for the sprig of gilt laurel and the accompanying smart copy of Milton's Poems.

She only stipulated that I should tell Miss Pringle of her resolution, or rather *my* resolution. I glanced at her in surprise. "You don't mean to say you are afraid, Helen?"

"No, indeed, Edy," she said; "who could be afraid of poor dear Miss Pringle? She always looks as if she were afraid of us. But I don't think she will believe me."

Well, I told Miss Pringle, who certainly was rather incredulous; but after a time I made her acknowledge that Helen had a chance. She dismissed me with a friendly pat on the shoulder, accompanied by the new and original remark that it would be quite an instance of the Lion and the Mouse.

This was rather more applicable in our case than most of the other similes which our friendship called forth; for I was not so very unlike a mouse, with my little pointed face, bright eyes, and quiet movements; whilst our glorious Helen had the tawny hair and golden-brown eyes with which we credit the conventional lion.

That sort of colouring nearly always goes with fine physical proportions, and Helen stood five feet eight in her shoes, and had the shoulders and bust of a young *contadina.*

Yet with all this height and breadth she did not look in the least too much for one's nerves. In the first place, she was a lady in all her thoughts and actions, perfectly natural and unaffected, with a nice voice and quiet ways. And then she was "finished off," as she said herself, so neatly; delicate little wrists and ankles, and fairy-small hands and feet.

I don't remember whether her features were beautiful; the portrait so deeply graven on my heart and memory is of a sweet frank face, with health and good-temper sparkling in its kind eyes, and curving pleasant lines around the mouth. I only know that although no doubt she was a handsome girl enough, she aged into a far lovelier old woman, with bright silvery hair, and the most exquisite calm and repose shed all over her. However, that is glancing much too far ahead, and it is not fair besides.

In these opening days of our life and love, Miss Ramsay was only sixteen, and I very little older. My few additional months gave me a great hold at that time over Helen. Whenever she disobeyed my advice, I brandished them verbally before her, adding, "So I ought to know." This formula was in constant use during that last school-term, for whenever poor, easily discouraged Helen announced that no ideas on her part were forthcoming for this dreadful "Essay on True Heroism," I insisted on her perseverance, adding that I knew she could do it if she tried.

Never shall I forget that essay, and the anxiety it cost me! We were not allowed to help each other, but still all my discourses *would* turn on heroic deeds and words; and I considered that some very fine things were said on the subject. Helen's great stronghold was an equivalent to "suffer and be strong," and this oft-used sentiment was brought into play more than once. However, she really turned out the best paper of the lot, which is not saying very much for the others.

I thought myself that Mary Wright's was the most interesting; but that audacious damsel had actually gone into the realms of fiction for her examples, and had collected thrilling and romantic episodes, chiefly turning on unhappy and heroic lovers. Miss Pringle's face changed from red to white, and she looked ready to sink into the earth with confusion as she heard this novelette—for it was really more like that than anything else—read aloud before the parents and guardians, as well as the pupils.

Dismal were her forebodings of Mary's future. Had the thing existed in those days, she would have prophesied, as a fearful fate, that the sinner would become a sensation novelist; but as it was, she could think of nothing more dreadful than that the girl would run away with an ensign. Poor Mary! she did nothing of the sort; she never wrote another line, married a country doctor, and lived the quietest and happiest life possible.

None of the "girl-graduates" ever performed a heroic action, as far as I know, in spite of the run upon heroes and the hero-worship which that essay called forth.

Helen's performance was correct, even to insipidity; and perhaps it was due to the revulsion of feeling produced by Mary Wright's romance that Miss Pringle, who gave the casting vote, decided that "Yours, my dear Helen, is the best example of English composition, and I have much pleasure," &c. &c.

When Helen took home her laurel spray and her splendidly bound book, Mrs. Ramsay seized on the occasion to declare that she meant to leave off parting with her daughter. The poor lady was very lonely in her large empty house, and missed Helen's delightful companionship more and more every time that the holidays ended. The fatal Monday of school-boy notoriety was only Black to Mrs. Ramsay, who was quite wretched when the time arrived to send the girl back to her school; and it was the mother who had to be consoled and comforted by anticipations of how soon the next holidays would come round, not the pupil.

Miss Pringle always took both Helen's and my joy
at returning to Holly House as a tribute to the
scholastic charms of that establishment ; whereas
the happiness of meeting each other there was our
great attraction to its prim precincts.

Helen invited me over and over again to come and
visit he·, but I was too popular a little personage in
my own quiet home to be spared for a single day
during holiday-time. The boys scouted the idea of
Edy's going away for a whole week, and thought me
a selfish monster if I mentioned the subject ; whilst
dear, gentle mamma—ah ! how long, how very
long it is since those days—said plaintively, " You
know, Edy, it isn't as if there were any more girls
to help me, but you really do get through so
much, and amuse the boys so well, that we can't
spare you."

I was very glad not to be easily parted with,
and made Helen quite envious by dwelling a good
deal on the duties and cares of an elder sister with
half a dozen school-boy brothers.

And yet many people would have envied Helen,
and not me ; for, so far as our dim earth-sight could
reach, her future looked calm and secure, whilst mine
was pretty sure to be full of cares and anxieties ;
but still I would not have changed fates with her for

the whole world.   She was an only daughter—indeed an only child now—for her brother had died some years before we met at Miss Pringle's "Finishing Establishment," and her mother only lived for Helen's happiness in the present, and Helen's welfare in the future.

Mrs. Ramsay's life was rather a dull one ; she was too perfectly comfortable and correct in all her circumstances and surroundings to lead anything but a monotonous existence.   She did not possess a poor relation in the world, who might have turned up unexpectedly with a startling tale of a new and crushing misfortune, to vary her existence.   Her means were ample and secure, and she had not even delicate health to amuse her.

When Helen was at school, therefore, her days passed slowly and heavily enough.   For about a month after her child left, Mrs. Ramsay used to go into the empty room every day, and sit down in the girl's low chair by the window, crying lonely tears until her maid or her housekeeper found her out and scolded her well.   Then she kept away until a few weeks before the joyful date of Helen's return, when she commenced happy little flutterings towards the beloved but forbidden chamber, and every order given inside or outside Holm Bush bore reference to something which was to conduce towards Miss Helen's comfort or her pleasure.

What wonder was it then that, in such an atmosphere of peace and plenty, Helen grew like a stately lily, and ripened in body and soul like a peach in the sunshine?

Sometimes I used to think she had not much depth of character, because, in spite of her really excellent spirits, she looked so placid. I was always in a ferment, with a thousand little cares of my own and everybody else's on my shoulders; and I strongly suspect I must have been a conceited little puss, who thought she knew better than anyone else. I quite enjoyed my sovereignty at Miss Pringle's, for all the girls, more or less, deferred to my opinion, partly because I was so quick at my lessons that I never fell into disgrace with the teachers, and partly because Helen adored and believed in me, and they all adored Helen.

But our happy, busy school-days came to an end soon after Miss Ramsay had distinguished herself, and astonished even her warmest admirers, by gaining the prize for English composition. In the letter which told me of Mrs. Ramsay's determination to keep her daughter at home in future, Helen said : " It is all the fault of that essay. I really should have liked to have gone back once more to Miss Pringle's, but mamma says if I am clever enough to write prize essays I need not return to school. Of course I am glad to remain at home for some reasons, but I shall miss you dreadfully, Edy; and neither you nor Mrs. Maude shall have one moment's peace until you promise to come and pay me a long, long visit." I did not go to Holm Bush just then, and one thing added to another kept Helen and me apart for nearly two years.

At last the younger boys left off having measles and scarlatina, and the elder ones began to pay visits to their own schoolfellows during the holidays.

Also, there came a pause in my constant copying for papa, as he took the first five volumes of his great biographical work, consisting of nearly everybody's memoir, up to London to be published; and mamma's only sister—a pale-faced, languid widow—returned from India, and I could depend on the new source of interest thus aroused at home, to keep my dear little pet mother from missing her active, elf-like daughter.

When I felt quite at ease about home duties and home cares, I wrote and told Helen that I could come now and pay her this long-promised visit; she seemed, by her reply, to be just as fond of me as ever; and never was there a warmer welcome given to a weary traveller than that which greeted me when I reached Holm Bush late one raw autumn evening, two years from the time when Helen and I had parted, with quivering lips and tear-stained eyelids, under the stately portals of Miss Pringle's Finishing Establishment.

I had only come about fifty miles, but I had been all day about it, for I had travelled with an old friend and neighbour by the Velocity stage-coach; and I wish that the luxurious young people of the present day, who grumble at everything, could have felt how even my young bones ached after that tiresome journey. I don't think we were so often killed in our travels as people are now, but there is this to be said, that, when an accident *did* happen to the Velocity or any other coach, there were no wires to flash the dreadful tidings all over the country in an hour or two, and so raise a momentary storm of pity and anger in men's breasts. No, we broke our necks or dislocated our joints in strict retirement, and without exciting any compassion except among our fellow-travellers. About a week, or often more, after a stage-coach accident had happened, a vague rumour would be whispered about, which in its turn took the shape and form of a short

newspaper paragraph ; this was immediately contradicted, and long after even the principal actors
had ceased to take an interest in the story of
their mishap, a certain portion of the truth was
administered homœopathically to the public.

CHAPTER II.

HOLM BUSH.

A FRIENDLY and amiable critic has just said to me, "But there's no Mr. Ramsay!"

I do not intend that there should be a Mr. Ramsay, for I never saw and hardly ever heard of him. It may perhaps be as well to state here, however, that he died soon after Helen was born, leaving, as he thought, a moderate *dot* for the baby girl, and a fine fortune to the sturdy three-year-old boy, of whom he was dotingly fond. The little fellow missed his father dreadfully, and showed his grief and his remembrance in a thousand touching ways. A whole year after, when the child sickened of the complaint which ended his short earth-life, his last baby words were an entreaty that his father might be told how sick Tony was, and how badly he wanted his dadda to kiss and make him well.

Helen told me all this when we first began to exchange our little domestic confidences. She was saying that she had never known a real anxiety or a grief, for this blank in her small home circle had been long ago filled up by the gracious healing hand of Time, drawing her mother's heart closer and closer to her own, year by year.

Now I have positively done with the long retrospective glance which possesses so much fascination for the old, and I will go on with my story, passing briefly over that first autumnal visit to Holm Bush.

The weather was bad: I remember it far more distinctly than the meteorological vagaries of last year; and I can hear now the dismal plash of the rain against the windows in Helen's room as we sat by the fire the night after I arrived. My first evening at Holm Bush gives me back only a dim, shifting scene of lights and flowers and gay colours; for my journey had so thoroughly shaken and tired me, that I could be conscious of nothing except the blessedness of rest and warmth and an early departure to bed.

Mrs. Ramsay was so deliciously motherly in all her ways that I did not feel in the least strange or shy with her; and when she came the first night to kiss me after I was in bed, she could not keep her hands from giving the bedclothes that final smooth and tuck which tells, more than any action I know, of a soft womanly nature. I don't believe the Ladies who want their Rights now-a-days, could do it if they tried.

A good night's sleep is Nature's own patent medicine for the young, to be taken in any quantity, and warranted never to fail in effecting a cure. I slept the clock round, as old nurses say, and woke perfectly strong and well again. Helen had charged me on no account to get up until she came to see me, and had given strict orders that I was not to be disturbed before I rang my bell.

It would not do to confess what time of day the clock hands announced when, after the tidy elderly housemaid—head chambermaids as they were called then—had answered my summons and drawn the thick curtains back, my lazy eyes travelled slowly, resting on each unfamiliar object by the way, towards the chimney-piece. I only know that I felt so thoroughly demoralized it seemed of little consequence now what enormity in the way of lying in bed was committed; so, instead of being startled or shocked to see the lateness of the hour, I merely said, "Tell Miss Ramsay I am awake, and would be glad to see her, please."

"I'll tell the mistress if you please, Miss," answered Martha. "Miss Helen, she's in the stables with Mr. Charles—leastways Mr. Kenneth, and she won't be in, not just yet, Miss."

"Have they done breakfast, then?" I asked, with some slight dawning sense of shame. Martha glanced at the clock, as if wondering to what hours I had been accustomed, and said, "Oh yes, Miss, times and times ago; but Mrs. Ramsay ordered breakfast to be served in Miss Helen's mornin' room whenever you was pleased to want it."

"Oh, that's next door, isn't it, Martha?" I inquired; "so I will get up directly. And I suppose I can go in there in my dressing-gown, can't I?"

"Yes, Miss, certingly," was Martha's demure reply, as she curtsied herself towards the door, and left me to get out of that delicious bed wherein I had found such stores of comfort and rest, as well as a fresh supply of strength and high spirits—that is, high spirits for me; but at my best I was a repressed little creature in those days, and had an absurd fancy that the more staid and undemonstrative I was, the more people would look up to me. It must have made me very uninteresting to strangers; but at all events it is a comfort to perceive that the damsels of the present day are not likely to fall into their grandmothers' errors. They can scarcely reproach themselves for prim steadiness.

I felt very small and lost, I remember, in that large room; my own tiny apartment at home not being much bigger than one of its spacious cupboards, but the fact was that the boys had accumulated such treasures in the shape of birds' eggs and birds' skins, and screens of feathers, little mats of imperfectly tanned mouse-hides, models and powder-flasks, that, as they outgrew the nursery, I gradually gave up one room after another to them, and had retreated to a last fastness, whose strength consisted in its cramped proportions.

As I went on with my toilette in the large room at Holm Bush I thought to myself, "Did I not see a young gentleman last night? Of course I did, tall and fair, rather like Helen herself. She has never told me anything about him: perhaps he has only just come;" and yet, saying this, I felt as perfectly persuaded as if Mrs. Ramsay herself had announced it, that Mr. Charles, "leastways Mr. Kenneth," either was now, or was going to be, Helen's lover.

I don't know how I jumped to that conviction, but I became quite certain that the affair was arranged; and by the time I had finished dressing, my speculations had reached the point of wondering where they would live. Near this of course, little Miss Absolute decided, shaking her neat head with its frightful bows of hair as shining and glossy as hard brushing could make them. I gave one more twitch to my huge *gigôt* sleeves, noticed with satisfaction that my waist was quite as high up under my arms as Helen's had been last night, glanced at my shoes to see that their broad ribbon sandals were crossed precisely at the right angle, and tapped at the morning-room door.

You see, dear reader, I had given up the wild notion of breakfasting in my dressing-gown. The idea had only sprung from the recklessness of finding myself in bed at nearly midday. With the shock of the cold water on my face, I had returned to the regions of common sense and propriety. Besides, I was so interested in thinking out the subject of Mr. Charles, and settling all his and Helen's future lives, that I found myself dressed as usual before I knew what stage of my toilette had been reached.

The door of the morning-room was opened, as my fingers touched its handle, by Mrs. Ramsay herself, who seemed delighted to perceive how completely, both in letter and in spirit, I had obeyed her injunctions to sleep well, and she now considered the only thing to prescribe was a good breakfast.

She was one of those active women who would really be much happier poor,—or we'll say poor-*ish*, —than rich, for she liked doing things herself, especially for those dear to her; and her household was unfortunately so numerous and so well drilled, that she never had the least scope for her love of movement and serving. Although it was quite foreign to my nature and habits to stand still and be waited on, I perceived that Mrs. Ramsay was so pleased to bustle about, that I gave myself up to her kind will, and walked about the room whilst she fussed over the arrangement of the fire and screen, a comfortable chair, and so forth.

I daresay you would not admire Helen's room very much if you contrasted it with the smart chintz boudoirs of the present day; but I felt thoroughly at home in it at once, and after all that is the highest praise you can give to any room in any house. No doubt, of a fine day, the view over the Park to the distant hills was a lovely one; but my first outlook only showed me driving rain, bending trees, and eddying flying leaves, through a blurred and indistinct haze of cloud and mist.

I turned towards the corner where Helen's harp

stood, securely fastened up in its stamped leathern case. "Ah, the idle puss, she wants Edy to play duets with her," I thought; but I asked Mrs. Ramsay if Helen practised steadily.

"N—o—no, not *very* steadily lately," she acknowledged; and the mother's deprecating air and faltering voice made me feel still more sure of the truth of my little romance : however, I said nothing, but went on exploring Helen's apartment.

She had collected all the most old-fashioned articles of furniture in the house—quaint inlaid chairs with spidery legs, marvellously upright sofas, and two or three really beautiful carved oak chests, but the greatest success was a narrow recess in one corner, which Miss Ramsay had filled with a tall Indian cabinet, on whose shelves was set forth an elaborate toilette service in filagree silver. The mirror itself had grown black with age and damp, but its frame was exquisite; and the chasing of all the bottles and pots for confection of roses, elder-flower-water, and what not, rendered them works of art. No amount of out-door bad weather could make that room look dull with its great beautiful pot of autumn flowers and its effective bits of colour, glowing out of an old red arm-chair or a table-cover contrived from a gay Indian shawl.

Suddenly I felt with a pang that, after all, it was the thought that Helen had taken pleasure in arranging these details, that she had lately sat in the old red-leather chair, and would perhaps come in directly to the circle of bright warmth around the open hearth, which constituted the chief charm of the room. If there was any truth in my idea about Mr. Kenneth, what would become of Mrs. Ramsay? Who would make up to me for the loss of Helen? One always thinks at first of the marriage of any one very near and dear to them, as if the tidings were those of death, not of happy love. "What shall I do without her?" is a sister's first thought, even when she is glad of the news so shily whispered.

I felt desperately anxious to know the worst at once, so I came back to the sofa on the large, though somewhat faded, Turkish rug before the blazing hearth. Mrs. Ramsay was standing with one foot on a quaint brass fender which shone like gold, and I felt sure, little as I had studied her face, that a new expression had come into it since we last met. She looked happy and proud, but there was a wistful tenderness in the deep blue eyes which had not always been there; I perceived also a slight flutter in her way of moving, and she started if spoken to suddenly. Indeed she shrank back as if I had struck her when, not being able to keep silence any longer, I asked quite abruptly,

"Who is Mr. Kenneth, Mrs. Ramsay? and where does he live?"

She answered my second question first, as if it had been the most important, and eagerly replied,

"Oh, quite near here, only a short six miles' drive, and a very good road."

"Who is he, though?" I repeated; and added, with a little acrimony, "I wish Helen would not go off with him the first morning I arrive."

"Dear Edy, you and I must both learn not to expect too much from Helen now," the poor mother replied, as she sat down next me on the sofa, and bent her head till it reached my shoulder. She could not go on, poor soul; though she was not actually crying, she seemed unable to find words in which to tell me the news I had already guessed. But I could not bear the suspense, so I said,—

"Is Mr. Kenneth the Cousin Charles I have heard Helen mention once or twice?"

"Yes, dear, the very same; he is really only a distant cousin, but both he and Helen have so very few relations on either side, that they always would have it they were quite near, instead of being truly very far-away cousins. We have seen a good deal of him the last year or two, since he came back from his grand tour, and we like him very much. He is so steady and nice, and very fond of Helen; and then his place, Dalethorpe, is quite close to this."

Mrs. Ramsay ended with what she considered her strong point, you will perceive. The most brilliant alliance in the world would not have found favour in her eyes if the suitor had lived a hundred miles away.

"Is Helen fond of him?" I inquired.

"Well, I suppose so; I hope she is, for she has accepted him, and they are to be married in the summer. Helen is in no hurry to leave home, thank God! and I tell Charles he can come here as much as he pleases. He is very nice to me about it all, and seems really quite sorry to take her away."

"Then why does he do it?" I asked, half-laughing, but still feeling very much inclined to cry.

I believe it did Mrs. Ramsay a world of good to find herself placed in the position of Mr. Kenneth's defender and champion. She raised up her head, and answered me boldly.

"How could I expect to keep my dear Helen always? She has every chance of happiness, so far as we can see. Charles is devoted to her and to me, and I don't think she could have chosen any one whom I should have liked better. And then, as I said before, Dalethorpe is so near. Charles has already settled that he will give *me*, as a 'wedding present' he says, a new sort of carriage, which I can use in wet weather as well as fair; and I daresay we shall meet nearly every day one way or another."

It was very lucky that Helen had not come in a moment earlier, when Mrs. Ramsay and I were apparently mourning together; now, as the girl entered, her mother went on saying, quite simply and naturally, with the most cheerful air in the world—

"Come and sit here, my darling; Edy wants to know all about Charles and you; I have been telling her how much in love with him I am, and now you must speak for yourself."

"Was the dear little woman much surprised, mother?" asked Helen, as she gave me a kiss.

Young ladies in those long-ago days were not nearly as demonstrative or gushing towards their female friends as they are now; Helen and I loved each other dearly, but we never made much fuss about our affection, and as for any school-girl talk about beaux or lovers, such a subject had never been mentioned between us. We chattered to each other about our homes and our occupations, our visions and our air-castles, but these had never a gallant in them : Helen's great project was to travel with her mother in France and Germany, but the same sad obstacle stood in her way which has kept us all at home lately. The War-God was then abroad, and his track was marked, as it is now and always has been marked, by awful sights and sounds of blood and tears.

I believe in my secret heart that I was the most romantic of the two, in spite of my prim manners; and I had cherished lately a faint hope that my favourite brother might some day meet Helen and fall in love with her. So he did, poor fellow, but not until long after her heart had turned into stone to all men and their love-vows.

Mrs. Ramsay went away to flirt with Charles, as she said, leaving Helen and me to our confidential chat, which did not come off then, however, for I have always noticed that whenever you are ordered to talk to anybody on any particular subject, it is sure to be the one passed most lightly over in the conversation. So we chatted about school news, of what had become of the "old girls," the marriage of the

drawing-master to the English governess, which
we considered a most suitable match—everything,
in short, but the topic nearest to my heart, and I
suppose to Helen's also.

I ate my breakfast with Miss Ramsay's help,
for she declared she had gained a fresh appetite since
her own meal; and then she proposed that we
should come down to the hall and play three-
cornered battledore and shuttlecock. I thought to
myself, despondingly, "She will be always wanting
to go and amuse this tiresome man now; I shall
never have her all to myself quietly, as I used to."
But I dissembled my selfish feelings, and agreed to
the plan with a good grace, even going so far as
to say I was anxious to be introduced to Mr.
Kenneth.

We found Mrs. Ramsay and the young gentleman
walking briskly up and down the big hall, and talking
about Helen or me, or perhaps both, for they stopped
and looked guilty as we entered.

Mr. Kenneth certainly had a look of Helen; he
was tall and well-built, with a nice frank face, but
it wanted the expression which Helen's dark eyebrows and lashes gave to hers. His eyes, too, were
blue—a good deep violet-blue, not a pale feeble
colour—in fact, they looked black at night. It was

more in their respective movements and gestures, the smile and turn of their heads, that the likeness lay. At all events he resembled Helen in the power of winning hearts, for I, too, fell in love with him on the spot, but only as Mrs. Ramsay did, you will understand—"*en tout bien et bel honneur.*"

It was a great comfort that awkwardness was out of the question even for the poor hero himself; he very nearly made me scream by the warmth of his hand-clasp, and I pitied Helen extremely if that was the usual strength of his greeting. Mrs. Ramsay seemed glad to sit down and rest, for the peculiarity of Mr. Charles was, that he lived always on his legs, unless he was on a horse's back. As for sitting in a chair and amusing himself with a book or a paper on a rainy day, he never dreamed of such a thing; he was irresistibly impelled to take just as much exercise in wet as in dry weather, only at present, in consideration to Helen, the "rampaging"—as they call it now—went on under a roof, for it was impossible for a woman to get out of doors.

The battledores were soon produced, and the triangle arranged, but after a few minutes' play I gave it up, for I was so short that I spoiled the game for the others. They had to change and lower their aim to suit my small stature, and the consequence was that the score never reached even two figures, so I joined Mrs. Ramsay; and of all the old-time pictures which linger in my memory none is more distinct than that of those two young people playing battledore that wet day. They both looked so healthy and so happy, so good-humoured and so big and strong. We really got tired of counting, and dizzy with watching the flight of the shuttlecock, long before they were inclined to give up.

During the remainder of the day Helen, Mrs. Ramsay, and I took it by turns to exercise Cousin Charles. We played bowls with him, Helen and I waltzed with him, for he had learned this fascinating mode of gyration during his tour, and had taught Helen, who in her turn instructed me. Altogether he was a most fatiguing lover to have, and I could not help saying, when she and I went upstairs at night, "Are you not very tired, Helen?"

"Well, yes, I am rather," she answered with a smile. "You see Charles has always been accustomed to a good deal of exercise, and indeed he tells me this is quite a sedentary life compared to what he generally leads; the worst of it is that he can't bear to do anything alone; mamma or I have to be with him always. It does not do us any harm, luckily, but I must take care and not kill you, my dear child."

"Now, Helen, it's all nonsense your calling me your child; remember I am older than you, and I'm sure I am quite as strong."

"No, you are not, dear. I am certain Charles would kill you in a week. Even I find him rather too much for me sometimes, but I do not suppose he will always be like this; he must have some men friends of his own to go about with. We don't know any men—any young men, I mean—whom we could ask to meet him, so he has no one to depend upon but mamma and me. However, he is going North next week, so we shall have some rest."

"Dear me, Helen," I said, "it's rather dreadful to be so tired by one's lover, is it not? Why don't you *make* him sit still and read sometimes?"

"Oh, I like him very well just as he is, Miss, and I don't want to begin to keep him in order yet. Don't you like him, too, Edy? He seemed to get on so well with you."

"Yes, he is very kind and nice, and I am glad he is not short; I was *so* afraid that if ever you married, your husband might be five feet nothing."

"Why so?" asked Helen, in some natural amazement.

"Well, I have always heard that people are attracted towards their opposites," I replied gravely.

" Then I shall begin to make myself miserable lest you should marry a giant or an ogre, Edy; but come, we had better say good-night, for Charles likes an early breakfast, and if the morning be fine I shall probably go for a walk with him before."

"I do believe that Mr. Kenneth is taking a brisk constitutional up and down his room at this moment, Helen. I can't fancy him lying down and going to sleep like a Christian."

" You are as bad as mamma, Edy; she always gives poor Charles the largest room in the house, so that he may walk about it if he likes whilst he is dressing."

"Is Dalethorpe very large ?" I asked; and this question beguiled us into quite a long conversation, in the course of which we touched on many things connected with the past and probable future of this episode in Helen's life—as old in its original features as the Creation, for our own love affairs are the only subjects of which we never tire in the discussion.

It was the first romance I had ever heard of, though, Heaven knows, it was unromantic enough. No tears, no scenes, no difficulties; all seemed smooth and pleasant and prosperous : Mrs. Ramsay pleased, Helen and Charles very much pleased, I suppose, and all the friends and relations on both sides perfectly satisfied. Yet I take just as much interest in a love-story now, even if its goal be the *bête-noir* of fashionable mothers—£300 a year—as I did in Helen's confidences of fifty years ago. Inexperienced as I was in such matters, I went off to bed with the firm conviction that, to borrow from the old French proverb, it was Helen who held up her cheek in passive content.

"We are not going to be married before the summer," she said. "It is so much pleasanter on account of the weather. Charles can be a good deal out of doors too, and I don't want to leave mamma in a hurry. Of course you will be one bridesmaid, and I will have Janet Parke for the other. We must get her here first, however, and teach her to waltz, for Charles has set his heart on having a wedding ball when we come back, and he will want plenty of partners, as he could not dance with me that evening, I suppose, and you will not be able to dance every waltz with him."

"Heaven forbid!" I thought; but I only answered pleasantly—

"Oh no, that would never do! Could not you teach the Compton girls before then?"

"I daresay. Good-night, little Edy, you look worn out, and I am a selfish monster to keep you up so late."

D

I have never told you yet how little these two years had altered Helen. She was still rather too placid and unformed in manner, but her mind seemed as simple and sweet as ever.

"Dear, bright girl, how happy Mr. Kenneth ought to be ; but oh, what will Mrs. Ramsay do ?" were my last thoughts, as I dozed off into a happy dream. Indeed, any fellow-guest of Cousin Charles would be pretty sure to sleep well, if being tired could ensure them a good night's rest.

Fortunately, he *did* go North in a few days, and, in spite of my admiration for his appearance and character, I enjoyed the quiet and repose of Holm Bush without its suitor ; and Helen, Mrs. Ramsay, and I spent a delightful fortnight together, for we girls had no secrets from the mother ; and dear Mrs. Ramsay declared she liked hearing of my boy brothers at home and their doings ; their talents and their scrapes. Helen certainly enjoyed these latter stories the most.

When I left, it was with the understanding should return on the 1st of June the following year, and remain at Holm Bush after the young people had started on their journey— for they meant to travel on the Continent—it being hoped by that time order would be restored. Mrs. Ramsay declared she should not miss her daughter half so much if little Edy was left behind. "We can talk about Helen, my dear, you know;" so that was settled, and everybody seemed satisfied.

CHAPTER III.

A WEEK BEFORE THE WEDDING.

WHEN next I saw Holm Bush it was in that fair time of year which is thus described in the most perfect of all idyllic love poems:—

"Lo, the winter is past, the rain is over and gone; the flowers appear on the earth; the time of the singing of birds is come, and the voice of the turtle is heard in our land."

In those days, when all the world was young, we used to have brighter summer sunshine than any which beams now—at least on me. Sometimes I think that this particular season, of which I am going to tell you, was the last summer belonging to my real girlhood; for, though I did not marry my dear kind old Mr. Baldwin for three years later, I never felt quite the same after I left Holm Bush; but this is anticipatory twaddle, and I must take you and myself back to the bright June morning on which Mrs. Ramsay, Helen, and I stood outside the hall steps feeding the peacocks, directly after our own breakfast.

It wanted just a week to the wedding day, and I was agreeably surprised to find that the woman, and not the mother, was uppermost in Mrs. Ramsay's feelings. She was in excellent spirits, full of interest in all the marriage preparations, and could only talk of Helen's purchases and plans and presents. I put these last, for in those old times wedding gifts had not become the heavy tax they now are. I am told that unhappy people of the present day who possess a large circle of friends and relations are in the habit of calculating this gilt mail—for the offering is generally of ormolu— among their yearly expenses, and putting it just after the assessed taxes.

Helen's godmother gave her an old-fashioned set of ornaments and a point-lace scarf; her god-father wrote a short homily on her new duties, enclosed with a bank bill for £100. Her school-fellows clubbed together, and sent a copy of Mrs. Chapone's Letters, which a private note written by that graceless Mary Wright declared was far from being their own choice. "'Waverley,' or even that charming, wicked Lord Byron's last new poem, would have been much more to our taste as a gift, dear Helen," she wrote; "but that old frump, Miss Pringle, would have this stupid thing bought for you. I hope you'll not read it much."

Helen herself seemed calm and happy; she was looking very handsome, but serious, and her manner to her mother was perfect; so full of tender devotion, and yet avoiding anything which might ruffle Mrs. Ramsay's cheerful serenity.

Whilst Martha was assisting me to unpack and arrange my clothes the night before, she had said more than once, "What a thing it is, Miss, that mistress do keep up so hearty. One would ha' thought she'd ha' clean broke her heart over losing of Miss Helen, but she do seem to ha' taken a new lease of her life and looks."

Mr. Kenneth, I heard, was not expected until the coming Monday, when it had been arranged for him to take up his bachelor quarters for the last time at the old Rectory near Holm Bush. He was to bring his best man with him, a Mr. John Saville, and they hoped to amuse themselves pretty well until the following Thursday—the wedding day. The Rector, Dr. Hall, promised to keep them employed during the forenoon with their fishing-rods, stipulating only that they should all be allowed to dine at the Hall every evening.

Poor man! how little he knew Charles Kenneth, when he proposed to require him to sit quietly on the grass all day long with a rod in his hand.

However, that was the programme; and accordingly on Monday evening the clergyman, the bridegroom expectant, and Mr. John Saville walked up to Holm Bush, about five o'clock, an extra-fashionable dinner hour in those times, and only adopted in compliment to the London lawyer, John Saville, whom report represented as being unable to dine earlier.

Girls then were pretty much the same in their little ways as girls are now, of course always excepting Girls of the Period, who belong to quite a different species. These poor creatures are really, I have reason to believe, the victims of enchantment, and must some day return to their true, beautiful natures. At present they seem to go on their restless course with the hearts of worldly old women, the manners of rude school-boys, and no morals in particular. But *my* faith, also, is large in Time, and doubtless this will all come right presently, and we shall have our own sweet rosebud girls back again.

It will not therefore surprise any old-fashioned

girl who reads this sketch, to hear that Helen and
I were dressed early, having taken particular pains
with our toilettes, and that when the three gentlemen arrived we were sitting in the cool shaded hall,
waiting to welcome them.

Mr. Kenneth looked as usual, in splendid condition,
in high health, and in perfect temper and spirits.
His manner towards Helen was all that a romantic
school-girl could desire, and yet it could not have
failed to satisfy the most prudish of chaperones. I
was the chaperone for the moment, and was warmly
greeted by the two gentlemen whom I knew, and
introduced to the one whose acquaintance had yet to
be made. This ceremony had already been gone
through in due form with Helen, and, acting of course
on Cousin Charles's suggestion, we all went out of
doors together and strolled up and down on the
lawn. That is to say, the Rector and I really
strolled, but the other three took what may fairly
be described as a brisk constitutional walk.

"Mr. Kenneth's love of movement must, if possible,
be more trying in summer than it is in winter," I
thought. "How flushed and heated poor Helen will
be, just when I wanted her to look cool and nice.
Tiresome man, I wish he would sprain his ankle."

But when Mrs. Ramsay had come out on the

threshold of the hall-steps, with the solemn butler behind her, his expressionless face peeping over her shoulder, and we had taken their appearance as a signal for us to come in to dinner, Helen's clear complexion had not gained even its usual sea-shell tint of pink.

Both Mrs. Ramsay and I had got into a way lately of gazing at our darling constantly, feasting our eyes, whilst we could, on the dear face so soon going away from its old home. A less sweet-tempered girl might have been fidgeted or bored by our looks, but whenever she met our eyes they always had a loving, tender glance for us. During this dinner, however, I don't believe Helen gave either her mother or me one smile or one look. Mr. Saville sat next to me and opposite to her, and it was on him that those large, serious, golden-brown eyes were turned whenever they were not gazing out of window.

Family dinner-parties were not more agreeable fifty years ago than they are now, and in this instance there were difficulties. My code of elegant manners for a young lady prescribed that I should hold my tongue. Helen was never much of a talker, one did not expect it of her; she was so sympathetic that a wealth of words would have de-

tracted from the great calm which always seemed
to shed itself around her.   Mr. Kenneth's conversa-
tional powers were nothing remarkable, though on
this occasion he was kept constantly speaking by
the necessity of answering Mrs. Ramsay's thousand
and one questions about Dalethorpe, when it would
be ready for them, &c.

The Rector and Mr. Saville also conversed a little,
but their talk was chiefly composed of question
and answer; and from the replies to all these
queries we, *i.e.* Helen and I, learned that Mr.
John Saville lived alone in chambers in Serjeants'
Inn, in the City of London; that he was unmarried;
that he was the eldest son of a poor man, had
numerous brothers and sisters; and finally, that he
worked very hard as a barrister.   He was too modest
to add that his life was one of daily self-sacrifice
and drudgery at a profession he disliked, but in
which his perseverance and his talents had already
won him a name and standing.

For the rest, he was a quiet, gentlemanly young
man, of middle height, with a face which expressed
both force and thought.   It might be described as
a face possessing a good deal of character, and one
which would be downright handsome if he lived
an out-door life, and had healthy browns and

reds in it, instead of a somewhat sallow tint. He
could but rarely afford himself a holiday, he said,
and was determined to make the most of the few
bright summer days stolen from his daily hard work.

I liked Mr. Saville the moment I saw him; his
open, quick look, which seemed to read your whole
character straight off, his grave, pleasant smile, and
simple unaffected manner, must have predisposed
any one to like him. Charles Kenneth was enthusiastic about him; and I think both Mrs. Ramsay
and I . felt a sudden increase of respect . for the
bridegroom's taste and judgment, when we found
that he could thoroughly appreciate such a man
as Mr. John Saville seemed to be.

Of course we ladies discussed the stranger whilst
we were alone in the drawing-room, but I remember
now that Helen said never a word for or against
him. In spite of the tedious length of dinner we
had yet a delicious hour or two out of doors before
we were summoned to the supper of those days,
preparatory to the gentlemen's departure.

I walked about with Mrs. Ramsay and Mr. Saville,
listening demurely to their conversation, which consisted chiefly of praise of Helen and Charles, first as a
solo and then in a duet. Mr. Saville said much of
Mr. Kenneth which was most comforting to a mother's

ear to hear; and of Helen he also spoke as a loyal gentleman might, praising her beauty, and warmly approving of his friend's happy choice. Such a topic naturally broke down most of the barriers which old-fashioned manners used to erect between recent acquaintances, and when we met again at supper Mr. Saville seemed to have made himself a place in the family. He was no longer the stranger to be talked to, he was the friend who found interest and amusement in all the little local and domestic subjects.

Helen, too, had recovered her gentle gaiety of manner, and was full of questions about the Opera, the Ring, and all sorts of fine places, of which Mr. John Saville professed complete ignorance.

"Yes," said Charles, "it's quite true, Helen; I never can get him away from his dusty old papers and stuffy chambers; I have hard work to drag him out for a walk now and then."

Mr. Saville smiled, and, with a glance at Mrs. Ramsay, said, "One walk with you, my dear Kenneth, counts as a whole week's exercise for any one else. I find it impossible to study the night after one of those excursions, there is nothing for it but to go to bed and sleep off the fatigue."

We all assured him we could easily believe it; and then the topic came up naturally of the next day's plans. I recollect it was settled that we were all to drive over in the afternoon and see Dalethorpe, which we did, and had a pleasant ramble among its beech and oak woods.

A few spring wild-flowers still lingered in the damp and shady places, and I well remember Mr. Saville gathering a bunch of harebells, blue and white, and presenting Helen and me each with a posy of the delicate blossoms. We both wore them that evening at dinner, fastened into the crossed muslin boddices of those days: I have not the least idea what became of mine, but it is not very long ago since I placed a little packet of those frail flowers, now only scentless fibres and dust, on a cold dead heart. The paper seemed yellow with age, and the date of this visit to Dalethorpe was written in discoloured ink inside it. The poor little parcel came out of an old-fashioned school-girl desk, on whose lid was scratched in letters, evidently formed by a child's hand, "Helen's treasures."

Looking back on it all afterwards, with the sight which can perceive flickering far away in the past that which should have been a beacon and a warning at the time, I wonder that neither Mrs. Ramsay nor I observed how changed Helen had become since that Monday evening. Instead of walking with Charles, she seemed to prefer a quiet talk with Mr. Saville, either in the library or under the shade of the avenue trees, where we generally strolled about after dinner.

On Tuesday night, when she came to give me her good-night kiss, I said, quite thoughtlessly—

"What do you think Mr. Saville told me to-day, Helen? That at first he merely thought you very agreeable and handsome, but that now he perceives you add a well-cultivated mind and a fine taste to—oh dear, I forget the rest! But my first thought was how delighted Miss Pringle would have been to hear this pretty speech, and my next that it is all owing to the prize for English composition! I was just going to tell him about that essay on true heroism when you and Mr. Charles came up, and I had not the courage to talk about it before your face."

I stared at Helen's change of expression in mute astonishment. The girl positively glowed and quivered under my words as if they had been the most ardent love-vows, instead of a disjointed and silly sentence, for I was too sleepy to be coherent. My eyes opened wide enough now to see her agitation, and I felt terrified at the effect of my nonsensical chatter.

"Was that all, Edy?" she whispered, bending down so as to hide her face by laying it in a coaxing way on my pillow. "Try and remember; I should like to hear what he said about me. Do you think he really likes me?"

"Good gracious, Helen, I think you must be mad!" I cried. "What earthly consequence is it to you what Mr. Saville or Mr. Anybody else says about you? Your cousin Charles thinks you perfection, and surely that ought to satisfy you. I never knew you were so conceited; and I would not have believed it if I had been told of your folly by a stranger. What would Mrs. Ramsay say if she had any idea that you wanted to know, forsooth, whether Mr. Saville really liked you. Go away, I am very angry!"

Of course I did not mean Helen to go away, but she took me at my word, and left the room at once.

My indignation lasted me as company for about a quarter of an hour; then qualifying reflections dawned on me, and justice became tempered with mercy; at last, in a girlish revulsion of feeling, I got up and stole barefooted through the morning-room to Helen's bedroom beyond it.

I gently tapped, but entered almost at the same

moment. Excited as I was, with my nerves strung up to a high pitch, it seemed to me as if my wildest imagination had failed to suggest any possibility so romantic, so unlike Helen's usual methodical calm, as the sight which met my eyes.

There, kneeling by her bedside, dressed just as she had parted with me an hour before, knelt, or rather crouched, a shivering, wailing creature, piteously moaning, and saying, "Oh, I cannot, cannot do it!"

At ·first I felt fairly frightened. I had never in all my short, practical life assisted at a romance. Helen's love-story was the only one I knew, and that had hitherto been all smiles and sunshine. What, then, was the meaning of this attitude, these tears, and, above all, this despair?

It does not always require a lifetime to learn the difference between the true and the false in human emotions, and I felt a belief, which seemed to amount to positive knowledge, that I was face to face with a great sorrow. The effect of this instinct was to make me feel how utterly useless our love and our sympathy is when we want it most. I question whether, if people would only acknowledge it, everyone does not feel on an emergency much as I felt then— frightened and helpless. Here was an emotion so violent as to change all Helen's usual habits and feelings, and I did not even know what it arose from, nor could all my love give me the least insight into her heart.

She probably did not find out that I was kneeling beside her, stupidly trying to pull away her concealing hands from before her face, for I had been thus employed some moments before she said—

"Is that Edy? Poor little thing, you can't help me—nobody can. Oh, what shall I do! Go away, Edy. You don't know how wicked I am."

"Helen, dear Helen, do let me call your mother; she will know what to do. How can I tell what is the matter if you won't speak to me? Pray let me go for Mrs. Ramsay."

"Oh, but mamma will hate me too: everybody will hate me—I hate myself; and yet what am I to do?"

It was such a relief to me to hear any words at all, in place of those dreadful moans, that my common sense partially returned to me, and I tried to assert my old habit of authority. I made Helen get up and sit on the edge of her bed. I brought some cold water and bathed her face and head. I found some drops she used for headache, and administered a double dose, on the somewhat dangerous principle that if a little is good a great deal is better;

and I finally managed, without any opposition, to get her into bed.

But my universal panacea for most human ills failed signally on this occasion. Helen's sorrow seemed only to have gathered strength for a fresh outburst, and so violent was the paroxysm that at last, being at my wits' end with terror, I pattered off to Mrs. Ramsay's room and begged her to come to Helen at once.

She naturally wanted to know what was the matter, but I could neither stay to explain the symptoms, nor had I any clue to their cause. I tried to persuade myself that Helen was only upset by my harsh words an hour or two before, but yet how unlike the girl I had known and loved as an elder sister might, was such susceptibility. Mrs. Ramsay, however, gathered from my paleness and agitation that something was wrong with her daughter, and this knowledge sufficed to arouse her in a moment. She followed me to Helen's room, and never can I forget her wild, scared look as we entered, and Helen's smothered screams and cries could be heard.

"My darling child, what is it? She has been dreaming. What can have put her in such a state? Oh, Edy, Edy, can't you give me any idea of what has upset her?"

"No, indeed, dear Mrs. Ramsay," I said, "I've been begging Helen for the last half-hour to tell me what ailed her, but she doesn't seem to know herself. She can't be so foolish as to have taken a little wee scolding I gave her just now to heart in this manner."

I tried to speak cheerfully, but I was really dreadfully frightened; scenes were not at all in my line or Helen's either. A sudden inspiration came to me that it would be better to go away and leave Mrs. Ramsay and her daughter together, so I said—

"I think I shall go back to my room, dear, and then you will be able to tell your own mother, who loves you so much, all about it. Why, I would tell my darling little mammy anything in the world, and surely you don't love your mother less, Helen!"

I stooped and kissed her throbbing, burning head, for her face was quite hidden, and I whispered to Mrs. Ramsay an entreaty to come to me for a moment presently, when Helen would be better; and then I took myself off with a heavy heart and reluctant feet to my own room, where I laid down on my bed, for I was very tired. I had fully intended to remain awake and watch for Mrs. Ramsay's visit, but sleep has never much difficulty in closing young eyelids with her blessed fingers; and so in about two minutes, as it seemed to me, after I had thrown myself on the bed, I was awakened by Mrs. Ramsay's kiss on my forehead, and started up to find the night gone, and a flood of sunshine streaming in through my open window.

"You must be very tired, my child, to sleep with such a strong light almost in your eyes, and I never heard such a noise as those birds make; it is really too much of a good thing."

Her composed words were much at variance with her wan, wretched face, and so was all the glory and beauty of a midsummer day-dawn. Ah! what a contrast they made—this light and music—to the great black cloud of sorrow and trouble which it did not require a prophet to tell me hung over us all, though I knew nothing of its cause.

"Dear Mrs. Ramsay, have I been asleep? How is Helen? What is the matter?"

I took her cold hands in mine, and instinctively tried to wrap her up, for she looked as shivering and cold as if it had been winter. She yielded to my efforts, and sat down on the bed. I drew my blankets and coverlet around her, and waited for her to speak. I should hardly have believed one night's wakefulness and worry could have brought such wrinkles and lines into a middle-aged woman's face ; its tint, too, was changed to a waxy yellow, all the bloom of health and happiness was gone, and as I tenderly touched her the forced composure gave way, her face worked as if she were going into a fit, and she threw herself into my arms, sobbing dreadfully.

"She is as bad as Helen, and I can't scold her," I thought in my despair, but I only cried, "Oh, do tell me what it is! How can I help if no one will say what is the matter with them?"

"You poor little thing, it is not fair to inflict all our troubles on you in this way," said Mrs. Ramsay, recovering herself by a strong effort. "Helen told me you knew, and had been very angry with her."

"Indeed I know nothing ; I only remember saying something about Helen's not caring for any one's good opinion except Mr. Kenneth's, but I was so sleepy I have forgotten what led to it. Besides, she never has minded anything I have ever said to her— not to go and break her heart over it in this way, at least. There surely *must* be something else the matter with her."

"There is a very serious thing the matter, Edy. Helen declares that no earthly power will induce her to marry her cousin, Charles Kenneth and, as if this were not bad enough, she is equally positive that no one but Mr. Saville shall ever be her husband. I have spent the whole night trying to argue her out of this resolution. You know how gentle and docile she is usually; well, I assure you that now nothing has the least influence. Why, the wedding is actually fixed for to-morrow!" shrieked poor Mrs. Ramsay, as the appalling proximity of the long-looked-for Thursday was "borne in upon her."

"Yes," I answered, in true Job's-comforter fashion "Janet Parke comes to-day, and everything is ready, and we shall have to set to work at once to send messages to put people off."

"But what am I to say, Edy? What excuse am I to make? How can we ever look poor dear Charles, or Mr. Saville, or anybody else in the face again as long as we live? Oh, Helen, Helen! you have never caused me a moment's sorrow until now, but I really believe this will be the death of me;" and Mrs. Ramsay, albeit the most untheatrical of women, wrung her hands and rocked herself to and fro, like any heroine in melodrama.

"I don't understand it all in the least yet," I said. "Has she taken a dislike to Mr. Kenneth, or has she fallen in love with Mr. Saville? It can't be his fault, surely; for so far as we could see he has never been anything but commonly civil to her. How unlike Helen all this fuss is!"

"Yes, that is just what puzzles me. I thought I knew my own child's heart and nature; and yet I declare I felt as if she were the veriest stranger talking to me last night."

"What is she doing now?" I asked.

"Well, I am thankful to say she has gone to sleep at last. I stayed till I was quite certain of that before I came away; she is perfectly worn out, as you may suppose, and the only way I could calm her in the least, was by solemnly promising that she should not be required to marry Charles to-morrow. Fancy Helen assuring me, and I could not help believing her, that if she were dragged to the church, she would drown herself before evening in the Mere yonder."

"Good gracious! she must be mad to say such things," I answered, much shocked.

"She is not in the least mad, my dear, only quite determined. Oh, how I wish Charles had never brought Mr. Saville near the place! Poor Charles, who will tell him this dreadful news! It will break his heart, I am sure;" and Mrs. Ramsay fell to sobbing and crying piteously.

" I will run down to the Rectory and leave a note, asking Dr. Hall to come here directly after his early breakfast, and we must see if we can bring Helen to reason, dear Mrs. Ramsay. And I can send a messenger to Janet Parke to tell her the wedding is put off. I feel as if it were a dreadful dream! Poor Mr. Kenneth, he is so good and nice, it seems very hard on him. I wonder what Mr. Saville will say to the news. Has Helen any idea that he likes her?"

" Not the faintest; she assures me that something you said quite accidentally, opened her eyes to the true state of the case; she laments most bitterly having brought all this trouble and misery on everybody, but she declares that she dare not marry Charles Kenneth, feeling as she does towards this other man. I asked her," continued Mrs. Ramsay, "whether she had not loved her cousin all this time, when she seemed so perfectly contented and happy; she said yes, she loved him then just as she loves him now, with a calm sisterly affection, springing from the knowledge of his many good qualities, but that if she had never seen Mr. Saville she would not have known what real love meant."

I was so perfectly ignorant myself, that bright June morning, of what real love meant, that I remember feeling somewhat scandalized even at the phrase, and, hastening to return to the region of commonplace, advised Mrs. Ramsay to go to bed, promising to get up and dress and watch Helen until it was time to take some steps towards accomplishing the change of plan.

But Mrs. Ramsay would not hear of my going to Helen, and she assured me that she was not at all tired, and much too wretched to sleep; that she would go back to her daughter's room and lie on the sofa there. Helen had made her faithfully promise not to ask her to see any one, not even me. As for the servants, not one was to be admitted into her room on any pretence. She could not bear to see any person but her mother, and the faithful soul hurried back to her charge, leaving me to carry out our hastily formed plans.

CHAPTER IV.

THERE'S MANY A SLIP, ETC.

IT was impossible to lie still or go to sleep again after Mrs. Ramsay left, so I got up and dressed, and went to the open window.

Nature is generally unsympathetic; and on that day, when a dull or a drizzling morning would have suited and soothed our hearts, lo! she was smiling and chirping and sparkling with all her might. I know well how often this feeling has been expressed in better words, but still the experience is so universal that no record of a great anxiety would be complete without the trite remark; and it really jarred on me so much, that I felt quite as if I were making a new discovery, and no one had ever felt or said the same thing before, when I turned away, sick at heart, from the lovely out-door sights and sounds, with the half-uttered words on my lips—

"How can the sun go on shining and the birds singing when Helen is so unhappy!"

Mrs. Ramsay sent me a little twisted note enclosed in another cover, which I took down to the Rectory as soon as I thought the servants would be up. I only found one sleepy housemaid opening the shutters, and she was greatly amazed to see me. I have reason to believe she suspected I had come to hurry, not to postpone, the wedding. At all events, she asked me if this was *the* day?

"No, indeed, Polly," I said; "but will you see that Dr. Hall gets this note the moment he awakes? It is of the greatest importance."

I did not want to be questioned, so I sped back again, and found that it was time to send off a messenger on horseback to Janet Parke's home, distant some fifteen miles.

My note to her was extremely laconic, and, as well as I can remember, ran thus:—

"DEAR JANET,—The wedding is put off. Helen is ill. Don't come to-day.

"Your affectionate friend,

"EDITH MAUDE."

I suppose if I had written ten pages I could not have stopped her more effectually, but it certainly

seemed a bald and disjointed epistle, though it was
the best I could compose.

Dr. Hall came up about nine, and his first cheerful
words made my heart ache with a sharp physical pain.

He told me that he had had quite a fight
with Charles, in which, however, he was nobly sup-
ported by Mr. Saville, because when the former
found that the Rector was coming up to Holm Bush,
he naturally wanted to come also, declaring that he
must be sent for about something concerning the
wedding, and that he certainly ought to have a voice
in the discussion. Dr. Hall added, that although
Mr. Saville had gone out fishing, Charles had
actually remained in the now deserted house, so as
to be near at hand if his opinion were wanted.

The worthy old Rector was looking in some dismay
at my agitated face, when a servant came to ask him
to step up to Miss Helen's room, where Mrs. Ramsay
was awaiting him ; and he told me afterwards that
he was quite prepared for some bad news from the
emotion he had seen me display.

He soon returned to the morning-room, and
certainly his very wig seemed standing on end with
blank astonishment. He asked if I knew of this
sudden fancy of Helen's ?

"No, indeed," I assured him.

"Did I think Mr. Saville knew of it ?"

"I felt quite sure he did not," was my reply.

"I cannot stop now," said the Rector; "the first thing to do is to go for Charles. I will tell him the news on the way up to the house, and then I had better go and find Mr. Saville, and send him back to London, for I presume Helen, mad as she is, and reckless of appearances as she has proved herself to be, will not want to see him just yet."

The poor dear Rector looked so heated and worried, that, without a moment's consideration, I proposed to go to the Rectory and bring Mr. Kenneth back, though I very nearly retracted my offer, which had been eagerly accepted, when Dr. Hall added—

"And you know, my dear young lady, if you see any really good opening, you might prepare the poor young man's mind—just a hint, you know."

Now I never give a hint. If I want to say anything disagreeable, I make up my mind, shut my eyes and say it; but giving hints is to me a detestable process, which never leads to any result save confusion. So I determined that if I could find courage to speak plainly, I would do it; if not, I should hold my tongue.

Mr. Kenneth's legs had found it impossible to keep themselves within the narrow bounds of the glebe meadows, and I met him striding briskly up and down the avenue.

"I thought I should be wanted," he said, "so I stopped at home; have you come to fetch me, eh, Miss Edy?"

"Yes, we want you, Mr. Kenneth; Mrs. Ramsay wishes to speak to you," I answered gravely.

Charles Kenneth was not the most acute observer in the world, but my pale, anxious face told of some trouble. With the sublime selfishness of lovers, who never think any calamity worth mentioning so long as the *objet aimé* is sound in wind and limb, he instantly said,—

"Nothing wrong with Helen? She's not ill, I hope? You've not come to tell me the wedding is put off, have you, Miss Edy?"

Was this a case for hints? I thought not, so I answered steadily, but said, with my own heart beating loudly in my ears—

"I have come to tell you something very dreadful, Mr. Kenneth. No one told me to say it, but I think I had better get my news over at once. Helen does not wish to marry you; she declares she never will do so, though she has a great regard for you."

Mr. Kenneth did not scream, or stamp, or roar, or conduct himself as heroes generally do; he did not even stop walking very fast towards the house, and he never said a word to me all the time until we reached the hall-door. Then, by a sudden impulse, stopping short he said,—

"Take another turn, will you, Miss Edy? I can't understand it. There must be some mistake. I suppose you can tell me as much about it as Mrs. Ramsay can, and perhaps you'll say it in fewer words. Have I offended my dear girl? Is she angry with me? I will go down on my knees to beg her pardon. Why, we've never had a quarrel in our lives. . Perhaps it's parting with her mother which has upset her; we could take Mrs. Ramsay with us quite easily if that were all."

Poor dear good-natured Charles! How could Helen find it in her heart to treat him thus, I thought. He is not very wise or very learned, but what a true faithful heart she is throwing away. I shook my head, and said—

"It's not that, Mr. Kenneth. Helen is not in the least angry with you; she is very fond of you, she says, but——" here I paused for lack of courage to say the reason. It certainly was not a pleasant thing to tell the principal person that his lady-love preferred some one else.

"But what, Edy? Do tell me at once, like a good girl."

I shut my eyes and stopped trotting by Mr.

Kenneth's side, for all my breath was needed for my news, and, with the courage of despair, I blurted out—

"She has fallen in love with Mr. Saville, I believe—at all events Mrs. Ramsay says that Helen vows she *will* marry him, and she won't marry you."

During my walk to the Rectory I had turned over in my much-troubled mind a hundred different ways in which Mr. Kenneth would receive this statement: in most of them he clenched his hands or struck his forehead, but never had my wildest imaginings prepared me for the real reception which my intelligence was to meet.

The clouds of anxiety and suspense cleared off his open, frank face instantly; a look of relief came into his big blue eyes; he burst out laughing, and said—

"What nonsense! she can't possibly marry Saville, because he's going to marry some one else. Why, he's as fond of Lucy Milward as I am of Helen, and that's saying a good deal. It was only last night he and I were talking of our future wives, and he said how much he wished that Thursday was to be *his* wedding-day; and added, poor fellow, that although his young woman and he might not look so imposing or be so rich a couple as Helen and I,

still they would love each other just as truly.
John Saville is the last man in the world, Miss
Edy, to carry off another fellow's promised wife in
this fashion, like a fox robbing a henroost. No,
no," said Charles, setting off at his best pace
towards the house, "if that is all that Helen has
got into her head we'll soon get it out again."

I never should have caught Mr. Kenneth up
before he reached Holm Bush, so rapid were his long
swinging strides, if he had not paused till I could
overtake him, when he said anxiously, but apologetically—

" I'm in such a hurry to see Mrs. Ramsay and set
all this nonsense straight ; but there's one question
I just want answered, Miss Edy—they've not done
anything to put off the wedding, have they ? Not
written any letters or counter-ordered the parson or
the carriage, eh ? "

"Well," I answered breathlessly, " I *have* sent to tell
Janet Parke not to come to-day, but that is all I know
of which has been done, except telling the Rector."

Charles looked vexed, and said—

" Why did not Mrs. Ramsay send for me at first,
before she mentioned this nonsensical idea to Dr.
Hall, or even to you ? I don't like any one in the
world to know that Helen ever did such a foolish

F

thing. I've never heard of her having whims or fancies, and I can't think what should have put this one into her head. The great thing, however, is to get it out as fast as possible, and above all, to be married to-morrow. We can do without Miss Parke, can't we? It does not make the marriage illegal, does it, having only one bridesmaid?"

I assured him that to the best of my belief bridesmaids were a superstition, and we reached the house in a few minutes.

Dr. Hall met us at the front door, and seemed much comforted to see how cheerful both Charles and I looked. He took the former at once up to Mrs. Ramsay, who was awaiting him in Helen's morning-room, and then came down rubbing his hands and saying—

"You seem to have managed very well, my dear young lady; our friend Charles appears sanguine as to the result of an interview with his cousin. I hope he'll be able to put everything right again. It would be such a pity if the match were broken off when the property joins this so nicely, and the young people seem so suited to each other. I must say I never expected my old pupil, Helen, to make such a fuss as this, and give us all a fright on her wedding eve."

I let the old man run on, for my heart was heavy

within me. As long as I was under the influence of
Charles Kenneth's reassuring voice and firm manner
I felt hopeful, but my courage departed with him, and
he also seemed to have left his good spirits behind
him when he came downstairs an hour or two later,
for his looks were anxious and troubled.

The midday meal was ready, and we all partook
of it with astonishingly fine appetites : the " we " only
included the two gentlemen and me, for Mrs. Ramsay
had returned to Helen's darkened bedroom, where I
was told that the poor girl lay in agonies of remorse
and sorrow for the trouble she was causing, but still
firm and unshaken in her resolution not to be married
the next day, nor indeed on any future day, to Mr.
Kenneth.

When we had finished eating, Charles proposed
that he and I should go and find Mr. Saville and
tell him the news.

"You see," said poor Charles, "I should like you
to hear what he says, because then you can go
straight back and tell Helen ; she knows you are
not so likely to bend things your own way as I am,
for it's not you who are going to lose her ; it's me
—God help me !"—and Charles's eyes filled with tears
as he brushed past me into the open air.

I lingered in the hall, fastening on my calash

before I joined him, so as to give the poor fellow time to recover himself, for I felt sure he was one of those men who regard tears as signs of weakness, instead of their being consistent with the strongest and most self-reliant natures.

We went a little way down the avenue, turned off into the Park, across a blazing open space, over a stile or two, until we reached a knot of old thorn-trees, on one of whose gnarled twisted roots John Saville was sitting, lazily whipping the stream before him for trout.

At any other time Charles would have been certain to laugh at his friend for this Cockney mode of enjoying his ease, and attempting to combine comfort and sport, to the spoiling of both: but even he was in no mood for jokes just then, and only said briefly—

"Come up here, will you, John?"—we were standing still under the shade of the pink-blossomed branches, but on the bank above him—"Come up here, there's a good fellow! I want to speak to you."

Mr. Saville obeyed the summons with alacrity, and in half a moment he had climbed up, stepping on the projecting roots, worn bare of soil by the wintry floods, and stood before us, looking a little ashamed of his former easy attitude. Never were honesty and uprightness more plainly written on a man's countenance than on John Saville's, as he confronted us that summer day, with a half-laughing yet apologetic air, picking off the dead leaves and little bits of twig and blossom which a passing puff of air had scattered over him.

Neither Charles nor I had any suspicions to be dispelled, and it was with the most genuine frankness and affection that Mr. Kenneth made a step forward, laid both his hands on his friend's shoulders, and, looking down into his eyes, said—

"Listen to me, John; we are all in a dreadful way, and the extraordinary thing is that you have been the means of getting us into the mess."

"I!" repeated Mr. Saville in great amazement, but meeting Charles's earnest look with equal fearlessness and frankness.

"Yes," continued his friend, "I know very well that you are not to blame, and you'll be as much surprised as I was, when I heard just now that Miss Ramsay entirely declines to fulfil her engagement; in fact, she says nothing will induce her to marry me to-morrow or at any future time."

John Saville's face showed the deepest concern and dismay, but being a man of few words he merely said, "Why?"

In spite of their intimacy and friendship and
perfect confidence in each other, Charles looked the
picture of embarrassment. He has told me since
that he wished me a mile away, feeling that my
presence added to his difficulty, but he bravely
gulped down his dislike of the subject, and, with a
faint, piteous attempt at a smile, said—

" Because she likes you best, dear old man."

Lawyers are not supposed ordinarily to have
speaking countenances, nor to indulge in an engaging
frankness of manner, even in private; but certainly
no school-girl's feelings could have lain more
transparently on the surface than did Mr. Saville's
on receipt of this intelligence. He started back
as if he had been struck, and looked around as if
his first impulse were to run away; then recovering
himself, he gasped in unpolite sincerity—

" But I would not marry her for the whole world !
I beg your pardon, my dear Kenneth, for being so
rude, but there's Lucy, you know; and even if there
wasn't, Miss Ramsay—'pon my soul, Charles, I don't
want to say brutal things—but really you know,
everybody's taste is different, she's quite charming,
but really——"

Honest John did not see his way out of the
colloquial difficulty at all. However, Charles and I

adored him for his bluntness and his non-appreciation of Helen's merits as a wife, and Charles, seizing his shoulder in a friendly grip, said heartily—

"Of course there's Lucy, the sweetest little woman in the whole world. I've told Mrs. Ramsay all about her, for Helen won't see me, and she has told Helen, but it does not make any difference; she only says, her mother tells me, 'Very well, then, I will never marry anybody.'"

"What do you think about it, Miss Edy?" said John Saville, turning to me. "Perhaps you would be good enough to tell me when Miss Ramsay first said anything about this—this most extraordinary idea? I hope it will come all right; it's impossible she can be in earnest."

I am not very good at telling a story, and I bungled dreadfully over this one, but Mr. Saville's experience in cases of reluctant evidence enabled him to divide the facts from my stumbling, incoherent details. He evidently thought the matter more serious when I had, as it were, stepped down from the witness-box, and he took two or three hasty turns on the grass before us.

How well I remember the whole scene; the glare of brightness, the faint sounds from a distant hayfield, the hum of busy insect life among the thick branches over our heads, and the lulling chatter of the brook as it hurried along "for ever and for ever." John Saville was pacing about like a wild animal in a cage. Charles Kenneth stood on the high bank, dreamily looking down into the water, and tossing from time to time a little bit of stick or a spray of hawthorn blossom into the swiftly flowing current. The two men seemed to have changed natures for the moment. Mr. Saville was eager and restless; Charles appeared only intent on childish enjoyment of his summer holiday—

Men and women of action have less to endure than creatures of thought; they get rid of some of the suffering by the mere power of movement; and it seems an instinct when calamity comes upon us to seek relief from our trouble in this way. John Saville's restless cogitations resulted in his saying briskly—

"Let us go up to the house at once, Charley, and I will see Mrs. Ramsay myself, or even, if needs be, Miss Helen, and explain how absurd the whole thing is."

We soon reached home, and John had an interview with our hostess, and afterwards with the refractory young lady herself, but he returned to us under the shade of the beech-trees, sadly crestfallen and dispirited. He flung himself down on the grass, viciously threw his hat as far as ever he could away from him, and said, in tones of the deepest vexation—

"It has been the most awkward and the most trying thing any man ever had to do, to tell a perfectly nice, good girl that you have no wish to marry her now or at any future time. I even explained to her all about poor little Lucy, how fond we were of each other, and so on; she seemed quite interested, and said, 'I hope you will be able to marry her directly, Mr. Saville; it must be very trying to both of you, this long engagement.' I jumped at the idea, and assured her we were going to be married in the autumn; and then, taking her composure as a good sign, I ventured to say a good word for you, Kenneth, told her your wife would be the happiest woman in the world, that my best wishes for the future of my favourite sister would be more than realized if I were going to give her to you, and a great deal besides to the same effect. She stuck steadily to the point of claiming her own freedom, whilst she did you full justice, but she vows she never will marry anybody."

We discussed the subject a thousand times over that long balmy evening; we talked of it whilst the thrushes and blackbirds sang vesper songs of love and thankfulness, as if their hearts were full to bursting with joy and happiness; we talked of it as their music gradually died away into the deep silent air, and allowed the last caws from the Rector's rookery to be heard. As the soft sunset splendours faded out of the sky, and rest and peace seemed to descend from heaven and brood over all the fair earth, the curfew bell rang out in cracked tones from the adjoining church tower, and poor Charles's hope and courage seemed to die away with the dying day; he threw himself at my feet, and buried his bright curly head in the folds of my cambric dress as it lay on the grass, just as if I had been his mother or his sister, crying—

"Oh, Edy, Edy, we were laughing at that old bell only yesternight, and I thought how glad I should be to hear it this evening for the last time. Helen said she liked the sound, and I told her that on a still evening, with the air from the north-west, we could hear it quite plainly at Dalethorpe. That was almost the last thing we spoke about, for I remember she turned away and went indoors. Oh, Helen, if you only knew how miserable you make me, I'm sure you would take pity on a poor fellow!"

I cried as if my heart were breaking, and could have almost echoed John Saville's muttered denunciation against the girl who had brought, by what seemed a mere caprice, so much trouble and sorrow into this bright young life.

"Don't give way, Charley, there's a good fellow," said Mr. Saville, as he dragged Mr. Kenneth up on his feet; "it almost kills me to see you like this. I'll tell you what I'll do," he continued, with a sudden air of resolution and self-sacrifice which changed both Charles's and my tears into laughter; "I'll go up to town to-morrow, see Lucy at once, and we'll be married out of hand. It won't inconvenience us in the least, for I can get a tidy lodging till we are able to afford to set up housekeeping. That will be the best thing to do, and then Miss Ramsay must surely come back to her senses, and it will all be right."

Charles, though sad at heart, smiled at his friend's attempt to persuade us that his own speedy marriage would be a tribute to friendship, not love, and he held out his hand, saying—

"Well, perhaps that would be the cleverest thing to do. I'm afraid it will be a great bore for you and Miss Lucy, but I dare say you won't mind it. I'll come up with you; there seems no use in my stopping here."

And so it was settled. We said good-bye to each other under the avenues, and the last I saw of the two friends was a glimpse of Charles's arm thrown lovingly round Mr. Saville's shoulder, school-boy fashion, as they slowly sauntered away into the distant darkness.

How sweet and balmy the outer air smelt as I ran home, and how hot and oppressive the house seemed. I never could bear the scent of roses ever since that evening, from the association in my mind of their perfume with the melancholy desolation of Helen's sitting-room. Already her wedding preparations were huddled out of sight, and the gay confusion of the last few days, the litter of dresses and boxes and all sorts of odds and ends had been tidied away with horrible primness.

I felt as if Helen had died on her wedding eve, and indeed she did not look unlike a fair corpse as she lay stiff and straight on her little bed, with her eyes closed and her hands clasped on her breast. She was only asleep, but Mrs. Ramsay came to the door, and said things were just the same. Helen would see no one except her mother, so I suggested that I had better go home next day, and Mrs. Ramsay agreed to this plan, saying—

" If ever we are happy again you must come to

us, dear Edy, but I never can feel the same after this conduct on Helen's part. Mr. Saville has behaved beautifully, and she has no idea now of ever marrying him; her great wish is not to be called upon to fulfil her promise to Charles. I am quite as sorry for him, poor fellow, as I am for her." And kind-hearted Mrs. Ramsay dismissed me with an affectionate hand-clasp and kiss.

I wistfully peeped at Helen, lying as I have described, and then the door closed for ever on our girlish love and confidence; we were always friends to the end of her life, but there never was quite the same perfect openness between us. It was very natural, but awkward for both.

CHAPTER V.

PICKING UP THE PIECES.

"AND after——," as Mr. Carlyle says.

I have put off telling this story until long, long after, that I might be able to say how they all lived and loved during the rest of their lives. John Saville and I are the only survivors of that tragic and yet absurd scene. He is a rich, prosperous man; a Q.C. and an M.P. as well, besides being entitled to write after his name a whole alphabet of initials bestowed by learned societies. I am not quite so rich nor so famous, but still the world has gone fairly well with me and I with the world; yet I listen eagerly for the call to leave it, not through ingratitude or cold-heartedness, but only from a longing for what it neither can nor ever was meant to give.

But perhaps it would be more systematic, if I went back and worked forwards to the present

time, instead of yielding to the temptation of beginning at the end, and harking back to that summer
at Holm Bush.

As I said in the last lines of my preceding chapter,
we separated on the day which should have been
'the wedding-day; Charles and Mr. Saville went up to
London, where the latter made such use of the
argument supplied to him by Helen's sudden fancy,
that the prudent Lucy Milward was silenced, if
not convinced, and allowed herself to be married
almost directly.

Charles bravely stifled his own sorrow, and helped
with counsel and purse in preparing a dimi-
nutive home for his friend and the bride. No one
dreamed of asking him to the wedding; I was
invited, but could not bear the idea of having anything more to do with my friends' marriages;
great therefore was my surprise to hear that Charles
had appeared at the ceremony, wished the bride all
happiness, slipped a note-case into her hand, with
bills on his banker almost equal in amount to the
whole of their modest yearly income, and then gone
off "for all the world like a fairy godfather," as the
bride's youngest sister, aged ten, remarked.

More than a year passed before I saw Helen,
but at last I went to Holm Bush, for I felt that

every month which slipped away added to the
estrangement and awkwardness between us. Mrs.
Ramsay took an early opportunity, after my arrival,
to beg me not to originate any conversation with
Helen concerning her broken-off marriage, but Helen
was wise enough to feel that it would be better
to speak of it at once, and so get the subject
over. She lamented, of course, having caused so
much confusion and unhappiness, but said that she
had borne her full share of wretchedness.

"And yet I felt all the time that I was right, Edy,
right towards Charles especially. It would have been
the deepest wrongdoing to have married him when
the sight of another man and the sound of his voice
had such power to move my whole being."

I could not help showing a little vulgar curiosity,
and inquired whether she had ever met Mr. Saville
since that memorable Tuesday evening.

"No, dear," she answered; "there has never been
any question of it yet, and I can only trust the
day may come when he will not dislike to see
me. Of course his feelings have been entirely with
Charles hitherto, and he positively dislikes me, but
I must hope he will get over that in time."

I had not courage to ask any more questions, but
Helen was quite unreserved, and told me all I wanted

to know. She acknowledged with a sad smile that Charles had never ceased trying to induce her to pick up the broken threads of their engagement, and go on with it from where she had so suddenly and vehemently rent and cast it away from her, last summer; but this, she said, could never be.

" My great difficulty is mamma ; dearly as she loves me, she seems to wish me to marry and leave her; I am sure her unselfishness is at the bottom of this strong desire. She has suffered so much herself, poor dear, from a lonely life that she wishes to see me married with plenty of fresh interests and cares before she leaves me; but I tell her that if ever I need them I can make them for myself."

I must confess that Helen seemed in my eyes to have improved in beauty and developed in mind since what Miss Pringle always alluded to as her " outrageous conduct." I no longer ruled her. Helen was gentle as ever, but that one act of self-assertion had established such a supremacy that she lived on the credit of it ever after. Albeit the most gentle and yielding of mortals, whenever in the years which followed Helen asserted, ever so gently, that she would or would not do such or such a thing, no one disputed her will. This must have been very agreeable to her, but she never appeared to notice it.

And so the time passed on.

Three years later I wrote to tell Helen of my astonishment at finding that a certain Mr. Baldwin, a well-to-do north-country squire, had actually asked little insignificant me to be his wife, and that I was going to live in Westmoreland; my only regret was my future home being so far away from my early ties, but as it turned out we never lost sight of each other, and were perhaps all the better friends that we were not very near neighbours. We often visited Holm Bush, and Helen and Mrs. Ramsay came to us.

I was matchmaker enough to allow Mr. Kenneth to pay his promised visit at the same date, one year, as the Ramsays had fixed for theirs; but I finally gave up all idea after they had left, that time, or constancy, or anything under the sun could ever alter Helen's decision regarding her cousin. He must have thought so too, for I did not see anything of him during several months, and then I heard from Mrs. John Saville, who had become one of my dearest friends, that Charles was at last going to be married to her sister-in-law.

"John's own favourite sister," she wrote, "who

was only a little girl of fourteen when he brought
her into his argument with Miss Ramsay as an ideal
wife for Charles. We are all so happy."

Helen also seemed thoroughly pleased at the
news, though Mrs. Ramsay lamented over it a little,
as was but natural ; however, she took comfort in
the suggestion that perhaps Helen might now feel
herself free to marry some one else if any other
suitor should present himself.

But suitors came and suitors went, and Helen
remained Miss Ramsay still. Not a melancholy
brooding woman, going about the world with her
head on one side, in honour of having had a
romantic history. Not a bit of it.

A cheery, hearty, healthy, and most beautiful
woman was Helen Ramsay to the last day of her
long life. For some years after Charles's marriage her mother claimed most of her time and
attention, and these duties increased day by day ;
but still she found leisure to do many a kind act
towards the three families of the Kenneths, the
Savilles, and the Baldwins. She was godmother
to one of each of their children, and the titular
and best beloved aunt of all. In sickness, in
sorrow, in perplexity, Helen was our mainstay and
support.

Gradually all awkwardness died away between John Saville and her, and the last light film of *gêne* disappeared, as Helen herself triumphantly told me, after she had nursed her rival, Lucy, through a terrible and dangerous illness. When the crisis was over and the silent doctor, who had not said one encouraging word for three days, whispered, "Go down and tell Mr. Saville she'll do now," Helen described with great humour how jaded and weary and ugly she looked as she stole downstairs to the dining-room, and found John Saville with the table littered by law papers to which he could not attend, striding up and down the narrow, dingy apartment—for a small dining-room, in an ordinary London street, has not an exhilarating appearance about three o'clock of a spring morning.

"I assure you he looked hideous, Edith (I had left off being Edy after my fifth son was born), and so did I," Helen used to say, "and I believe we liked each other the better for being both so ugly and we shook hands most heartily, and he thanked me and so on, and we've been the best friends ever since. What do you think was the first thing, the ungrateful man, he told Lucy? That Miss Ramsay had altered very much, and that it was little dark-eyed women like herself who wore the best after all."

John Saville was wrong, however. Helen only altered as spring alters to summer, and summer changes to autumn. There was no winter for her; no frost or snow, no biting winds. Her noble, generous nature grew and strengthened each year, and kept her heart and her face ever beautiful with the highest beauty—that which is born of expression.

I believe all the young Saville and Kenneth boys—and they were neither few nor far between—fell in love with her one after another as soon as they were old enough to appreciate her stories. My boys raved of her to me for weeks after they had paid their annual visit to Holm Bush, and the girls loved her just as well.

Who gave them their first dolls, their first ponies, their first guns, their first ball-dresses?

"Aunt Helen!" would cry a quarter of a hundred voices. She helped the boys with their commissions, the girls with their trousseaux, and she never wearied of her labours of love and joy-giving. Other people's children arose and called her blessed. To Charles Kenneth she was always a queen among women; nor did his sweet, lovely little wife ever object to this homage on his part. John Saville ended by adoring her, and so did Lucy.

And so that is the end of my wedding story, which is a comedy after all; and as two out of the three heroines have married—for I assure you both Lucy and I considered ourselves heroines at that time— my motto is not so inappropriate as it would seem to be at first sight.

II.

A STUPID STORY.

II.

A STUPID STORY.

CHAPTER I.

LOVE'S YOUNG DREAM.

I FIND it quite impossible to introduce Monica Treherne, my first walking lady, at so early a stage of this chronicle. I say impossible, because she was not born when her uncle that was to be, Sir Ralph Scudamore, came to live at Scudamore Chace, or, as it was generally called for short, "The Chace,"—in the ugliest part of the ugliest county in England.

Of course everybody wondered why he should leave, with orders for it to be let to the first offering tenant, his beautiful place in Kent, where wood and water, softly rolling downs, and hills standing out against the sky-line, made up a fair and homelike scene. That is to say, his few and scattered neighbours at the Chace wondered; for, as it happened, the parish was singularly deficient in those local newsmen, or rather newswomen, who busy themselves in inventing a dozen different reasons for everything which doesn't concern them. In this respect you will agree with me that it was highly favoured, blessed among parishes; but then, on the other hand, never was so unpromising a neighbourhood for the promulgation of gossip. The estates were large and tolerably unencumbered, so there was no letting of ground for villa-building or breaking up of old properties, which had been held together for generations, into independent farms or Liliputian manors.

However desirable this state of things may seem on paper, its practical effect was to render the whole place intensely dull. So great were the distances in this particular shire, that in paying an afternoon visit it was necessary to consider wind and weather as much as if the expedition had to be undertaken in a balloon. Consequently there were unusual difficulties in the way of a self-elected dispenser of local intelligence.

The county newspaper congratulated itself and its public on the fact that Sir Ralph Scudamore had seen fit to change his place of abode, and to take up his residence at the ancient seat of his race and family. The editor of the said journal, being a man of sanguine mood and romantic tendencies, drew at the same time a brilliant and highly coloured sketch of the future, with Sir Ralph himself standing in the foreground, dispensing a liberal, open-handed hospitality.

Not one of these Barmecidean prophecies ever came true, and at the time they were uttered Sir Ralph had been quietly settled at home for more than a month.

He would have said that the word home could never again be applied to any human habitation as far as he was concerned. If lofty rooms, filled with convenient and handsome furniture, make a home, then Scudamore Chace deserved the name; but, fortunately or unfortunately—it is hard to say which—they don't. Home is like heaven, a condition, not a place; and the happiness which formerly made the Kentish house a very heaven of home-content and joy had gone out of Sir Ralph's life for ever and ever in this world.

During three years, which seemed now like a bright momentary flash of light amid a lifetime of darkness, there had been a Lady Scudamore; but already the recollection of her pretty face and gentle manners was waxing pale and dim, for children who

were babies when she was laid with prayers and tears
in the old family vault in Kent hàd grown up into
young men and women.

This was what made Sir Ralph's sudden freak
of coming to the Chace the more extraordinary.
If he had betaken himself there, to its grey
solitude and silence, twenty years before, in the
first weeks of his great, lifelong desolation, no one
would have wondered; but why should he go now?
He was not a person, however, for all his courteous
ways, to be lightly questioned; nor was there any man,
luckily for himself, who felt it his duty to inquire.

Certainly no one would have suspected that the
cause of the sudden change in Sir Ralph's plans
arose from the offered visit of his favourite and
newly married niece. But so it was.

Edmée Scudamore (all the women of that family
bore fanciful names) had been rather a pet with her
silent, grave uncle. As a rule he did not en-
courage visits even from near relations, but more
than once the orphan child of his dead brother
had announced her intention of arriving with a
mission to " cheer up Uncle Ralph." I don't know
about the success of the cheering-up process, but
Sir Ralph endured her presence, which was more
than he did that of others.

A year ago, however, Edmée had married a certain
Colonel Treherne, a gallant soldier and a loyal
gentleman, grave and serious beyond his years,
who had escaped all the wiles of maids and matrons
at home and abroad, to fall head over ears in love
with Miss Edmée at first sight. He declared it was
her name which attracted him ; be that as it may,
they were married, and living as happily as the
prince and princess of any fairy tale, when Mrs.
Edmée took it into her curly head, one Midsummer
morning to invade Sir Ralph's solitude.

Colonel Treherne objected for the first time since
his wedding-day, and declared that he could not
possibly go, uninvited, to any man's house. Edmée,
being in a softened and yielding mood, compromised
so far as to write a few days beforehand to her
uncle ; and it was as well she did so, for by return
of the post came a letter from Sir Ralph, telling
her that he was going to live at Scudamore Chace
for some years, but giving, at the same time, a not
very cordial permission, rather than invitation, to
Edmée and her husband to pay the offered visit a
little later, and at the Chace, instead of in Kent.

Now the real truth, as Sir Ralph confessed long
afterwards, was that he simply could not bear to
be reminded of his own vanished happiness; to see

its light shining in the eyes of others, amid the scenes and places where those three blissful years had fled so rapidly away.

Edmée was no longer a child for whom the schoolroom, or at most the library, was sufficient accommodation. For Mrs. Treherne, the gay young bride, the drawing-room suite must be opened and inhabited, so the tyrannical old housekeeper declared; and even in the stable department Sir Ralph was reminded that what was good enough for him would not do for "the Colonel, let alone Miss Edmée!"

Not that Sir Ralph was in the least stingy. Anybody might buy anything they liked for Mrs. Treherne's comfort or convenience, so long as it did not recall to him his former profuse purchases for his own fair girl-wife. He feared that if he wrote and told Edmée what anguish it gave him to picture new-married people, full of life and love, walking about the rooms as sacred to him as shrine to pilgrim, her susceptibilities might be wounded, and some coldness might grow up between them. So he suddenly resolved to uproot himself from what had been his true home, and betake himself to a gaunt, desolate, rambling, stone house, which was little more than a name to him.

Once there, the housekeeper reigned supreme. She

summoned to her aid upholsterers and other birds of prey from the nearest country town. Between them they brushed up a wing of the mansion, and made it garish with chintz and paper, taking care of course that there should be connection between the style of the old building and their decorations ; and, after about a month of incessant bustle and fuss, they announced that suitable rooms were ready for the reception of Colonel and Mrs. Treherne.

Ever since his arrival at the Chace Sir Ralph had felt unutterably wretched. A thousand times had he been on the point of starting off for Kent, and taking possession of his former dwelling-place once more.

Not only was the Chace a very wilderness of comfortless large rooms, but his few and far-between neighbours hardened their social hearts, and would not be dissuaded by coldness or shortness of manners from paying him visits and sending him invitations to dine and sleep. At all events, the Kentish squires had learned better than *that* long ago, and there he was sure of being left alone with his garden and his books.

Edmée had impressed upon her husband that he was not to be chilled by the scant welcome they were likely to meet with at her uncle's hands; and when Colonel Treherne attempted to remonstrate at being forced to intrude his company on any one, Edmée's argument was, "I am sure it must do him good to have us in the house; and as for his manner, I hope, sir, you would not lay yourself out to be pleasant to strangers if I were to die."

Contrary even to his own expectations, Sir Ralph found the greatest consolation and happiness in the society of his niece and her husband. Indeed, he took to the latter so thoroughly and entirely that Edmée affected to suffer agonies of jealousy, and ended by announcing that she had married only to please her uncle.

The fortnight's promised visit doubled itself; then Sir Ralph was induced to take a gun and go out with his stately nephew-in-law on what the newspapers call the Feast of St. Partridge. To these poor feathered victims succeeded some excellent pheasant shooting in November, and so it came to pass that the old housekeeper received a long notice to fit up a south-west room for a possible nursery.

Strange to say, Edmée took the greatest fancy to the Chace—not only to its grey solitude, but even to the flat, ugly country around. Everything looked beautiful to her when viewed through the rose-coloured spectacles which happy young wives wear;

and she herself proposed that, instead of going
back to her pretty house in Mayfair, she should
wait at Scudamore Chace till with the snowdrops
and crocuses should arrive the anxiously expected
baby-boy.

It has always seemed to me as if it must be good
to die in spring, when every twig and bud speaks
to the aching hearts left behind of that Resurrection
and Life, the thought of which they cling to so
desperately.

The first fresh green tints were on the larches,
the thickets had laid down a snowy carpet of wood
anemones, and all nature was upheaving with a
new life, putting forth its utmost powers to protest
against the rigour of cold, death-like Winter, when
Edmée Treherne went home to the angels.

The long-looked-for heir was only a dark, ugly little
girl, who had been christened Monica three weeks
before her young mother left a world which the
spring-time of year made beautiful even around
Scudamore Chace.

Edmée had lived long enough to notice that,
whilst Colonel Treherne was content to postpone the
display of his strongest parental affections until a
future occasion, when it could be more fittingly
lavished on a young gentleman, poor lonely Sir

Ralph, as desolate at five-and-forty years of age as if he had been Methuselah, took the greatest fancy to the reddish-brown baby. All his own belongings, including Edmée, had been fair, and he seemed to like this little dark intruder upon her brother's rights, who, by the time her mother's lovely blue eyes were closed for ever, had learned to look out on her fellow-creatures from a pair of great big black-fringed and beady orbs.

"I give her to you, Uncle Ralph," said poor fading Edmée one day. "Nurse says she will be very big and strong, and I hope she'll be healthy, and not cause you any trouble. I don't think her father would quite know what to do with her. You will always live here, won't you? And you must show her all my favourite places and walks; she will soon be a dear little companion for you, and you will be able to talk to her about me presently," concluded Edmée, with that pathetic horror of being forgotten which we all feel.

Now that my heroine is born she shall at once assume her proper rank and station ; and indeed she took upon herself to wield, metaphorically speaking, a sceptre of dominion long before she had left off unclenching her wrinkled fists or sucking her fat thumbs. By the time she was twelve years old she had reduced her subjects to the most slavish subjection, Sir Ralph himself setting an example of unquestioning obedience to her will.

"What an odious child!" I should say to myself at this part if I were reading these pages; but Monica was really very nice in every way, and not in the least imperious or spoiled. This uncommon and desirable state of things was due chiefly to Miss Alicia Edmonds, who had been summoned from a life of what is called genteel poverty (whatever that may mean) and third-rate society at poor, pleasant, much-abused Brighton, to preside over Miss Treherne's education with an eye to possible chaperone duties in the future.

A heroine should have her rights, though she be still in her minority, and therefore Monica's face shall be sketched at once, so that all men and women may know what latent good looks sometimes lie hidden in ugly babies.

From a most unattractive, weird-looking, brown infant, Monica had grown into a picturesque gipsy of a child, the apple of Sir Ralph's eye; for Colonel Treherne had acted according to his wife's wishes, and given up the baby completely to her granduncle's care. As Miss Treherne grew older she gave promise of much beauty, but it was a constant wonder from whence the little girl derived her Italian cast of countenance.

As she stands before me now she is precisely like the pictures one sometimes sees of a Roman peasant girl. There is the same grand type, telling, in the falcon glance and shapely limbs, of an ancestry which once ruled the world. There are the level eyebrows, distinctly but not coarsely marked on the broad low brow, from which the hair is drawn back so as to show to advantage Monica's one vanity, her exquisite ears. The dark eyes, now only bright with a girl's fearless innocence and happy ignorance, must look upon love and suffering—in fact, must look upon life—before their full depth and beauty will come to them. The little straight nose, with its finely-cut sensitive nostrils, carries out the ideal *contadina*, and the fault of that type of girl is also the fault in Monica's face. There is something unsatisfactory about the mouth, but at twelve years of age we may reasonably hope for improvement in this feature.

Until Miss Alicia's arrival, Monica had been her great-uncle's sole companion, but after that fashionable and noisy lady appeared with half a hundred boxes at Scudamore Towers there was naturally a change in the order of things.

Now Miss Edmonds is not going to be either a monster or an angel; she will neither marry Sir Ralph nor murder Monica. Long ago I think I knew some one exactly like her, and on the whole she was a very agreeable acquaintance, though I am not sure I should have liked her for an inmate of my home.

However, Monica was not so much afraid of her as was Sir Ralph; the loud voice, flowing in ceaseless talk, which jarred on every nerve of the recluse, could tell most charming stories to children, and Monica, whose knowledge of the fairy world was sadly limited, sat at her feet entranced for hours. She never could decide whether it was most pleasant to listen to Miss Alicia's stories of goblins and ghosts, giants and fairies, by the fireside in winter, or to wander over the heathery moors, and sit under the ancient trees with her governess, and hear endless romances of knights and squires, and ladies fair, all of the olden time.

Miss Edmonds was exceedingly good-natured, though it may seem a paradox to add that she could also be exceedingly selfish; but so it was. With wonderful talents and resources of intellect she was utterly frivolous and narrow-minded, and in spite of a certain dash of affability, a very little of her society went a long way, as poor deafened Sir Ralph found to his cost. At first Miss Edmonds made his very eyes ache by the brilliancy of her cheeks and her gowns; but when she discovered that the smarter the toilette the more Sir Ralph avoided her, she went into the other extreme of dowdy shabbiness.

On the whole, things jogged on pretty comfortably, though Sir Ralph failed to detect any very marked improvement in his beloved Monica's manners or accomplishments; but still the child seemed healthy and happy, so his life's desire was in process of being fulfilled.

Colonel Treherne's visits to Scudamore Chace were rare. Indeed, he went there solely to see the old man, of whom he was really fond—for, strange to say, he resented Monica's being so unlike his beloved wife. The child had evidently gone back to a distant foreign ancestress of his own for her type, especially for her complexion, which resembled a ripe apricot in the summer time, when the sun and wind seem to bring out its rich glowing tints. He did not really care a bit about her, but he showed as much affection towards Sir Ralph as if he had been his father.

It is needless to say that Miss Alicia Edmonds, too thankful to have another auditor, bloomed forth like a rose, and dressed like a bride, in her efforts to subjugate the stony-hearted parent of her little pupil; but whilst she was wasting her strength in vain struggles to attain unto the impossible, she felled, bound, and captured a youth whom Colonel Treherne had brought with him on one of his visits to Scudamore Chace.

This susceptible young officer's name was Raymond Talbot, and his degree that of a cornet in Colonel Treherne's regiment. His years were few; in fact, he had only reached his eighteenth summer. He was very big and clumsy, whilst there are no words in the English language strong enough to express his shy awkwardness.

I am aware that it is hardly fair to introduce my hero in this embryo stage of his existence, when as yet his moustache was not, nor had he won for himself golden spurs on battle-field or in lady's drawing-room; but what can I do? It would come to the same thing in the end, for a hero's past has always to be rapidly sketched, and I prefer dealing with the present.

Miss Edmonds was half bored and half flattered by her lover's attentions. Like all really shy people, he fluctuated between the extremes of bashfulness and familiarity, but at whichever stage he had arrived

he was equally tiresome to her. Sometimes he behaved to the queen of his heart as if she were a rough
schoolboy, and as such to be challenged to feats of
strength and speed; and at others he stared (perhaps
at her wonderful colouring) and sighed until Colonel
Treherne could have kicked him.

"I cannot think what has come to that young ape,"
observed his commanding officer to Sir Ralph one day
after a particularly trying dinner; "he used to be such a
nice lad, so fond of his profession and with no nonsense
about him, and now he's making a perfect fool of
himself with a woman old enough to be his mother."

"Grandmother," put in Sir Ralph, with a malice
born of aching ears and over-taxed politeness.

"His father, poor Dick Talbot," continued Colonel
Treherne, "was one of the nicest fellows that ever
lived; he's left a whole lot of youngsters, and I
thought I would look after this one and keep him out
of mischief, and now he seems determined to make
me lose my temper with him before we leave."

"What a pity he does not make up to Monica if
he must be a fool," said Sir Ralph; "I like the boy
myself, and I could take my oath he has no real harm
about him; with all his uncouthness you can tell he is
a gentleman, and by and by he will be an uncommonly fine fellow, you'll see."

"I'm sure I hope you're right, sir," said the Colonel, pulling savagely at his pipe: "about his turning out well, I mean. He's the last person in the world I would choose for Monica, however; in fact, I don't see why she should be in a hurry to settle at all. She has everything in the world she can want here, and I'm all for her stopping with you as long as possible. When she's a little older and more up to those things——" here the Colonel gave a flourish with the poker, being in the act of mending the fire, which flourish was intended to include love and marriage, and all such youthful follies, "you'll see I'll take precious good care who I bring down here."

"I intend Monica to have what is called every advantage," replied Sir Ralph gravely; "she shall see plenty of people to choose from. I have no idea of bringing up the poor child to a future life of solitary misery and loneliness, nor am I going to make her waste the best years of her life in nursing a melancholy old man."

Colonel Treherne grunted, and would perhaps have continued to express his unambitious views for his little daughter, if he had not been exasperated to madness by the sight of poor Miss Edmonds, in a pink silk dress festooned with black lace, Spanish fashion, and with an attempt at a mantilla thrown gracefully over her head, strolling up and down the lawn. On one side clung Monica, gazing across her instructress at Master, or rather Mr. Talbot, and evidently listening intently to every word he was saying, whilst that gallant and gigantic youth stalked on the other side of his lady-love with an air of intense spooniness disposed over his whole person, even as seen from a little distance.

"Hang that boy! Why doesn't he stop with us and have his pipe and glass of grog like a man, instead of dangling after that old woman!" exclaimed poor worried Colonel Treherne.

If Miss Edmonds could but have heard him!

"Well, I'm not at all sure that the lad is not much better out in the open air this fine evening," replied Sir Ralph drily; "he knows that hard words break no bones, so let us hope that soft ones don't either. We'll ring for lights and tea in the drawing-room, and then they will all come in; it is rather late for Monica to be out."

CHAPTER II.

REVENGE IS SWEET.

POOR little Monica met with a great deal of snubbing in those days. Her father snubbed her, though unintentionally; but whenever Monica was alone with him, and felt called upon to make conversation, she would, instead of prattling whatever nonsense came into her head, as she did to her beloved uncle, cudgel her brains for five minutes in hopes of inducing them to furnish forth an original remark or a wise question. The result, as may be expected, was utter folly; and the little girl stood corrected or reproved so often during these dialogues that at last she took refuge in silence, and was talked at by both governess and father for being a sullen and huffy child.

But Monica was so unhappy at Raymond's treatment that she could not find room in her heart for

any resentment towards others.   Not that she resented the young gentleman's neglect or his rudeness
—she only grieved over it.   With scarcely any companions of her own age, the girl clung to Raymond
—who, in spite of his substantial stature, was but
a schoolboy at heart—and would fain have introduced him to her favourite haunts, and made him
free of all her little outdoor mysteries regarding
squirrels or magpies or even kingfishers' nests.

Had it not been for his infatuation about Miss
Alicia, Raymond Talbot might have proved a pleasanter associate for the forlorn child, but he certainly,
at this stage of their acquaintance, behaved very
unkindly to her.   Not only did he flatly refuse to
have anything to do with her, to take her out for
a ride or a row during the long summer days, but
when the little girl came down to dessert he would
take care to move his chair as far away from her as
possible, and never once was known to speak or
look at Monica, who sat next her old uncle, eating
strawberries and biscuits, dainties which seemed to
have suddenly lost all their flavour and sweetness,
and thinking, "Why, oh why, does he dislike me
so much?"

The real truth was that Raymond perceived by
some mysterious instinct that Monica had fallen head

over ears in love with him, and like many of his sex
he resented this encroachment on the order of things
which has existed since the days of Adam and Eve.
Men generally like to think that they take the initiative in such matters; though I daresay if the truth
were known, the object of their lordships' preference
has herself gently suggested the first idea of her
superiority, but of that they are of course profoundly
ignorant. Monica, poor child, had not yet studied
these little feminine wiles, or she would hardly have
shown so plainly her adoration of the gawky youth
who was a king and hero in her loving eyes.

To me there is something inexpressibly pathetic
in a child's vehement love-fancies. It always speaks
of a heart starved of its proper food, and craving
with a desperate hunger for what alone will satisfy
it. Whoever heard of a girl with plenty of brothers
and sisters at home, or school-girl friends and cousins,
with constant demands on her time and thoughts,
caring for the companionship of a rude, rough hobble-
dehoy—for, alas! those are the only terms in which
to describe Mr. Raymond Talbot as he appeared
to unprejudiced eyes at that time.

But poor lonely little Monica did care. Of course
she knew nothing whatever of the symptoms of her
malady, as they affect grown-up people; yet for all

that she was quite as blind as the beautiful Titania herself, and, had an opportunity presented, would have shown a devotion equal to Lady Rachel Russell's.

In the meantime all her pretty touching little efforts were repulsed by her hero, who muttered that he hated forward girls, and Monica had no one who could understand what she felt, to turn to for comfort under Raymond's harsh speeches.

Once when her heart was very full and sore, she laid her head upon Sir Ralph's knee, and sobbed forth an incoherent detail of her grievances; but alas! it was no consolation whatever to be patted on the head and told "Never to mind, Raymond has a very bad taste, my pretty; Uncle Ralph thinks Monica very nice, and so does papa." Now, unfortunately, the child knew perfectly well that her father considered her a somewhat blowzy country girl, and she felt that he was always drawing unfavourable contrasts between her and his fair dead wife, so she refused to be comforted.

That very evening Monica appeared at dinner in a pair of mittens belonging to a former mistress of her old nurse, and carefully hoarded by that worthy as a treasure of fashion and beauty. These talismans were at least thirty years old, and were awful in their gaudy hideousness. They reached half-way up to Monica's elbows, and hung in wrinkles about her shapely hands. Embroidered on them, in gay unfaded silks, were bouquets of roses and forget-me-nots, and, literally armed with these decorations as weapons of conquest, Monica came, more cheerfully than usual, down to dessert.

The effect of this early appeal to the mystic influence which most women believe lies hidden in finery, was enough to disgust her for life with aught but sober greys and browns. Colonel Treherne actually shuddered, and groaned aloud. Kind Uncle Ralph concealed his smile by kissing the top of his pet's head, as she took her place beside him, and he murmured, "What have we here? how smart the little woman is to-day!" Whilst Raymond, the obdurate, gave a glance of the deepest disgust at the unfortunate mittens, and, turning to Miss Edmonds, said in a deep solemn voice, "If there is one thing on the face of the earth more odious than another, it is a little girl who dresses herself up."

This was too much for Monica. She snatched off her cherished decorations, thrust them into her pocket, whilst, with crimson cheeks and flashing eyes, she said, "It is more odious to be rude, I am quite sure; and you are very rude, sir, now and always."

If Monica could have kept this up there is no doubt that Raymond would soon have relented, but alas for the inconsistency of women, especially when in love, her righteous wrath vanished as she spoke, already she repented of her severity, and, flinging herself into her uncle's arms, sobbed forth bitter complaints regarding Raymond's treatment of her. The moment, however, Sir Ralph said to the young gentleman, "I really think, my boy, you might be a little more kind and patient to Monica; she's not used to harsh words or looks, and I don't see why you need teach her that there are such things in the world," that instant the damsel dried her eyes, and, transferring her reproaches to Uncle Ralph, declared that Raymond was perfectly civil and kind to her, and that she knew she was often very tiresome.

Poor little Monica! The love sorrows of so youthful a heroine are apt to be tedious, so your faithful friend and biographer will inflict them no more on your possible future acquaintances, but will pass quickly over these early days and present you again to them.

Monica "is not seventeen, but she is tall and stately."

She is in full court dress, and is making a profound curtsey, first to a long looking-glass between the windows of a London drawing-room, and next to Sir Ralph Scudamore, who stood by criticising her toilette in all its details with an anxious eye, lest any one should detect flaw or fault in the appointments of his cherished grand-niece.

I was there, too, that day as an old friend of the family, and Sir Ralph appealed to me for an unprejudiced opinion. It was very difficult to know what to say. Milliner and florist had done their work well, and produced a costume simple as any worn by Arcadian shepherdess to uninitiated eyes, but, financially speaking, it might as well have been made of cloth of gold. Monica was standing before me perfectly dressed, in high health and spirits, and yet she did not look nearly so handsome in all her bravery as she used to do in her out-grown frocks down at Scudamore Chace, or scampering on pony-back over the wild country around that place in an old grey linsey habit and a sailor hat. The fact is her beauty was of the true royal kind, grander when seen under apparent disadvantages. She looked so much older than her seventeen years, and her skin was of that creamy white which is sure to take a yellowish tinge under a flood of spring sunshine.

I felt that I liked her much better in her every-day home beauty, but still it was not difficult to praise her as she stood before us, looking so simply anxious for our approval. Miss Edmonds was unable to resist the opportunity of saying spiteful things, for every young and beautiful woman was regarded by that spinster as her sworn foe, to be vanquished wherever encountered.

"Dear me, Monica, how yellow you look," she observed. "What a pity you should be obliged to wear white! At all events I should have covered myself up a great deal if I had been you."

Now Miss Edmonds never did cover up her lean brown neck and arms from the public gaze. We all wished she would, but nothing could induce her to do so. Not long before Monica's presentation I had met Miss Edmonds at a party attired in a glistening white satin dress extremely *décolletée :* the decorations of this sheeny garment were knots of bright blue velvet, so it surprised me to observe what I thought was a band of *brown* velvet around her throat, and on this band rested a string of large mock pearls. As the evening wore on, I perceived that the dark-coloured velvet grew wider and wider. At last my curiosity overcame my discretion, and I ventured nearer to see— oh, shades of vanished youth and beauty!—the pearls had originally been clasped around a neck of artificial but snowy whiteness, through which they had rubbed this band of the natural, underlying material for themselves.

Yet this was the critic who found fault with Monica for showing a neck and arms, not dazzlingly white indeed, but soft and dimply with all the beauty of a seventeen-year-old girl.

"Is everything as it should be?" asked Sir Ralph, disregarding Miss Edmonds' candid remarks, and turning anxiously to me.

I affected an air of judicial impartiality, the gravity of which was much impaired by Monica's making little faces at me all the time I surveyed her; and at last I declared that, to the best of my judgment and belief, she was perfectly arrayed.

So Monica went off with a light heart to her first Drawing Room, and returned enraptured with the grace and beauty of the lovely Danish lady who was just then smiling her way into the hearts of men, women, and children. She had not been long among us—only a few months, in fact—and this was her first Drawing Room, as well as Monica's.

"Nearly every one was in white," declared Monica, "and we all looked like brides. As for the Princess, there is no one so charming. Oh, how I do hope she will be happy amongst us all, away from her own people! Don't you, Uncle Ralph?"

"I do indeed, my dear, with all my heart. It was only yesterday I thought of her as I was listening to my favourite old glee, and heard you all sing in the chorus—

> " Never harm, nor spell nor charm,
> Come our lovely lady nigh."

Monica shrugged up her little shoulders at such old-fashioned gallantry, and said, "Oh, I'm not at all afraid of spells or charms hurting her, but I hope she will be able to perceive how much we all love her, and be comforted for leaving her own land."

"Don't be enthusiastic, Monica," remarked Miss Edmonds; "I have always told you it was ridiculous. Nobody is enthusiastic now-a-days. The Princess is all very well, and she is a sort of fashion at this moment, but still you need not rave about her. For my part I don't like the way her hair is dressed;" and Miss Edmonds instinctively put up her hand to smooth her own tresses; "you are never happy, Monica, I observe, unless you have somebody to rave of. Do you remember what a fuss you used to make about that Mr. Talbot, and he never cared a bit for *you* after all?"

This was said with a little conscious simper, 'which made me long to box Miss Alicia's ears.

"Mr. Talbot was at the Drawing Room to-day, but I did not speak to him," replied Monica sweetly and gently, possessing her soul in patience; "but now I will go and take off my smart things and come down to tea. You will stay, won't you?" she continued, turning to me. "Pray do: I feel just as I used when I had been to a pantomime in the daytime long ago; it was all very brilliant and delightful, but still it utterly upsets and demoralizes one, and I shall be good for nothing but gossip during the remainder of the day. Uncle Ralph, you must take me for a long ride to-morrow, and then I shall be quite right again."

Uncle Ralph's eager assent was so completely a matter of course that the young lady did not even wait for it, but departed to return in half an hour, "clothed and in her right mind;" at least she entered the room very sedately, and said to me, "Shall I send a message that I am tired, and Uncle Ralph is out, or shall we let him in and give him some tea?" I looked bewildered, I suppose, for Monica laughed, and held out to me daintily between her finger and thumb, a card with Mr. Raymond Talbot's name, regiment, and present address inscribed upon it.

Before I could answer, Miss Edmonds called out with great eagerness, "Let him in, of course, Monica. Why not? You are always so selfish. Poor man, he would be so dreadfully disappointed;" and Miss Edmonds took up a position near the door where she could bestow a first and most friendly greeting on the gentleman who now entered.

Monica had entrenched herself behind her tea-cups, and stretched forth a hand to be taken and bowed over with an old-fashioned and courtly grace which sat well on so youthful a gallant as Mr. Talbot.

He had improved immensely; not alone with the improvement of manner which comes from living in good society, but with a deeper progress born of travel and adventure and a life of self-reliance, for Colonel Treherne, in despair at the boy's long-continued phase of cubbishness, had sent him out to India in a cavalry regiment. There he had seen a little service, and had even shared in a short, brilliant campaign—one of our little wars of which we must only hope some one is keeping a chronicle; for unless their history be written, Mr. Raymond Talbot's excellent services will be forgotten by the time he is a middle-aged man.

Colonel Treherne did not intend to banish his young friend for ever and aye; so, as soon as he

judged from the tone of his own letters and those
of the captain of his troop that he had learned
wherein true manliness consisted, he availed himself of the first opening to purchase him his step in
one of the Household regiments. Mr. Talbot had
worn, therefore, his cuirass and tall boots for the first
time to-day.

Miss Edmonds attempted, as usual, to monopolize
the attention of the young soldier; she shrieked a
string of questions at him, and would not allow
Monica to say a word, but that damsel appeared
well pleased at being ignored; she promptly availed
herself of some inquiry of mine to rise from her
sofa and show me the flower or book in question,
and actually left Mr. Talbot ruefully gazing after
her, and trying to respond to one of Miss Alicia's
numerous and tender restrospections.

I am a very bad story-teller if I give you the impression of any awkwardness on Monica's part. She
was perfectly graceful and self-possessed, but she
showed Mr. Talbot plainly that she considered his
visit as paid to Miss Edmonds rather than to herself, and that therefore it was more in kindness than
in discourtesy she withdrew both herself and me into
the next room for a short time.

When we returned, it was easy to see we were

welcome. Miss Edmonds was still vociferous, but cross, and was in the act of giving her former lover a graphic sketch of what a failure she considered Monica's first grand toilette had been that day. She was not in the least discomposed by the young lady's entrance, for, to do her justice, her remarks were quite as candid before people's faces as behind their backs, so she continued to dwell on Monica's shortcomings.

Mr. Talbot, however, seemed in an agony; he looked appealingly at me, and regarded his former love with deep disgust; at last, as if to stop the unflattering turn of the conversation, he said—

"I saw Miss Treherne at the Drawing Room to-day, but I did not recognize my old acquaintance at first. The Colonel pointed you out to me, and then I remembered you directly. At all events, Miss Treherne, your father was satisfied and pleased with your *début*: I am sure you will not think me impertinent for saying as much."

"No, indeed," said Monica, simply; "I am very glad to hear that papa liked my dress. I saw him too for a moment, but Lady Brentwode had a bad headache and wanted to come away early, so I had not time to speak to him."

Raymond looked much cheered at these words, and brightened perceptibly. Poor fellow, he thought for

a brief moment that it had not been then the intention of Miss Treherne to ignore so completely as she
had done their former relations.   His satisfaction
was but of short duration, for Monica continued with
great calmness and decision—

"I noticed papa talking to you, Mr. Talbot, and I
knew you at once, but I did not suppose you would
care about resuming your acquaintance with Uncle
Ralph and me, so I left you alone."

Monica said these somewhat uncivil words without
the slightest dash or sparkle of coquetry to soften
their severity, and the consequence was that Mr.
Talbot felt directly that his youthful want of taste
was going to be visited upon his head, and he
immediately gave himself up to the direst apprehen-
sions of possible vengeance.   However he was
sufficiently master of himself, in spite of the way his
heart thumped against his cuirass, to reply—

"I am sorry you believe I could be so ungrateful,
Miss Treherne.   Sir Ralph was always tremendously
good to me, and I am not likely to forget the Chace.
Why, I used often to think of it when I was in India ;
and you would not speak so cuttingly about not
resuming our acquaintanceship if you knew how
anxious I am that Sir Ralph would only give me the
chance some day of running down there again."   '

Miss Alicia took this entirely to herself, and simpered sweetly, and answered with enthusiasm—

"Oh, I'm quite sure Sir Ralph will be delighted to see you some time this autumn. How nice it will be to take our long walks together again;" said the lady, appealing to her former attendant upon those expeditions, but alas! he could not feign rapture at the prospect of future rambles with one, whilst his whole soul was fixed on obtaining a kind word in the present from another.

Monica considered evidently that Miss Edmonds had done all which hospitality demanded, and nothing more was said on the subject of past or future visits to Scudamore Chace. Mr. Talbot was still young enough for his face to have an inconvenient tell-tale way of expressing his emotions, and as he left the room he gave Monica a pathetic, imploring look, a look which plainly said, "Be merciful to me;" but Monica's calm countenance did not relax, and I rather agreed with Miss Alicia, who had observed the look, and remarked with asperity—

"Upon my word, Monica, you seem to me to be giving yourself all the airs and graces of a grown-up young lady rather soon; you have been downright rude to that poor young man, just because he does not admire *you*, and ever since you were presented two or three hours ago you have been behaving as if you were thirty years old, instead of a girl who ought still to be in her school-room. I told Sir Ralph I didn't think you would do any good with your masters when once you were out, but he had some absurd fancy about your going to this first Drawing Room of the Princess. Such nonsense! as if it would not have been much better to wait another year."

Miss Edmonds' speeches always seem long when written down, but she delivered them with such rapidity that even this one appeared to be the briefest remark.

Monica only said gently, " I hope I was not rude; Uncle Ralph would not like that." And we all separated.

CHAPTER III.

HE THAT WILL NOT WHEN HE MAY,—

IF there was only a little more common sense in the world, it is quite certain that both our money difficulties and our love troubles would be greatly diminished; but the supply of novels would fall off immensely, for once you admit the existence of an element of common sense into your story, adieu to dramatic situations and heartrending episodes!

However, in these instances, the follies which are here chronicled are not of my invention, for all my silly young people actually lived and loved, quarrelled and made friends.

If I were capable of inventing anything I should certainly invent Common Sense, but as I cannot do even that, I must content myself with a slight sketch of the troubles and tears which Miss Treherne insisted upon bringing into her own life and the lives of others, by a persistent course in what may be briefly described as *contrariness*.

When Sir Ralph consulted her about asking Mr. Talbot down to the Chace that autumn, she carefully concealed from him her anxiety that the invitation should be given and accepted, and the kind old uncle thought to himself, "She is quite cured of childish fancy, and although *I* like this young man better than any one I have seen, still if he does not care for my darling it never would do to give her the vexation of renewing the old difficulties." So he said one day after dinner to Colonel Treherne, when they were settling their plans for the autumn, "I think I shall get you to bring Raymond Talbot down with you on the 12th. I have half promised that he shall have a look at the old place again, and he seemed to like the idea."

Colonel Treherne did not like the idea at all, though he was very fond of his handsome subaltern; but he was too thoroughly a gentleman to consider that any degree of relationship or intimacy gave him a right to dictate to Sir Ralph who was to be asked to his house, so he concealed his disapproval of the proposed invitation, and merely said—

"I've no doubt he would be delighted, sir, but you must not let him be any plague to you on my account; he has got lots of friends now, and ought to be able to get along well by himself. It is not as in the old days, when I did not like to let him out of my sight, and used to bring him down to the Chace to keep him out of mischief."

Sir Ralph chuckled at some recollections which presented themselves at these words, and said—

" I don't know about the mischief. What a row he made when I told him I thought he was behaving like a fool about Miss Edmonds! Upon my word I could have a good laugh now, when I recollect how cut up he was after you had pointed out to him that she was older than his mother. Do you remember what a help it was to us, her happening to catch a cold in her head? I think I see Raymond's face now, when he came down from a visit to her dressing-room one morning. She did not wish him to come up, I must say—it was he who insisted ; but, oh dear, how woebegone and disenchanted he looked ; and Monica made it worse by asking him with great sympathy if he thought he had caught Miss Alicia's influenza. Good gracious, I wonder if we were all such fools when we were boys ?"

Now Colonel Treherne remembered all these scenes perfectly well, and he winced, for there was a strong suspicion growing on him that they would

be enacted all over again shortly, but with a different lady-love, who would not change as if touched
by a wicked fairy's wand into a wrinkled old hag,
if even she caught a cold, nor could any superiority
of age be urged against her; so that there seemed
every probability of his *protégé's* second attack at
the Chace being worse and more hopeless than the
first. But still he did not see his way towards
preventing it by stopping the invitation, and said
therefore—

"Of course, Sir Ralph, you must do just as you
please, but I don't know why you should bore yourself by having Talbot for the grouse."

"It isn't merely for the grouse I would have him,
Treherne; it's for Monica. You may well look surprised at my turning out an old match-maker, but
I confess I should like that to come off some day,
and Monica is all right now, I'm quite sure; there is
no fear of her giving her heart away for nothing
in return this time. It's rather the other way, I
fancy."

"I can't imagine why Monica should marry at all,"
replied her father, "at all events not for ages. What
do girls get by taking all the cares of housekeeping
and bothers upon themselves when they ought to
think of nothing but nonsense? Why, half of them

die, like poor darling Edmée. She would probably
have lived long enough if I had not been a selfish
beast;" and the Colonel stretched out his hand for
the old Madeira, more to conceal his emotion than
for any flavour he expected the wine to have.

"Edmée was very happy," Sir Ralph said gravely;
"if Monica is as fortunate in being as much beloved
as her mother I shall be satisfied, and so would she,
even if she had to pay the same price for it;" and
the two lonely, bereaved old men, with the one strong
sympathy between them, the memory each of a
youthful bride fading away when all else on earth
was blossoming into beauty, gazed mournfully into
the fireless grate, for Monica declared that even a
wood fire in London made an early August evening
stuffy.

"It's so nice to talk by," poor Sir Ralph had
vainly pleaded, and certainly the unsympathetic look
of the fireplace soon stopped the conversation given
above, and the gentlemen returned to the drawing-
room, and to Monica's singing and flowers, and girlish,
bright surroundings.

In a day or two after this, the whole household
moved itself back to Scudamore Chace, and it is hard
to say which enjoyed themselves most, Sir Ralph or
his grand-niece. Unlike the young lady described

by Mr. Pope, she was delighted to get back to her country home, her big dogs, her rides and walks with her uncle.

The only one of the party who may be said to feel as did poor, bored Zephalinda, was Miss Edmonds; but even she found solace in unpacking and arranging her clothes. It is hard to understand how fine dresses and velvet mantles and fashionable bonnets could have been such a comfort to her when she knew that their style and splendour would be wasted upon both Sir Ralph and Colonel Treherne, but so it was. She regarded her clothes with a sort of respect as well as the deepest admiration ; and, inconsistent as it may seem, she was at once the most talented and the most utterly frivolous person possible.

An accomplished musician, a charming artist, well read, of highly cultivated literary taste, she yet preferred spreading her numerous garments out in a room (if any apartment could be found large enough to hold them all), and contemplating their various beauties, to any other amusement under the sun, except perhaps an interview with her dressmaker. I only dwell upon this because it was so strange ; in a fool it would have been natural, but in such a clever, accomplished woman it was a perpetual puzzle to me.

K

Monica's attention was, however, distracted from Miss Edmonds' wardrobe by little anxieties of her own. She wished much to find out whether Mr. Talbot had been invited for the grouse shooting which was to begin the next week. First she determined to try and elicit the required information from her former *gouvernante*, who remained with her as a sort of *dame de compagnie*, so she betook herself to Miss Edmonds' apartments.

Things were rather reversed at Scudamore Chace; the heiress of all its lands slept in a low-ceiled, draughty, and somewhat uncomfortable room, which had been a sort of supplementary playroom for her on a wet day. To Monica's eyes it possessed the charm of having a staircase of its very own, opening on the terrace, so that she could be out as early as she pleased, for this young person was a very gipsy in her love of freedom and open air; indeed she has been known to reply to strictures on this favourite room that she preferred it "because it was so like out of doors," and it certainly was a temple of the winds. Latterly, the young lady had been prevailed upon to allow screens and heavy curtains to be placed so as to break the violence of the gales which swept through her apartment. Its furniture was simple to plainness, and the few tokens

of youthful taste had chiefly belonged to her poor
dead girl-mother, and were therefore somewhat faded
and old-fashioned. Miss Treherne herself had con-
tributed several foxes' heads and brushes to the adorn-
ment of her walls, and Miss Edmonds had made
a life-sized sketch of her favourite dog's head
for her. There was a portrait in oils of Sir Ralph
with a splendid Russian wolf-hound by his side
over her chimney-piece, and that was the most
valuable object in the room.

Miss Edmonds had also selected her own apartments for herself, and, not being guided therein by
any other consideration than that of ample space
for the bestowal of the objects nearest her heart, she
had preferred rooms at the back of the house with
no view to speak of, but with a whole corridor of
wardrobes outside them. In her dressing-room the
light was good for her looking-glass, that was all
she demanded of Fate. The rooms were luxu-
riously fitted up with sofas and arm-chairs, but
each article of furniture was covered with a gay
silken skirt or a precious filmy garment; so that
when Monica appeared on the threshold she was
forced to remain standing there, so as to be out of
the way of these draperies. Miss Alicia was
anxiously examining an exquisite blue satin tunic

and she turned to her startled visitor, saying vehemently—

"I *hate* that odious Raymond Talbot. Look what he has done to my lovely gown! Awkward booby! why did they not keep him out in Burmah, or wherever he has come from? I am sure he is not fit to mix in society. It was half your fault too, Monica; you spoke suddenly to your father just behind me at supper the other night, and this is the consequence. That great idiot, young Talbot, jumped like a nervous housemaid, and spilt all his claret-cup down my skirt. Oh, how I hate him!" and the afflicted lady burst into tears.

As I said before, Monica had come into Miss Edmonds' room, or rather as far as her threshold, on purpose to see if she could find out whether this very delinquent were invited to the Chace or not. She had sought diligently in her own mind for various excuses to mention his name, and, behold, here was the subject ready prepared. She did not mind hearing him abused by Miss Edmonds, for was it not an opening for defending him?

"What a pity," said Miss Treherne, cautiously stepping between a lace burnouse and a velvet train; "he must have been so sorry to see the mischief he had done."

"I don't think he minded one bit," snapped the injured lady ; " he mumbled something about hoping he had not hurt it, and then began bothering about our going to that flower-show next day. I remember it so well, because I thought how heartless he had grown. He has never been the same person since he came back from that place. I never saw any one so changed, so dis-improved. I will have nothing more to say to him, great awkward booby!" and Miss Alicia rubbed the injured satin tenderly with some stuff out of a little bottle.

"It ought to be a lesson to us all to be very careful what we wear when he is here," said Monica with great gravity.

"Yes, indeed; I shall make it a point to find out beforehand if he should be coming, and we'll put on our oldest and ugliest dresses, Monica, and I will tell him why. *That* ought to make him ashamed of himself, I should think."

Miss Edmonds lost no time in inquiring of Sir Ralph that very day whether this destroyer of blue satin tunics was to be permitted to have future opportunities of perpetrating his ruthless ravages. She did not only ask the question, but she aired her grievance in such strong and expressive language that Sir Ralph was perfectly deafened, and felt half afraid of confessing that the monster in question was actually coming to Scudamore Chace in a few days, and he said deprecatingly—

"You see, I asked the poor fellow before I knew of this dreadful crime. Never mind, Miss Edmonds; it was a great shame, I declare, but young men are so thoughtless, and he'll be very sorry some day, I have no doubt. But in the meantime, as it certainly was partly Monica's fault, you will oblige me by ordering from her dressmaker another—another—thing, just like the one they have managed to spoil between them."

Miss Alicia's eyes sparkled and her face reddened with pleasure beneath its company complexion, at the idea of her beloved garment coming back to her in all its original beauty, and she forgave Mr. Raymond Talbot on the spot.

Monica also blushed and smiled a little shy smile, but it was with pleasure at hearing herself joined with the delinquent in that word "they," and she blessed Miss Edmonds' gowns, especially the blue satin tunic, for having been the cause of the momentary alliance. When she descended to earth again after her flight into the airy heaven opened to her by hearing her uncle not only say Raymond was soon coming, but speak of him and her as "them," Miss Edmonds was saying gaily—

"And you know I have an old black silk which I shall wear every day when he is here, Sir Ralph, but Monica had better look out her brown holland pinafores to wear over her good gowns—don't you think so, dear?" she graciously inquired of the girl.

Sir Ralph's quiet, mournful eyes, for all their want of practice in observing young maidens' glances, had noticed Monica's bright blush and smile, and he said fondly—

"No—no; my little woman" (Monica was very tall, as it happened) "must wear nice dresses every day, just as she always does. I can't have her shabby or dowdy for all the awkward young Guardsmen in the brigade."

"Dear me, Sir Ralph, I am sure they are not all awkward, and even Mr. Talbot may improve," said Miss Alicia, who was now in perfect charity with all men; "and I was only in fun about the pinafores, for I don't think Monica has worn any since Mr. Talbot was here last, and he used not to notice then how she dressed, I fancy."

"I dare say he won't know any better now," said the young lady in question—though she knew perfectly well she was telling a fib—as she rose from the table and stepped out on the terrace, feeling herself unequal to carry out her assumed calmness before her old uncle's eyes.

If ever there should be a committee appointed by the House of Commons to inquire into and put down young people's falling in love with each other, because all the colonies are over-populated, and if it came to pass that I, as one of the oldest inhabitants of this planet, should be examined before that committee as to what constituted the first and most infallible sign or symptom of the disorder known under the name of love, I should unhesitatingly answer " Deceit."

The moment young people—or even middle-aged ones, who ought to know better—begin to care about each other, that very moment they give their minds to concealing the fact from their friends as well as their enemies. The trouble they take to do this is extraordinary, but generally thrown away; which fact, again, may be accounted for by the spectators retaining some faint memories of their own wiles and falsehoods.

Statistics will prove that I am right, and that lovers, no matter in how early a stage of their passion, invariably insist on covering Cupid up, as it were, with a heap of leaves, so that no one may suspect his existence. But though they work quite as hard as did the villains of our nursery tragedy, they are always found out ; for it is not an inanimate little corpse they have to conceal, but a rosy mischievous boy, who betrays his hiding-place, and constantly requires a fresh lie-leaf or subterfuge to hide .his smiling face.

So it was with Monica. She had never, no, not for one moment, ceased to love her first boy-friend. She had felt, with an instinct above all knowledge, that he would come back to her some day and love her even as she loved him. She could give no reason for this belief : one cannot always do so about other creeds ; but she could have answered as simply as the typical Eastern maiden in the great Song of Songs, "I am my beloved's, and he is mine."

On every other subject she was frankness itself to the loyal old man who had been both mother and father to her ; but never since the day of the mittens, five years before, had she mentioned the name which was always in her thoughts and prayers, which came floating before her eyes as she gazed on a beautiful view, or made music itself more melodious to her ears.

If any one had told her she was deceiving Uncle Ralph they would have encountered a passionate denial of their words, but that would not have made the statement less true.

Of any one else, man or woman, old or young, Miss Monica was most free in expressing her opinion; but when Uncle Ralph ventured to inquire whether she did not think Raymond Talbot a fine fellow, she had replied, with as little truth as elegance of expression—

"Not particularly."

Uncle Ralph, however, was merciful; he too had been young, so he only said softly to himself, "I should not have asked her."

CHAPTER IV.

WHEN HE WILL, SHALL HAVE NAY.

So Raymond Talbot came back to the old scenes and the old faces, but in spite of the gay French *chanson* he did not return to his old love. Truth to tell, that lady no longer desired his attentions, when she discovered that they might possibly endanger the safety of her beloved dresses ; so he was free to haunt Monica's footsteps, and to gaze on her face when she was singing, and to do all those absurd, idiotic things which we think so wise and so delightful when they happen to ourselves, but which on-lookers find so utterly uninteresting and stupid. The old, old comedy has only charms for the actors therein, it bores the audience to death ; therefore I will be wise in time, and spare Monica's pen-and-ink friends a precise account of those happy, silly, autumn days. Enough of summer lingered in the morning air to allow of outdoor rambles, and just the first chills of winter made the evening fireside idyllic in. its snug warmth and sociable chat.

Sir Ralph Scudamore thoroughly liked and trusted Raymond Talbot, and he was willing to give him his grand-niece to wife. The old and the young man had many and many an anxious talk on the subject. I know it is against all the laws of romance to proclaim it, but the fact is that the young lady had no confidante, nor did she ever mention to living ears the secret of her heart, whilst the unhappy lover talked of nothing else to Sir Ralph. The burden of his tale was always the same, " I cannot tell whether she likes me ;" and, easy as it may seem in theory, it is very difficult in practice to ascertain this point if the damsel be determined to conceal it.

Far be it from me to say *why* Monica would not give look or word upon which the most sanguine of his sex could build the faintest hope. I only deal with facts, and am obliged to give her mood as I saw it ;—saw it with surprise, not unmixed with anger, for in spite of strict watch and ward Monica had traitors in her camp. School her face as she might, her colour would come and go, her eyes would flash with joy before the long, dark lashes remembered to mount guard over them. From a thousand little signs I, remembering the days of my youth, felt sure that she loved the man to whom she would not vouchsafe smile or glance beyond what strict courtesy demanded. Though they were constantly together, Monica took care they should never be alone; and at last poor, much-tired Raymond was driven to confess to Sir Ralph that despair was rapidly taking possession of his mind.

"Have you never tried to find out in any way whether the child cares for you at all?" demanded Sir Ralph at one of the many consultations.

"She won't let me, sir. I did once whisper, 'Monica, I'm so fond of you,' but I think she did not hear, for she never said a word."

"Well, it was rather a difficult speech to answer," said Sir Ralph, laughing; "for, you see, it was not exactly a question, it was more of a statement, wasn't it?"

"Perhaps so," answered the rueful suitor, "but it is always the same; she is perfectly nice and kind to me, but she won't let a fellow say a word about anything else."

"Dear me," said Sir Ralph mischievously, "I don't know much about these sort of things, but I should have thought it would have been so easy to get upon the topic of when you were here long ago, and then you could naturally say such nice things about always having cared for her, even in those days."

"Oh, no ! Sir Ralph, I couldn't indeed, for that is just what has done all the mischief, my having been such a blind dolt and idiot at that time. Don't you remember how I used to snub the poor child if she came near me ? Ah, she was fond enough of me then ! What would I not give for her to come and put her dear little brown hand into mine now, and look up in my face with those wonderful eyes of hers, and beg me to take her out for a walk ! "

"Well, it would not be quite the thing at present, I am afraid ; besides, she probably thinks she might meet with the same repulse ; that is to say, if you did repulse her—I forget ; " said Sir Ralph artfully, for he remembered perfectly having observed Monica's ill-placed affection in those old days.

"Repulsed her ! of course I did, brute that I was," answered Raymond, kicking the logs of wood on the hearth with his boot-heels. " I only wish you or the Colonel had knocked me down every time I spoke crossly to the sweet little angel. How could you let me behave in that

way to her? I don't wonder she hates the very
sight of me."

Sir Ralph laughed softly to himself at the recollection of Monica's lovely shy happy face that morning, when they were together in the sun in front of
the house for a few minutes alone. It would not
do for him to say too much; all this suspense and
misery were rather good for his young friend, he
thought; it would be certain to come right in the
end. Besides, I am not at all sure that he did not
on the whole enjoy the idea of Monica's revenging
herself on her former tyrant. He remembered the
girl's thoughtful face that morning as they stood
looking out from the wide expanse of moor to the
purple hills stretching away on the horizon, and he
felt, with that knowledge born of past experience
and present love, that it was not hatred which had
brought that deep look in her eyes, which had curved
those soft smiling lines around her sensitive, mobile
mouth. So he hardened his heart, and shook his
head as he answered—

"Yes, you certainly were very unkind to that
poor child at that time; she was so fond of you
too, fonder than she has ever been of any one,
except me."

Raymond started up, all hope and joy again.

He seized Sir Ralph's hand and shook it rapturously.

"Thank you, sir, you've done me a world of good. I do *not* think she cares for any one else, that is my only comfort."

And the scales of his heart, which had been weighed down to the ground by despair and accusing memories, flew up to the ceiling with only airy hopes and dreamy wishes to balance them. Poor Sir Ralph had learned by this time how delicate is the lover's equipoise, how slight a word or a thought suffices to disturb it, so he took advantage of this reaction to break up the conference.

Monica, artful little puss, had heard her swain's awkward whisper; to her ears no words had ever been so sweet, but she must have agreed with Sir Ralph that the sentence was rather an unanswerable one, for she made as though she heard it not. Every day added to the difficulty of the position; she had kept silence so long that it became hard to speak, and yet the time was flying fast. It seemed to go still more rapidly after Raymond, having duly consulted Sir Ralph, announced that he and "some other fellows" were going to shoot lions in South Africa. He had come to this resolution in one of his fits of despair at Monica's wilful misunderstanding, and Sir Ralph honestly thought it best for all parties to carry out the scheme.

"My darling is so young," mused the old man tenderly, "and it would be so dreadful for her to make any mistake about her own feelings. Perhaps I have been wrong in thinking she cared about this boy; at all events he will only be a year away, and if they like each other we'll see about it when he returns."

During the last week of Mr. Talbot's visit, the tables were rather turned upon the young lady. Colonel Treherne came down to the Chace, and entered eagerly into Raymond's plans, talking incessantly of the delights of the expedition and of its details. He was great on the subject of guns, of explosive bullets, of all the weapons with which man arms himself when he is intent on invading solitary jungles or forests, and making war to the death against the defenceless dwellers therein.

The Colonel was not actuated solely by a sportsman's enthusiasm; he wished to detach his daughter from the young Guardsman, or perhaps one should say, strictly speaking, the young Guardsman from his daughter, though he was not as much deceived by Monica's wonderful and incomprehensible acting as were the others. He knew that he had forfeited all

right to a decision about her choice; he observed
with surprise the strong sympathy and friendship
which had always existed between his subaltern and
Sir Ralph, and he felt certain that the old man would
gladly consent to receive him as Monica's husband.
Colonel Treherne was more ambitious than Sir
Ralph, and particularly disliked the idea of an early
marriage for his daughter; he therefore hailed with
delight the idea of Mr. Talbot's setting forth to deal
death and destruction to inoffensive lions. At all
events here was a respite, and he would trust to
chance for further help in the matter.

Raymond was still young and full of the spirit of
adventure; besides, he grew rather tired of the hopeless attempt to induce his lady-love to acknowledge
that he was dear to her; one moment he would feel
sure that, in his own phraseology, it was "all right,"
but the next moment would see him calling himself
a conceited ape for fancying such a girl could care
two straws for him.

Of course, in obedience to the law of perversity
which governs our being, the more he turned to his
rifles for consolation, the more Monica came out
from behind her entrenchments of maiden pride and
stately shyness. But even as a rabbit rushes back
to its hole if you turn your head towards it, so

did this young person retreat rapidly behind her ramparts if Raymond looked at all happy. Perhaps it was really revenge, and not either shyness or pride which influenced her manner; for, as this is not a tale of fictional feelings, I may say here, once and for all, there is no manner of doubt but that Miss Treherne only loved Raymond Talbot now; loved him with all the strength of her warm, impulsive, devoted nature, and had never taken away the heart she gave him so entirely when she was still a mere child. The moment she saw him at the Drawing Room she felt that her reward had come, and that his heart flew to her feet. Had she possessed a mother to go to with her first great joy, Master Raymond would have been spared a good deal of suspense, and Miss Monica many a heartache. She had neither mother nor friend, however, to counsel less reserve; she remembered with needless agonies of remorse and shame her frank advances of former years, and determined to conceal from him as long as possible that she loved him every bit as much in the present as she had done in the past. Day by day she thought with secret delight that the trial was nearly over. Surely enough had been done now to avenge former slights; at last the garrison of the little beleaguered .

heart might march out with all the honours of war, and let the enemy enter

"Breathing and sounding beauteous battle."

Alas, and alas! whilst she was already preparing a treaty of peace, with very easy and delicious terms, the stupid, faint-hearted enemy raised the siege to all appearances, and seemed now only intent on beginning a fresh campaign, against lions.

Monica could not say a word; it was all her own fault, but what comfort was to be extracted from that reflection? She dared not go and complain to Sir Ralph, as in days of yore; besides, of what could she complain? When first the idea was broached before her about the South African expedition, she had perversely approved of it, though a sudden physical pain, a contraction of the heart, might have warned her not to tax her powers of dissimulation too far. Her father fell naturally into the way of talking of the affair as a settled thing; as if Africa were no further off than Ireland, and lions were as defenceless and easily-bagged game as land-agents.

So it came to pass that Raymond Talbot was to depart on a cold, grey day when all nature wore an air of desolation, which exactly accorded with

Monica's feelings. It was a good-bye for a year which they were saying under the portico of the Chace, with the dog-cart waiting and Colonel Treherne saying nervously—

"Now, look sharp, Talbot; you're running it very fine as it is.—Do you think she'll do it?" he asked anxiously of the groom, referring to Firefly, who stood champing her bit and wondering when these farewells would be over.

"Oh yes, sir," replied that worthy, with great want of tact, for the Colonel's look might have warned him to speed the parting guest; but Robert had been young himself, and even now did not like to be hurried, "if so be that he had a mind for more last words with pretty Susy up at the farm."

"Oh yes, sir, lots of time, she'd do it in the five-and-thirty minutes easy, and we've more nor that."

Thanks to Robert's sympathy with all true lovers, Raymond felt he had time for another good-bye. His heart utterly refused to accept Monica's impassive farewell, which ought to have satisfied her father's mind, but didn't, being a trifle overdone ; he turned back with his foot on the steps for one more look, if haply the dark eyes might be kinder than the voice or the little cold hand.

Oh desperation, no Monica was there! Colonel

Treherne had gone round to the other side of the trap, Sir Ralph stood on the threshold looking wistfully at his young boy-friend, who was leaving his sight perhaps for ever. Miss Edmonds remained rather in the shade, with a somewhat bored and absorbed expression of countenance; for was she not debating whether forget-me-nots or ivy-leaves should be brocaded on her next black Lyons silk? Past these individuals Raymond dashed like a lunatic: a happy inspiration made him look in at the library door. There was Monica, leaning her poor little head against the high, carved mantelpiece, and crying as if her heart were broken, which, indeed, it wellnigh seemed to be.

If ever it became necessary to argue about the advantage of action over thought, this moment might go far to prove it. Raymond dashed up to the sobbing girl, caught her in his arms, covered her streaming face with kisses, whilst he murmured, "Oh my darling, my darling, you do like me a little, then?"

Monica was so afraid of any uncertainty remaining in his mind on this point, that she managed to gasp out, "Yes I do, very much." This blunt avowal brought on such raptures and such frantic embraces, that she was already beginning to feel it was possible to have too much of a good thing, when Sir Ralph put his kind old head in at the still open door, and said gently—

"Time's up, my boy. Yes, I see, it's all right. Go now, there's a good fellow. Of course I'll take care of her." This last was in answer to Raymond's instantly assuming airs of proprietorship, and entreating Sir Ralph to be good to his newly-acquired treasure.

Raymond does not know to this day how he got into the dog-cart, nor did he notice his Colonel's glum face. Robert the groom perceived the situation at a glance; he did not permit himself to make a remark on wind or weather, or horseflesh in general, till the station was reached, and his fingers had closed upon Raymond's reckless tip, when he said, "Thank 'ee, sir, here's wishing you safe back for good. I'll take care of Miss Monicar, sir, out ridin' and such like; you may depend on me—good-bye, sir," by which the young officer perceived that Robert knew just as well what had happened as if that last unexpected and heavenly parting had taken place *en plein air*.

From Southampton the happy lover despatched enough correspondence addressed to the Chace to fill a Blue Book. There is no need to allude to Monica's share of the budget. Unfortunately I cannot invent, as Mr. Trollope would do, a love-letter so charming as

to drive to distraction all mortals who have to write
daily two sheets of twaddle to their absent beloveds.
I must therefore content myself by referring every one
to their own experience of similar epistles, and ask
them to imagine how incoherent, and rhapsodical, and
nonsensical, and generally delightful Monica found her
first letter from Raymond Talbot. Sir Ralph's might
almost have passed as a *billet-doux*, except for its
length. It was filled with expressions of the wildest
gratitude and the most devoted affection; but so
confused were the tenses and pronouns, that it became
hard to decide whether Sir Ralph or Monica was intended by such phrases as "the sweetest angel," "my
lovely flower," and similar nonsense. Colonel Treherne's letter had just a glimmering of reason and
common sense in it, though it also diverged into
ecstatic ravings towards the end. He was forced,
however, to keep his opinion on lovers in general, and
this lover in particular to himself, for Sir Ralph and
Monica together were too strong for him, and Miss
Edmonds treated the whole affair with supreme
contempt.

"Why, the man must be mad," she declared; "it
was but the other day he was frantically in love with
me, and wanting me to run away with him. He has
only made up to Monica because I have not taken

much notice of him lately. I daresay it is merely in a fit of pique that he has proposed to her. Ridiculous girl! she is much too young to marry any one. She has no idea of dressing herself, and she wears her hair in such an absurd manner, no one believes it is her own. She ought to cut half of it off."

"I only wish to heaven, Miss Edmonds, you had kept the fool of a boy tied to your apron-strings a little longer," said Colonel Treherne, "until Monica was well out of his way. She might have gone abroad with her uncle next year, and the whole thing would have died away."

"He is not a fool of a boy at all," replied Miss Alicia, affronted; "he used to have a great deal of sense, and he was tremendously in love with me, poor fellow. Certainly he has gone off a good deal lately, and he has taken, you know, to spoiling people's gowns. Did you ever hear what he did to my lovely blue satin tunic?" And the injured lady commenced a long story, from which Colonel Treherne escaped speedily.

In each of these letters, written on the point of departure, Mr. Talbot had detailed his movements and plans, declaring that he would give worlds to be "off" the whole thing, but that he was afraid of being tremendously "chaffed" if he gave up the excursion at so late an hour. It is needless to add that he vowed

and swore he would return to England the very
moment he could escape from his companions; and
the lengthy epistles ended with an entreaty to
Monica, and also to Sir Ralph, to write to him by
every mail.

I am sure there must be a Mr. Grundy somewhere,
and that he influences men just as his mythical wife
is supposed to keep us women in order.   What other
reason, save dread of ridicule from his brother officers,
or fear of his motives being suspected, could have prevented Raymond from turning back and returning to
Scudamore Chace?   One would have thought that
he was a convict, to judge by his deep depression at
leaving his native shores, and yet nothing but the
magic which lies in the idea of unknown opinions
held him to his purpose.

When he and I were talking of that voyage the
other day, I confided to him, with a frankness worthy
of Miss Alicia, that he seemed to me almost an idiot
to have left Monica for lion-hunting before anything
was settled, and just as he had made her confess her
real " sintimints."

" You very nearly lost her, sir," I concluded, " and
a jury of ladies would certainly have brought in a
verdict of ' served you right.' "

Raymond had learned enough of strategy to know

the importance of carrying the war into the enemy's country, so he replied—

"And pray, madam, do *you* never do anything you don't like, just for the same undefined reasons, because you seem pushed into it by unseen hands?"

"That is quite a different matter," I answered, "and not at all a case in point. Women often do those sort of things, partly because they are more amiable than men, and partly because it is less trouble to say yes than no; but that has nothing to do with your going away and leaving a beautiful girl before it was all settled," I concluded vaguely.

From which conversation it will be gathered that Raymond did go on his lion-hunting expedition leaving Monica "her lane," as the dear old Scotch song has it; but perhaps my readers will hardly believe me when I say that for nearly two long years no letter, no scrap of writing reached Scudamore Chace from Mr. Talbot. News was received from others of the party, in which he sometimes figured as an ardent sportsman but an odd moody man, and there was no word of his return.

Of course the whole thing was a stupid mistake, but it very nearly killed Monica Treherne all the same; so I may be excused for a degree of tartness in my subsequent conversations with the young Guardsman.

CHAPTER V.

ALL'S WELL THAT ENDS WELL.

SUSPENSE îs as trying to readers as it is supposed
to be to its unhappy victims, so we will have none
of it. Instead, therefore, of describing the growth of
Sir Ralph and Monica's gradual conviction of Mr.
Talbot's fickle unworthiness, we will skip the two years
which have intervened since that misjudged but
foolish youth drove away from the Chace with the
full intent of finding himself back there as soon as
might be.

That is one advantage which stories have over
the trials and troubles they narrate ; you can always
get over the disagreeable parts quickly, and linger
on the pleasant memories. Poor Monica would fain
have disposed of her days of anxiety, her sleepless
nights of conjecture, in this summary fashion; but
alas! it was not to be. Each week had to drag

itself drearily round from Sunday to Sunday, each month exacted its full measure of hours of miserable brooding. The moors were purple and golden again with their sunset splendours of the year for the second time since Raymond left, when both her father and her grand-uncle agreed that "something must be done."

Love never feels its utter helplessness until it tries its might against death, and it had come to this, that whilst Sir Ralph was holding his darling back to earth with passionate prayers, with all that wealth and skill could do to restore wasting health and strength, Monica seemed gradually fading away; dying, simply because she did not care to live.

Who can wonder at it? who can marvel that she should have so little spirit? More than two long years—well-nigh a thousand days—of utter silence, silence as deep as the grave on Raymond's part, had come and gone. And the reaction was so great. To his departure had succeeded a few weeks of intense bliss; she had been quite willing to let him go, had even rejoiced in the solitude of those first days of deep joy; then had come a time when it was a renewal of happiness to be able to talk about it to her sympathizing old friend and uncle. Next a happy flutter of expectation as the date arrived on which the mails were due, a transient shadow of disappointment as it passed without bringing her a letter, and then an arraying of facts and statistics, both geographical and arithmetical, to prove that it was quite impossible for Raymond to have written by that mail.

When the next packet came in, and the next, and still no letters reached Scudamore Chace, accident was held responsible for the delay. Monica gradually became pale and silent, but Sir Ralph's tact and delicacy prevented his watching her closely, so he could not, and Monica would not, answer when the great London doctor said, "And how long has this been going on?" "This" meant a short dry cough, loss of appetite, and a blooming country lass changed into a sickly, hollow-eyed, melancholy girl.

Oh how I wish heroines in fact could be as ill as they are in fiction without losing their beauty; but they cannot, alas! Monica was quite plain at this date, and Miss Edmonds perpetually pointed out the sad falling off to every one. She did not mean to be ill-natured, for, so far as her self-absorbed and unsympathetic nature allowed, she was kind to the girl; but she could not refrain from proclaiming her convictions that Mr. Talbot had never loved Monica, had only cared for her in fact, and that therefore Miss Treherne was little better than a fool for fretting herself to death about a boy who did not know whether you had on a black or a white gown.

"I would have more spirit if I were you, Monica," said Miss Edmonds with energy. "What is the use of losing your health and such good looks as you ever possessed, for the sake of a great gawky young man? Pray, did I lie awake and refuse my food because he chose to flirt with you after having really loved me? *I* knew he could never care for anybody else, so you've only yourself to blame."

"There must be some frightful mistake, my darling," was Sir Ralph's more consolatory argument. "What is the use of love, if you have not faith? They go together, my pet, in things human as well as in things divine. We shall know all about it some day, and then how Raymond will scold you for your want of trust."

"Ah, no, Uncle Ralph! he will have to forgive me for it; I shan't be here for him to scold," said Monica, with that sort of inexplicable attraction which the thought of death often has for the young and fair. It is the old and the wretched who seem to cling to life, in spite of their infirmities and troubles.

She dared not utter these speeches before her father, for his tardily awakened affection and anxiety took the form of crossness, and he would lecture her severely for her wicked carelessness of life, and end with such frantic abuse of Raymond as made Monica shudder.

But two years of this suspense, of these upbraidings, even of these consolations, was killing her—there was no doubt about that, so now uncle and father were taking counsel together if haply some way out of this labyrinth of misery might be found.

"The scoundrel is not dead, I know that," said the Colonel savagely; "I heard from Bertie Arbuthnot the other day, and he mentioned that Talbot was far and away the best shot of them all, and that he seemed to care for nothing else but hunting. I saw Greville's letter to Bertie, and after saying what I have told you, he goes on to speculate about the reason of Talbot's selling out and remaining in that wild country. He supposes that he must have quarrelled with his people, or got into a scrape or something of the sort, for he seemed to be only one degree less savage than the lions he hunted, and quite as disagreeable. I hope he's wretched," added the Colonel; "it's the only comfort I could have."

"Poor boy, I am sorry for him, in spite of all that's

come and gone; and yet how completely he has thrown his happiness away. At all events there appears to be no other woman in the case, that's a great point; what can there be so very fascinating about lions to make him give up Monica ? "

" Give up ! " growled the Colonel; " I only wish Monica would give him up. I'll tell you what, Sir Ralph—I cannot stay at home and follow Monica to her mother's grave over there. I'll just put myself on board the next Cape steamer and go and give Master Talbot a piece of my mind. Don't let Monica think that I am going to fetch back the fellow — of course I will take care of her dignity; but I should like to ask him face to face what he means by writing those letters two years ago, and then never letting any one have a line from him afterwards."

Sir Ralph considered a little, for aged people are as deliberate in their mental as in their physical movements, and then said: " I am not at all sure that would not be a good thing to do, Colonel. But Monica ought to know nothing about it ; she is so worn with anxiety that the additional suspense would kill her, I am certain. Have you thought what you could say to Talbot if you did find him ? It might be a very awkward meeting for both of you."

M

" I'll take care he shall find it as awkward as I can make it. Awkward! it is much more awkward for Monica to be in this state. Good heavens! when I think of her now, with her sallow face and great melancholy eyes, and remember what she was even a year ago, I can't answer for what I shall say or do to the fellow if I catch him."

" You must remember, Treherne, that I don't think Monica acted quite wisely at the beginning. I did not know it at the time, for she did not tell me until some months had passed, but it seems that about six months or so after he sailed, and when yet there was plenty of time to repair any little quarrel, she wrote him a most vehement letter, not only upbraiding him for his silence ever since he left England, but telling him that she felt so wounded at his neglect and indifference that she declined to have anything more to say to him : it must have been, from her own account, a most cruel and final dismissal, and yet she evidently expected him to write again and make it up."

" Oh, well, all I can say," replied the candid father, " is that she must be as great a fool as he; but still, you know, we cannot sit still and let the child die ; besides, she must have been very much provoked to write in that strain."

"Monica is so dreadfully sensitive," said Sir Ralph, "I know, for she told me herself that the reason she was so icily cold to Talbot for such a long time, and would not let him say a word to her until just at the last, was because she used to make such a fuss about him when she was a child. She must have kept a sort of debtor and creditor account with herself of all her affectionate speeches and artless regrets at his indifference in those old days, and made him pay her for them twenty times over afterwards. What other girls look upon as the merest trifle, is in Monica's eyes a tremendous event. She can't get over all those kisses at the last moment, and, ridiculous as it may seem, I do believe she looks upon herself as thoroughly disgraced, though it has not been known that they were ever engaged."

"Well, it is better she should be the romantic goose she is than like the others." By this Colonel meant the other young ladies of his acquaintance. "However, I really think the best thing I can do is to go and look Raymond up, and see what it means. At all events, it will be something to do."

This was rather an unequal division of suffering, for Colonel Treherne took change of scene and sea

air and all the excitement and bustle of the voyage
for his share, and left to Monica and her uncle the
dreary task of watching and waiting. It had been
judged better, almost at the last moment, to tell the
girl of her father's errand; indeed there were impracticable difficulties attending its concealment.
Truth seldom or never hurts a sick person, suspicion or deceit is far more dangerous, and Monica
certainly brightened up after the Colonel had started.
Her face lost in some measure its terribly listless
look, and her large haunting eyes were not so hopeless in their expression.

"You are still very ugly, Monica," said Miss Edmonds, frankly; "but if you would not wear black
you would look much less like a ghost than you
have been doing lately."

Monica actually smiled a little pert smile, and said,
"Don't ghosts wear white? surely I am too yellow for
that? I have been obliged to wear black lately, you
know, on account of my mourning for Uncle Ralph's
sister, and I am afraid of lilacs just yet; what do
you think?"

By which words it will be seen that Miss Treherne
was reviving. She still had moments of deep depression, during which she sought her beloved old
uncle's society, just as a girl goes to her mother with

her first heartache, and confided to him her conviction
—her firm belief—that Raymond Talbot had changed
his mind, and that her heart was broken. Together
Sir Ralph and Monica went patiently over the same
ground again, and yet again, for love knows no
weariness; all the old doubts and fears were
brought out of their hiding-place in that poor
aching little brain, to be met and vanquished for
the moment by Uncle Ralph's tender cunning and
heart-taught sophistry.

It was an immense comfort to the old man to
find she would talk about her trouble, for he felt
then that she was permitting him to help her to bear
its burden. Over and over again had he formerly
besought her to speak to him on the subject, but she
had always said simply, "It is not a thing I can
talk about, even to you, Uncle Ralph; I am too much
ashamed of myself." Now, the very fact of her
father's caring about her sufficiently to take so much
trouble on her account, proved that life still held
great stores of love, and she volunteered to whisper
to him as a parting consolation, "I will try to get
better, dear papa, I will indeed. Don't put yourself
in any danger for me." Whether Miss Treherne
meant peril from lions or from lovers remains an
unexplained mystery to this day.

And now my story is drawing very near to its close. I wish I could invent a more dramatic conclusion—say, a scene of treachery and frustrated villany. Alas! I cannot; it is all quite true, and it is only I who am in danger from the vengeance of all the Post-office authorities at Natal.

When Colonel Treherne reached that port his astonishment began, and he lived in a state of wide-open-eyedness for long after. His first surprise was to see Raymond Talbot step on deck from the earliest pilot-boat (he had been told, it seems, through other sources of the Colonel's meditated trip), and to hear him say whilst he seized his hand and squeezed it as if it were a lion's throat—

"For God's sake, Colonel, tell me what it is all about! Why has Monica thrown me over in this way; and why doesn't she answer my letters? It is at least eighteen months since I have had a line from her. I've written by nearly every mail since, and she blew me up sky high for not writing at first; why I wrote and wrote no end of letters."

This speech put the Colonel's mind quite at ease, so, instead of answering poor anxious Raymond's questions, he looked at him, but his glance was so friendly and so frank that the young man's worst fears departed like ghosts of dead horrors as they

were, before a summer's day-dawn. The two men
stood there grasping each other's hands and looking
in each other's faces; feeling without any more
words that all heaviness had departed, and the joy
which morning brings had already come. But what
a night it had been! and darker for Mr. Talbot
even than for Monica! No wonder he had taken
furiously to lion-hunting, and many a widowed
lioness had reason to curse Miss Treherne from the
depths of her royal and bereaved heart.

During Monica's worst fits of depression she had
never fancied that any other woman had stepped in
between her and her lost love, but Raymond suffered
tortures of jealousy, and imagined nothing less
than that Monica was long ago married. He
remembered that wild moment in the library, he
lived over and over again its ecstasy, until he felt
her soft lips on his own, as eager to give as he
to take their kisses; and then he pictured her telling
another man—whom Raymond would have killed
as ruthlessly as he would a wild beast—that she
had never loved before. He said afterwards that
he dared not come home, dreading that his fears
were true.

"What a fool you were not to ask!" said the
Colonel.

" But I did ask ! " cried poor Raymond ; " I asked you, I asked Sir Ralph, I implored Monica to tell me: not a word, not a line have I had since that last bitter letter from her. I have a sort of feeling it has all come right, Colonel," continued the young man, half-sobbing with excitement, " and yet, upon my word, I don't see how."

It is not only women who like to play the cat and mouse game. Men are very fond of it too when they have a chance, and Colonel Treherne seemed to take a mysterious pleasure in torturing poor young Talbot in return for what he had, even so unintentionally, made Monica suffer; so he shook his head and said sententiously, " Monica is very ill." Raymond looked wildly around him as if he intended to jump into the sea, and swim straight off to ' England, home, and beauty ; ' and the Colonel further added, by way of a shake to his wretched victim, " We've none of us had one letter from you since you left—no, not a line ; I don't know that Monica will ever get over it—I don't, upon my word."

I need only ask any young lady or gentleman who, in default of better reading, may be skimming through these pages, to imagine what their feelings would be if they heard that their love had been brought to the brink of the grave through supposed indifference on her or his part, when their conscience absolved them from having kept silence. In other words, I ask them to fancy finding their letters, one and all, lying in a heap at the General Post Office, never having travelled any further.

Yet this was Raymond's case. Like an Englishman, his first impulse was to abuse the Post Office authorities in St. Martin's-le-Grand. It was only at Colonel Treherne's suggestion that just before putting themselves, their luggage, and a large bale of trophies on board the next mail steamer, the travellers inquired at the ugly wooden building which sheltered Her Majesty's mails at Natal, whether there were any letters for Scudamore Chace. Yes, there were, a good many; and, after much signing of printed forms, they were produced—over a hundred in number!

The clerk declined to receive the contents of the huge vial of wordy wrath which Mr. Talbot forthwith uncorked and proceeded to pour on his head in a stream of frantic reproaches.

"It wasn't me, sir, that's all I know. As fast as these ere letters come, Mr. Tomkins says they ain't properly addressed, and they can't be forwarded like that, and he puts them in here."

"And where is Mr. Tomkins?" roared the two gentlemen with one terrific voice.

"Gone up country," promptly replied the clerk.

If it were a falsehood, let us hope he was forgiven for it on the spot. After a few more thunderbolts and threats of exposure, of writing to the *Times* (as if *that* menace had terrors for a sub-clerk in Natal), of vengeance on Mr. Tomkins and his descendants unto the third and fourth generation, Raymond and the Colonel took possession of the packets and packets of thick envelopes addressed in Mr. Talbot's somewhat illegible scrawl, to Monica, to Sir Ralph, and to Colonel Treherne himself.

"What! I came in for my share too," said the Colonel, with his somewhat grim smile; "fancy my having to read all that," he continued, holding up a large blue envelope as broad as it was long.

"Ah, that has got one for Monica inside," said Raymond, half shyly. "I thought perhaps she was going to be married, and that it might bore her to get a letter from me, so I just enclosed it under cover to you, and asked you to give it to her, if there was nothing of that sort in the wind."

"Look here, Raymond," said the Colonel, as they walked out of the Post-office with their pockets bulging out in all directions, "we'll keep these, and if we get safe home we'll have some fun out of them. Goodness knows, we have been dismal long enough."

But Raymond could not imagine the possibility of fun whilst he did not know whether Monica were on earth or not. One mail had come in, bringing a letter from Sir Ralph, in which he said all he dared to say with regard to Monica's improved health. " It may be only a flicker, Slater says," he wrote, " but I hope and believe it's more than that. She still looks fearfully fragile, and her cough worries her a good deal, but I hope everything from good news."

The travellers telegraphed from the nearest point at which they could command the blessed wires, and never, since we tamed it for our use, did electricity convey such winged words. Colonel Treherne toned down Raymond's first wild message, but it still bore sufficient internal evidence of a lover's hand to arouse the sympathy of the clerks at the various stations, who remarked to each other, " I say, Jim, this one must go on, mustn't it, sharp ? " So it flashed over hill and dale, by mountain and river, by highways and byways, until it reached its destination, and told Monica that Raymond Talbot had never ceased to love her, and that both he and her father hoped to arrive at home in a day or two.

Miss Treherne's great anxiety now was to conceal from one of the travellers how ill she had been, and in pursuance of this strong desire she forced herself to eat and sleep, so as to collect in ever so small a degree her scattered resources of health and strength. I do not know whether she was more perverse than ordinary young women, but now her highest wish seemed to be to prevent Raymond Talbot from discovering that his silence and fancied desertion had brought her down from the heights of youth and beauty,—down to the very entrance of the valley of the shadow of death.

A shy, coaxing word to Sir Ralph was enough to enlist him on her side, and to impress on him that he was not to betray to Raymond the reason for her failing health. "You may say we thought his silence rather odd, you know, uncle, but you must not say anything more ;" and Sir Ralph promised at once, too happy to hear her speak of illness and unhappiness as things of the past.

Miss Edmonds was more difficult to manage, and scolded Monica well for the fuss which had been made, ending by saying with many sobs—

"I am sure I am very unhappy, and yet no one cares for my sorrows. It is so dreadful to live among people who think of nothing but trifles. Just fancy, Ophèle has sent me over a purple bonnet to wear with that light blue silk dress, and declares I

ordered it. As if I *could* order such a thing. Oh
dear, what shall I do?" and the afflicted lady wept
genuine tears of sorrow.

Monica had already lived long enough to know how
different is each man or woman's standard of grief or
joy. To Miss Alicia, a blunder on her milliner's part
was as real an affliction as Raymond's silence had
been to herself, so she comforted her with the same
true sympathy which I have heard one man express
to another on the subject of a corked bottle of wine
or a missed shot at a bird.

I hesitate to describe the meeting of Raymond and
Monica, for in truth it was very unsatisfactory. Miss
Treherne's shyness and perversity came to the surface
at first, and it was her father who received the most
rapturous welcome. But the Colonel was shrewd
enough to guess that, like many another woman,
she was lavishing all these caresses on him in pay-
ment of the present he had brought her, for lack of
which she had well-nigh died.

"You sly little puss, what are you smothering me
for? Go and tell Master Raymond that you are glad
to see him, and don't choke me;" and then the
wretched man demolished all Monica's webs of deceit
by saying, "How much better she is looking, eh, Sir
Ralph? Why, she is getting quite fat. You would

hardly believe, Talbot, what a ghost she was when
I left England."

I do not know whether the people of other
nations are less awkward in moments of strong
emotion than we are. Certainly such a meeting
as this one, so far from 'making amends,' as the
song saith, is a sort of thing to be dreaded and
avoided as much as possible. Each person's heart
is quite full, and their tongue quite silent; they have
schooled their faces to express absolutely no feeling
at all, and every one is disappointed with every
one else. This was especially the case at Scudamore Chace during the half-hour in question, and
each succeeding moment seemed to freeze up more
thoroughly all expression of real feeling.

At last after they had been driven to discuss the
just completed voyage, Raymond suddenly started up,
rushed off into the hall, and returned bearing a good-
sized leathern bag in his hand, which he proceeded
to unlock with great deliberation. He then crossed
the room to where Monica was seated by her father's
side on a sofa, knelt down, and emptied the contents
of the bag at her feet.

Such a crackling and rustling was heard as these
unfortunate letters simultaneously arrived at their
destination! And yet you could hardly hear the

noise of the paper avalanche for the peals of laughter which rang through the room. It was a capital and complete justification; no further explanations were needed; there they all were, and Raymond availed himself of his momentary advantage to whisper, " I behaved better than you, after all, Monica, for I did write, you see; now you have never written me a line for a year and a half; there is no heap of letters waiting for *me* at any post-office."

" Why did I not get them ?" inquired Monica, very naturally, but feeling herself vanquished; and then Colonel Treherne and Mr. Talbot told the story of their interview with the clerk, and detailed their plans of future vengeance against Mr. Tomkins, none of which happily were ever carried out, for they had all as much as ever they could do preparing for the marriage.

It took place very soon—in fact before poor Miss Edmonds could get her costume over from Paris for it. Raymond had proposed that it should be solemnized the next day, declaring that some other accident might happen to make Monica hate him again.

" Just as if I had ever hated you," complained Miss Treherne; "you know very well it was you who used to hate me."

But Raymond utterly refused to believe that he had ever been so blind or so insensible. I, as his friend and biographer, cannot altogether bear him out in that statement, though I am prepared to endorse the "happy davy" which Robert volunteered to take at the servants' wedding feast, to the effect that there never would be a happier couple than "the Capting" (a brevet rank conferred by Bob) "and our Miss Monicar."

III.

A SCOTCH STORY.

III.

A SCOTCH STORY.

CHAPTER I.

GIVE ME BACK ONE HOUR OF SCOTLAND.

TIIERE is almost always one standard topic of conversation in an out-of-the-way country neighbourhood. Generally it is some piece of local gossip to which the good folk delight to return again and again, for newspaper news is very foreign politics to the rural mind, while the farmhouse romance or the village mystery becomes always more fascinating as it grows older.

Births, marriages, and deaths among the small circle are only, so to speak, flashes in the pan. The babies bloom into lads and lasses; the brides wear out their wedding finery; the dead are buried out of sight, and their place knows them no more. What a satisfaction, then, to have one "strange story," one real genuine wonder, the delightful inexplicable details of which can never lose the gloss of novelty!

Such a topic I found fully established at Lough Shellach some years ago. It was my first visit to the Highlands, and I was fortunate enough to be independent of wayside inns, and even of those dens of discomfort, shooting-boxes, and to be agreeably housed in a thoroughly Scotch home. There I learned first how to breakfast, and next how to walk; there I discovered, during a wet summer, the fallacy of waterproofs, and how much better it was to get wet than to be kept dry by a mackintosh. There I found out the amount of exercise it is possible for a human being to take when, having had ten hours of mountain climbing during the day, we used to send for the piper after dinner and dance reels and strathspeys till midnight; and, lastly, I made up my mind that the Scotch pony is the missing link between the monkey and the horse, combining the activity of the former with the strength of the latter.

My friendly hosts, the Keiths, lost no time in telling me the history of all their neighbours—not that they had any neighbours in our southern acceptation of the word—but I soon learned to look upon twenty miles as hard by. There was *rather* a sameness in these stories; if the people at the great house in question were rich, it was to be regretted that they spent very little of the year at home; if they were poor, they were apt to shut themselves up and be unsociable, so the result was much the same in both cases. But to this somewhat sweeping rule were two exceptions; one was Glenthorne, where the Frasers lived with a large family and small means, and the other was Strathmore, the newly-purchased property of a great West India merchant.

Nowadays there is no such thing as wealth to be found in those lovely but ruined islands of the Caribbean Sea. Our new blood, the men who come home and buy up acres upon acres of Scotch property, have sought and found their fortunes at the Antipodes, have known when to cease speculating in sheep and land, to give over buying and selling farms as large as English counties. They have resolutely turned their backs upon the lands which lie beneath the Southern Cross before the tide of prosperity has ebbed away from them. Not to all is this wisdom given; it is so hard to stop rolling the golden ball, and to answer a tempting investment with "Le jeu est fait;" but those who hold on, in spite of signs and warnings, repent their rashness to this day in dust and ashes of spirit.

Thirty or forty years ago young men generally sailed Westward Ho! following the wake of the heaven-led Genoese sailor who found those glowing, sunny lands for us, and who lived to regret, long ere he died, that his wonderful discovery had brought so much misery and desolation on his bronze-coloured fellow-creatures.

Seldom did these adventurous youths return ; their home-place knew them no more ; a nameless tropic grave under a cedar tree was too often their quiet resting place and the end of all their feverish visions of wealth and splendour.

More fortunate or less self-indulgent, however, had been old James Munro, the master of Strathmore. He belonged originally to the class which is the thews and sinews of Scotland, and answers to our English yeomen farmers. His father had owned a small holding on the very estate which was now the son's, but the soil was poor and times were bad ; so, although the family was small, for James had only one sister, Elspeth, he could not bear, as he said himself, to leave life as he found it, and an unconquerable spirit of enterprise and adventure sent the lad forth at eighteen years of age to try and better his fortunes, or rather the fortunes of his family. His hope was to win the means of affording his father some luxuries in the extreme old age which he hoped he might reach, and of giving his little sister the good education she could only have by his help.

But although the outlines of this sketch of the future remained unaltered, the picture when actually filled in retained but few of the lights and shadows which James Munro's boyish fancy had painted. He carried out his programme, inasmuch as he achieved the success which is won by steady hard work and self-denial, but even this did not come to him till the middle of his life.

By that time his father was sleeping under the rowan trees in the hill-side churchyard, and Elspeth had only so far bettered herself that she had married a shepherd on the neighbouring property, who bore the same name as her own. Her husband was steady and frugal, and when he died a few years later, he left Elspeth sufficient means to enable her to give their only son Malcolm good schooling.

Elspeth herself had that innate love of learning, that quick perception of what is best in a book or a person, and that true refinement of taste and feeling which I myself have met with in the wife of a Scotch shepherd. I am not drawing on my fancy for the sketch when I try to show you what Elspeth was; for one of the most perfect ladies I ever knew, a lady in heart and soul, in outer manner and in inner feeling, occupied just such a position as Elspeth did in those distant days.

Malcolm was her only child, and on him all the affection and devotion of her nature concentrated its strength. She not only sent him to the excellent, village school, where his thirst for knowledge made him welcome as springs of water in a dry land to the schoolmaster's heart; she not only worked with him out of lesson-time, encouraging and helping him on with his studies, but she gave her boy the higher education which only a mother can give. She planted in his baby heart seeds of a noble, wide creed; she taught him his duty towards his God and his fellow-man, and she showed him the beauty of love and truth. The boy learned these lessons faster even than she could teach, and at eighteen, Malcolm Munro, in face and figure, in heart and soul, in his cultivated mind and fine perceptions, was a youth whom any mother might have watched setting forth on his life-journey with tears of hope and pride in her eyes.

Elspeth felt all this, but she was tempted to mourn

over the lowliness of the first opening which presented
itself in Malcolm's career. It was only that of "house-
boy" at Mr. Fraser's, the laird. Elspeth had a little
of her brother James' upward tendencies, but,
woman-like, her ambition was solely for her heart's
darling. Earthly joy and sorrow could but touch her
through her son, and it was for his sake that she
hesitated about accepting the laird's offer.

Mr. Fraser had often found occasion to call at
Elspeth's door, and he had always been struck by
the air of refinement and even of elegance which
characterized the simple arrangements of her cottage.
An artist's eye would have rested lovingly on all
the homely details. Small as was the house-place,
if you passed it by in summer you would feel inclined to linger and rest in its calm, cool shade, with
the scent of Elspeth's beloved flowers and the hum-
ming of the bees outside to lull you to sleep; if you
looked in of a cold winter's forenoon, the bright
warmth of the ingle-nook, and Elspeth in her home-
spun gown, spinning and singing by the fire, made
a picture which you found constantly recurring to
your recollection during the day.

It was no wonder, then, that Mr. Fraser asked
Elspeth, seeing that Malcolm was growing from a
fine lad into a handsome youth, what she was going

to do with her boy. Elspeth told the laird that she
had always kept up an affectionate intercourse with
her brother James in his West-Indian home, and
that he had frequently of late asked her the same
question by letter. The poor mother, whilst she
related this, looked with pathetic wistfulness at the
laird, as much as to deprecate his proffering her the
good advice of sending her son away to his uncle.
Mr. Fraser's tact and kindliness of feeling prevented
him from offering any such unpalatable counsel at the
moment, though he secretly felt that of course
Malcolm's chance of rising in life lay in his uncle's
hands, and that it must come to a parting between
mother and son sooner or later. He at once kindly
suggested that the youth should come to them
for a time.

"It is not far off, and it will break you in a little,
in case you make up your mind to let him go to
foreign parts, Mrs. Munro," he said; "besides which
I don't fancy Malcolm has had much practice in
turning his hand to odds and ends of work, and he is
sure to find such knowledge useful. It won't do to
trust only to bookwork, when you have to seek your
fortune in a new country, you know. One must learn
how to use one's hands as well as one's head, and you
had much better send him up to us for a few months

at all events to look about him. I shall be very glad of his help now and then with my accounts, for old James is getting rather slow (he might have said the accounts were coming in too fast for old James), and Malcolm is a great hand at figures, I hear.

In her inmost heart Elspeth felt a wee bit affronted at Mr. Fraser's offer, but she was too much of a lady to show offence where only kindliness was meant; besides which her common sense told her there was truth in some of Mr. Fraser's words, and so she contented herself by thanking him and promising to talk it over with Malcolm. Much to his mother's surprise the lad closed eagerly with Mr. Fraser's offer, and Elspeth looked keenly at his sparkling eyes and mantling cheeks, as he begged her to arrange matters at once for his going to Glenthorne the following week.

" It is not that my boy is glad to leave me," she thought; and then quick as a flash along electric wires darted the cynical old philosopher's query. Elspeth's gentle mind did not exactly ask itself plainly " Who is the woman ? " but before her memory rose a picture which had been deeply stamped on it two years before.

She remembered a summer holiday at Glenthorne in honour of the eldest son's safe return from Indian battle-fields, and she saw the fair and only daughter of the house, Marjory Fraser, dancing with the best-conducted lad in the neighbourhood—her Malcolm. She saw, with eyes which glistened at the recollection, as they had glistened at the time with pride and love, his splendid figure in the most picturesque of manly dresses; his fine open face, instinct with feeling and thought ; his bare head—for he held his bonnet in his hand as he danced with the young lady —covered by a mass of bright short curls. She remembered Marjory's sweet shy grace, and the utter momentary forgetfulness of differing rank or station which had evidently come upon them both, and what wonder was it if her woman's wit and mother-love combined, told her in an instant the secret of Malcolm's readiness to be house-boy or anything else at Glenthorne ?

Elspeth was too wise a woman to oppose or argue against a plan so acceptable to her son. She felt that he was by nature at once too proud and too noble to do anything underhand or treacherous, and for the rest she trusted to the daily working of the scheme to disappoint and disgust the young man with it, and to send him back to her, prepared to seek a fresh start. In this calculation she seemed for a time destined to be disappointed. Each Sunday afternoon brought Malcolm to visit her, and they had a long, loving chat together; every time they met she saw the light of happiness and content shining in his clear eyes. He never wearied of telling, nor she of hearing, how, instead of being called on to give menial service in the house, he was Mr. Fraser's right hand, going over the farm with him, seeing people on business, arranging papers and accounts, and so on. " It is quite true, mother," he would say, " that I have a great deal of everyday useful knowledge to learn, and that is just what I am doing at Mr. Fraser's, and yet I'm helping him also there is no doubt."

Malcolm had too much delicacy to add, and Elspeth was too little of a gossip to wish to know, that the more he learned of Mr. Fraser's affairs the less he liked them. Outside it was all calm and peaceful, open-handed hospitality to all comers, generosity to friends, handsome allowances to the sons of the family, but within was confusion and scarcity of money. Malcolm could not bring to Mr. Fraser's aid any knowledge of the pecuniary shifts by which a shadow of prosperity may be kept up long after the substance has melted away; but he was able to detect overcharges and irregularities in the never-diminishing, always-growing, heaps and heaps of bills and accounts. Mr. Fraser also found it a great comfort to have Malcolm's ready sympathy and quick intelligence to go to for consolation ; whilst the young man's cultivated mind and innate good breeding made him an agreeable companion at all times.

The summer and autumn passed away thus uneventfully, when one November morning, more than twenty years before my story should begin, Mr. Fraser came down to his early breakfast intending to go out with Malcolm on the hills, and found instead a letter on his plate—a letter of farewell and grateful thanks from his young secretary. The poor boy could think of nothing more original than to write these hurried and incoherent lines and leave them on the table, from whence they were transferred to Mr. Fraser's plate by the servant.

Malcolm, though the least vain of young men, would have been flattered to know how desolate and blank Mr. Fraser's face became as he read the hasty words, telling that he, Malcolm, had made up his mind to join his uncle in Jamaica, and had started on his journey. He did not attempt to offer any explanation of his conduct, but in spite of the evident hurry of the letter, Mr. Fraser felt its tone of manly dignity and independence, and respected the request conveyed in it that he would speak as little as might be of Malcolm's departure, even to his mother.

In the course of a day or two the laird went over to Elspeth's stone cottage expecting to see her in a dreadful state of grief, and, truth to be told, dreading a scene of tears and sobs, questions and suggestions, but nothing of that sort ever happens exactly as we anticipate ; he found Elspeth, certainly with purple eyelids and quivering lips, but composed and guarded in manner. She received Mr. Fraser as usual with simple cordiality, and although she did not avoid the subject of Malcolm's sudden departure, Mr. Fraser felt it best not to say, or rather to ask, too much about it. For his part he had absolutely nothing to tell. Up to the last day of October the young man had gone on quite as usual, spending his whole time with his master, and the next morning he had departed, as it seemed for ever. Elspeth briefly acknowledged that in the first instance he had come straight to her cottage, arriving there in the wintry moonlight just before dawn, but after their talk, when, as his mother touchingly said, " he showed her his whole heart," he had started again for the nearest seaport, with a well-filled purse and a comfortable kit.

She seemed to realize the truth of the proverb about excuses being accusations, for she offered no apology for her boy's sudden departure, merely saying he had convinced her that it was the wisest thing to

do, and begging Mr. Fraser to respect their wish for
silence on the subject. This seemed a small thing to
promise, and the laird went away with a lightened
heart respecting the wisdom of the step, but still
feeling much mystified as to its cause.

From that time to the date of my first visit to
Lough Shellach twenty years had come and gone.
They had brought changes and chances, chiefly for
evil, to the Frasers, and but little difference to
Elspeth's quiet life. Gradually the broad lands of
Glenthorne had melted away, acre by acre, until there
was nothing left except a few fields round the house.
The moors were let to a rich Australian, the salmon-
fishing to a retired cotton-spinner, but the high rents
they paid barely kept down the accumulation of the
heavy interest on the mortgages. Of course all the
countryside knew Mr. Fraser's affairs quite as well as
he did himself; and even I, a Southron, and a visitor,
grew to feel the liveliest interest in the fallen fortunes
of the home party at Glenthorne. Doubtless this
universal sympathy was due as much to the peculiar
charm of the Fraser family, as to mere vulgar
curiosity. Never did people bear misfortune so
bravely and so cheerfully. They contrived to hit
the happy mean, and neither to weary their friends
by constant regrets and references to the past, or to

disgust them by reckless indifference to the present. Then they had no false pride or morbid sensitiveness. They accepted all their neighbours' good offices with a simple heartiness which was delightful ; and they found themselves even more popular in adversity than in the open-handed days of their prosperity.

This brings me to the end of my chapter. It is true I have not yet alluded to the local mystery; but, inexperienced as I am, I feel it ought to have a place of honour at the head of a new page. Besides this sense of what is due to the Unexplained, I tell my little story as I should like it told to me ; that is to say, I have tried to sketch distinctly the outline of the past history of the principal characters in this slight comedy, so as to save you the trouble of tracing it out for yourselves as the tale proceeds.

CHAPTER II.

AN observation made during dinner on the first
evening of my second visit to Lough Shellach
had, as I remembered, been hazarded on a similar
occasion two years previously.

Some one said then, and indeed I had often heard it
said before, "How charming Marjory Fraser is! there is
no one like her:" then would come a moment's pause,
and either the speaker's own voice continued, or
another person would take it up,—in any case the
remark was quite sure to follow,—"I wonder she has
never married!"

This was the signal for a multitude of conjectures,
of speculations, of decided, well-built reasons, which
crumbled into ruins at the·next breath; of probable
prosaic or romantic causes which only existed in
their inventor's imagination. Everybody contradicted

everybody else, in all politeness of course, but still gave a flat denial to the truth of the last statement. Even the young ladies on their preferment, who spoke of Marjory as "quite old"—and indeed she was thirty-six (fancy a heroine of thirty-six! what shall we come to next?)—agreed that she was neither prim, nor cross, nor spiteful; nor did she possess any of the evil qualities with which the conventional daughter of St. Catherine is usually credited.

I often think it is the men who ought to feel envious and angry when they see how many of the most thoroughly agreeable and beautiful women in the world they have been unable to lure into the house of bondage! But they are not supposed to care, whilst we poor spinsters go down to posterity as examples of baffled ambition. At all events no one could say *that* of Marjory Fraser, for although, especially latterly, she lived a quiet and retired life, she refused many offers more or less desirable. Her own solution of the mystery was contained in the words, "What would Papa do without me?" But the handsome old laird used to scold her well if this reason ever came to his ears, and scouted the idea of any such selfishness on his side, declaring loudly that he wished his Madge to marry, although she was the apple of his eye.

I should not have been a true woman if I had not felt great anxiety, the first time I listened to all this talk concerning Marjory Fraser, to see the lady who contrived to interest her neighbours so much without giving the least cause for an ill-natured remark. So after dinner I heard with secret satisfaction that we were going the next day on a boating excursion to the head of the loch, ostensibly to catch fish, but really to spend a whole happy idle holiday out of doors.

Scotch people seem the most gregarious in the world, and always like to enjoy themselves in company; therefore, although the Frasers lived nearly eight miles off they were bidden to this picnic; and it was arranged that we were to be joined by the party from Glenthorne a little higher up the loch. I would fain linger over the details of that delightful water journey; I would fain let memory touch with loving faithful fingers each happy moment, especially the happiest of all, when, after the bustle of settling ourselves in the boat was over, the first vigorous strokes floated us out from the shore, giving us a fuller view of the beauty of sky and water, and of the distant hill-tints; but if I have made you feel one quarter of my impatience to see Marjory Fraser you will not thank me for delaying to word-sketch by the way.

I remember that, although generally too lazy and too selfish to be in the least curious about my neighbours' affairs, I leant forward to look at the picturesque group which came in sight after we had rounded the second headland. It did not require the obtrusive loud sigh of my next neighbour, a gigantic but susceptible artilleryman, to tell me that Marjory Fraser was of the party; nor, although there were other ladies among the group, did I need to inquire which was she.

"Pray, how did you know?" a carping auditor inquired the first time I told this tale *viva voce.*

Well, I didn't know, I guessed, and guessed rightly. I felt that, according to the fitness of things, no one else of the party before us could or ought to be Marjory, except the lady who was lightly jumping off her shaggy pony as we suddenly turned the corner and shot in sight of the Glenthorne contingent. We could hear her clear ringing voice, the voice which is distinct without being loud, as she said, "Too late, sir;" and we could see by the laird's outstretched hands to whom the laughing little reproach was addressed.

I want to make you see the bright group as my eyes saw it that lovely autumn morning; but I don't know at what part of a picture an artist begins to paint. My instinct leads me to commence with the foreground, as that is what seems to arrest the attention first; and then as one looks, all the harmonious details of the composition gradually make themselves seen and felt.

To begin, then, according to this theory, with the striking figure of the laird. He had his back to us, and his arms extended towards Marjory and her pony. The Highland dress is quite as becoming to old men as to young ones, which is one of its many advantages; and we used often to declare that Mr. Fraser looked as if he had stepped out of one of Scott's novels or Landseer's pictures. Although his face was rugged in feature, and even in these holiday moments showed deep lines of care and anxiety, the kindly glance of his honest eyes, and his sweet genial smile, made a new acquaintance, as I was, feel like an old friend directly; and one only needed to see him with his daughter by his side to perceive how chivalrous was his devotion to her. There was a Mrs. Fraser in the world; a perfectly amiable, contented, and harmless woman, whose existence everybody forgot.

It was rather ridiculous to find that in speaking of the Glenthorne party, none of them excited any interest or special mention except the laird and Marjory, which omission generally led strangers to

suppose that the family circle began and ended with
these two. Great therefore has often been the surprise to hear of a house full of younger brothers, but
the public interest refused to centre on any one
except Marjory. Of course I cannot tell what was
in her heart, but in spite of the attention she excited,
her manner seemed perfectly simple and unconscious
—that was its great charm ; with all its polish and
finish she gave you the idea of being almost a child
in freshness of feeling and keenness of enjoyment.
Like her father, she was tall and firmly built, but
her perfect and unvarying health kept her form
as slender and her step as elastic as it had been at
twenty years of age.

Even in my individual limited experience I have
known faces which improve as they grow older, and
it was easy to believe that Marjory Fraser's was one
of that class. " How handsome she is ! " I involuntarily
exclaimed. " Yes, and she grows more beautiful
every year," answered the big artilleryman, mournfully. This was quite true, as I afterwards found
out for myself, when a longer and more intimate
acquaintance with Miss Fraser taught me that a
pure fresh heart and a noble elevated soul can, as
it were, win the enemy, Time, round to their side,
and cause his every touch to beautify and improve,

instead of hardening or destroying the lines of a fair sweet face.

It is quite as difficult to paint her portrait in words as it would be to paint it in colours, for the highest kind of loveliness is ever the most subtle. She was neither dark nor fair; that is to say, that, whilst her complexion was transparent and delicate as the tints on a spray of apple-blossom, and her eyes blue as her. favourite ribbons, the dark eyebrows and long, almost black lashes prevented her from being called a blonde. Then her hair had caught the best tints from both raven and auburn locks; it rippled away in dark shadows, whilst the high lights shone in the sun like the red, red gold of the old ballad.

Perhaps, inasmuch as form is more than colour, her features ought first to have been described; but miniatures are not in my line, and I cannot limn for you the shape of her nose or the lines of her mouth. All I know is, "her smile it was the sweetest," and as she and the laird came towards us, I felt an unwonted and warm sensation in the region of my heart, similar I suppose to the emotion which was changing the stalwart gunner by my side from a fine frank young man into a blushing awkward schoolboy.

Marjory's dress of Lowland plaid was brightened

by a scarlet petticoat, and the ends of a ribbon which matched gleamed here and there among the plaits of hair which showed beneath her simple little hat. Without going into a milliner's details I should like to convey to you some idea of how nice she always looked. I, for one, never could admire an ill-dressed woman, and in spite of her quiet life far away from towns and shops, Miss Fraser's toilette, whilst it possessed an individuality of its own, gave no occasion for disparaging remarks from fashionable visitors.

Poor Mrs. Fraser! it is always her fate to come last. She was just getting out of a little rough carriage when I perceived her, and the other members of the family were superintending the unpacking and transferring to our boat of an ample quota of provisions. Then there was a little knot of gillies and ponies and dogs, which had fallen naturally into picturesque attitudes, their quiet neutral tints standing out deliciously from the rich background of purple heather.

The scattered birch trees were already showing golden threads among their slender drooping branches, and, higher up the hill, patches of whin and bracken broke up the heather into lovely masses of colour. Overhead, little flecks of vapoury cloud sailed in a deep blue sky; a sky of that cobalt blue which misguided people believe exists only in Italy, but which I have often and often seen in the Highland heavens, quite late into the autumn too!

There was another boat for the Glenthorne party, but everybody wanted to come into the one wherein Miss Fraser had taken her seat. Not only did my tall neighbour and I keep our places with a pertinacity which I fear must have looked like rudeness, but before her younger brothers embarked I saw them glance wistfully round, and heard them say, "Where is Madge?"

Before we had been an hour on the loch, I too was completely *"sous le charme;"* and yet it is so difficult to make you understand exactly wherein Miss Fraser's strength lay. She was not the most beautiful woman I had ever seen, she was simply the most loveable. Without being either the wisest or the wittiest of her sex she was perfectly agreeable. A ruined Highland laird's daughter is not in a very grand social position, yet we all hung on Madge's smiles and words :—

> "A Queen by right of nature she,
> More than a Queen by name."

Never since the days of Boccaccio had a lovely charming lady ever found herself elected, by such universal suffrage, to be the sovereign ruler of whatever society she found herself in.

Before my visit to Lough Shellach ended, I too had learned to think it strange that such a girl, or rather such a woman, should have been left unwon for twenty years. The most perplexing thing in the affair was that no tradition existed of an unfortunate attachment, or a blighted affection, or anything which could account for Madge's determined refusal to leave her home and her father, for good, as the saying goes.

She had been often on visits in England for a few months at a time, and more than once the elder members of the family had travelled on the Continent; but from all these mild dissipations Madge returned as heart-whole as ever. In spite of her natural, unaffected manner no one except her father had ever dared to question her on the subject, and to his attempted inquiries she replied (so he said), by a kiss and the unvarying formula, "I don't wish to marry anybody, papa; if ever I do I'll come and tell you directly."

With this promise the laird was forced to content himself; he must have secretly rejoiced at his beloved companion not being in a hurry to leave him, though he used often to say, "It's very hard

on me, Madge, everybody abuses me, and thinks
me a selfish old beast, who won't let you leave
him ; whereas you know, my darling, it would be
the proudest day of my life on which I gave you
away to some nice fellow. I must say I should like
him to be a Scotchman though, but that shall be
just as you like, my pet," Mr. Fraser would add
hastily, lest Madge's decision might be influenced,
as it always was, by his lightest wish.

One evening at Lough Shellach I took up a little
portrait, a vignette photograph, of Miss Fraser, which
had been done at Naples. In some respects it was
perfect; the *pose* of the head, the beautiful expression
even of the eyes, were faithfully reproduced, and
yet it was not a likeness any one who loved Madge
would wish to possess.

"It is like her," I said to my hostess, "and yet
it is very unsatisfactory ; what is wrong with the
picture ? "

"Ah! you don't know Marjory's face so well as
we do," answered that lady, "or you would see
directly where the fault lies, but it is exactly like
nature. Have you never noticed when Marjory
is quite silent and thoughtful how very, very sad
and drooping the lines around her mouth become ?
One does not observe it so much in real life, but

this photograph is exactly like Marjory as I have seen her sometimes in church (kirk was what she really called it), or listening to music, or sitting silently looking at a beautiful view."

Of course this hint was quite enough for me. "Then there *is* an unfortunate attachment after all," I thought, and immediately inaugurated a series of artful and apparently innocent inquiries which were unhesitatingly answered, and from which I gathered that Marjory had always been observed to look sad unless she were talking or laughing.

"Always?" I persisted.

"Yes, ever since I can remember her, and that is about twenty years ago. She was just recovering from a low fever when we first came here. She had caught cold at the beginning of that winter, and they were very anxious about her, I remember, for some months. She was growing fast, and looked very delicate. She certainly was not nearly so pretty, so lovely I mean, as she is now, but the first thing I observed in her face was that sad droop of the mouth if it was silent. In those days of course she was more reserved and less taken notice of than is the case now; therefore, the mournful expression has always been there, and never quite outgrown."

So you see I was no wiser at the end of my long, delightful, autumn holiday than I had been at its commencement. At last I grew reconciled to the wonder of Madge's hard-heartedness, and agreed with my hostess, who used to say—

"I am tempted to hope that Marjory Fraser will never marry now, for what should we do without our standard subject of speculation and of interest? Some day I will write a book entirely on the theories which I have heard advanced about her and her affairs, poor girl. The most romantic, the most idiotic, the most plausible reasons have been assigned for her resolution, and after all I believe it is simply because she has never seen anyone whom she prefers to her father. Dear old man! I don't wonder at Madge being so fond of him."

CHAPTER III.

MALCOLM MUNRO.

THE Highland year appears to me to consist of only two seasons — autumn and winter. The summer is not really summer at all, for there are not three evenings in either June or July when a fire is unacceptable, and as for spring, the less said about that the better. But then on the other hand, a Scotch winter is much more to my taste than the corresponding English season ; at all events, one knows what one is about, and there are none of those death-giving changes and chances— one day mild and the next, a hard frost—which victimize us in the south. The individual does not however exist, who, having once spent a fine autumn in the real Highlands (even on the west-coast, if he does not mind rain), is not haunted all his life long by pleasant memories of happy days, and a burning desire to go north again, "When the bloom is on the rye."

Such was my case I know; and year after year I shook the dust of cities from off my weary feet early in August, and turned a joyful face towards the "Noble northern land." Sometimes I went west, and sometimes east; oftenest westwards, for there lay Loch Shellach, and near Loch Shellach lay Glenthorne, and Glenthorne held Marjory Fraser.

I used often to reproach the kindly chieftainess of Loch Shellach for the unvarying silence she preserved in her letters about our beautiful Madge, but she used to defend herself by saying—

"No, I will not tell you anything about her when I write; I choose that it shall all be fresh and new to you when you come to see us. Marjory Fraser is the great interest of the place, and I am not going to lose the advantage of having something new for you instead of recurring to an old subject; besides, I had nothing to say. All goes on the same at Glenthorne, Mrs. Fraser has been ill, and Madge was kept at home a good deal after you left us last year. It happened to be just that gay time I told you of at Christmas, when Mr. Munro came home and took possession of Strathmore. You remember having heard long ago that he bought the place, and it has been kept in good order ever since, so when he came back from the West Indies the other day he had nothing to do but walk into it. Naturally, we made a little fuss about him, for we are not what you call snobs in this part of the world," continued the lady, with a toss of her comely head; "we are very proud of our self-made men, and James Munro was once a small tenant-farmer's son on the very estate which he now owns."

"Is he a nice, pleasant person?" I inquired, with true feminine vagueness.

"He is perfectly gentlemanly and quiet, and his manners are simple and unaffected, but his health is not good, and he excuses himself from entering much into our little society on that ground. I fancy he has been used to live alone a good deal, and I don't think he cares much to see any one except his sister, who is also a Mrs. Munro, you remember."

"Yes, I remember perfectly—Elspeth you called her, I think; does she live in that nice cottage still?"

"She lives in the same spot certainly," replied Mrs. Keith; "but it has been so added to and improved by degrees that you would hardly recognize it again. You know it is, after all, the place where she and her brother were born, and her son also, for poor Munro, her husband, never took her away from her father's house. As Mr. James Munro's circumstances improved he sent money home to his sister, and she has always laid it out in beautifying and improving the old homestead. The original cottage and even the garden is still there ; but it is now the perfection of a small comfortable house. James Munro often goes to see her, and seems to like Shiel-dag better than his own place."

This little conversation revived my slumbering interest in Elspeth, and I took an early opportunity of suggesting that we should go and pay her a visit. To ask was to have at Lough Shellach ; so the next day found us jogging along the narrow steep road, which after many ups and downs, winding over heathery moors, and dipping into lovely, lonely valleys, brought us at last in view of Elspeth's—or, as she was universally called, old Mrs. Munro's— dwelling place.

It was the sort of delicious home-like abode which one cannot help coveting with an exceeding great desire, especially if it is beheld on such a day as I saw it ; its garden glowing with flowers and fruit, for here they both grew together, adding much to the beauty and richness of colouring around; its stone walls tapestried by a profusion of creepers,

some of which were losing their summer green, and
showed splendid reds and browns among the glossy
ivy leaves. Through the middle of the garden
hurried, with noisy chattering ripple, a little burn,
and the music of its waters chimed in with the
hum of Elspeth's bees. As our pony's feet disturbed the afternoon silence, a couple of splendid
collies, with frills erect and pointed ears, sprang out
upon us, but the highland pony was too well used
to these noisy greetings to be disturbed by them;
shaking his head as though he would say, "Don't
be foolish, it's all right," he continued the even
tenor of his way and landed us in front of the
porch.

A stout, red-haired servant-girl came out, but she
was not equal to the occasion, and merely ' stood
staring and smiling at us, dropping from time to time
a welcoming curtsey. We inquired after Mrs. Munro,
who did not wait for the tardy movements of her
freckled mistress of the ceremonies, but appeared
herself in the porch. What a picture she made as
she stood there, with her old-fashioned cap and
short-waisted, scanty-skirted gown!

Elspeth's manner had always been perfectly free
from vulgar hurry or confusion. I believe that if
Her Majesty had paid her a visit, Elspeth's quiet

graceful dignity would have known no change. On this occasion her welcome of us was perfect, and although she was now an old woman with white hair and a much-lined face, her figure was as straight and as strong as when I first saw her. Inside, the living-room of the cottage, as I prefer still to call it, was as unlike a conventional parlour as could well be imagined, with its well-used books, its jar of flowers, and Elspeth's knitting on the table, and a spinning-wheel in the corner. I must not yield, however, to the temptation to linger over our visit ; we both agreed, as we talked during our homeward drive, that there were few people with whom it was so pleasant to associate as Mrs. Munro; Mrs. Keith added,—

"Her brother is quite as nice, Keith likes him immensely ; he is coming to dine and sleep at Lough Shellach to-night, so you will be able to judge for yourself, and we shall also see another member of the family. Mr. Munro asked leave to bring a relation who was going to live with him ! I have no idea who it can be ; perhaps it is a woman ! I hope the individual, whoever it is, won't disenchant us with the Munro family. Elspeth and her brother are so charming that it would be a thousand pities if they set up some stupid, far-away cousin to spoil the pleasure of going to see them." Then as she waxed warm with her fancied wrongs, Mrs. Keith whipped up the pony and said quite indignantly, " I daresay this relation will turn out to be a horrid vulgar school-girl, who will want to flirt with the boys, and who will say with a giggle that Marjory Fraser is quite an old maid."

"Perhaps she may be a niece," I suggested; as if nieces as a rule were less objectionable than cousins.

" No, she must be a cousin," persisted Mrs. Keith, " because there's only Elspeth, and she has no children."

" Poor thing! then she must have lost them," I replied, " for I certainly saw a little heap of children's toys in that old-fashioned glass cupboard, and they must have lived some years, too, for many of the things were only fit for a big child."

"Oh, yes, now I think of it, Elspeth had one son; but I don't know what has become of the lad, I never saw him. I fancy there's some mystery about that boy, he went away suddenly, I believe; at all events Elspeth never speaks of him, so no doubt he is dead."

" But Mrs. Munro does not look unhappy; her face is thoughtful if you like, but not in the least sorrowful."

"Ah, well! he may have been more plague than profit, as the poor people say, and he may have died long ago, and she has forgotten him probably."

It is needless to say that buxom, prosperous Mrs. Keith had never lost a child herself, or she would have known that a mother *never* forgets. The tiny infant, the dear, engaging, little child, the fine promising youth, all live eternally enshrined in a holy and secret place within the mother's heart. Their memory is kept ever green, ever watered by tears; but as years pass on the bitterness may be washed away and it may heal over, but the smart of the wound is always there.

We had at all events quite determined that the relative who was to take up an abode at Strathmore was a female, probably an objectionable one, and the last words Mrs. Keith said to me, as we separated to dress for dinner, were—

"Now don't be late; Mr. Munro is sure to come early on account of the bad roads, he always arrives in daylight. There is no post-bag to keep us writing letters to-night, and I wish you to have a good chat with the dear old gentleman before the others are ready; and," she added dolefully, "I may want you to help me with that odious woman."

But when I came down an hour later there was

Mr. Munro in the library, and, standing at the window, looking out, I presume, at the lovely sunset colours over the loch, was a tall, broad-shouldered man with his back towards me. Mr. Munro and I did not require any formal introduction to each other, and he only waved his hand in the direction of the stranger, saying something which I could not catch. I looked round the room for the lady of our imaginations, and, not seeing her, said blandly, "I hope your cousin is not very tired, Mr. Munro, the roads are so bad about here that they rather jolt a lady if she be not used to them."

How dreadfully mortified I should have been, had any suspicion occurred to me that James Munro took this speech to mean a querulous complaint against the rough country roads. I who pride myself on never finding fault with what can't be altered, who always pretend to enjoy discomfort, to be supposed to complain of a Highland cross-road! It would have been too much for me, and happily James Munro only looked a little surprised and said, "He can answer for himself, but I don't think he minded it."

The tall gentleman at the window could not refrain from an involuntary glance at the reflection of his substantial figure in the glass as he assured me he did not feel the least fatigue.

Now I have always found that explanations are a mistake. It is much better to stop at one's first blunder than to plunge into a quagmire of, "I thought," and "I had no idea"; so although I felt extremely like a fool and turned very red, still it was wiser to refrain from explaining that I fancied the relative had been a young lady, and I contented myself by a little bow, but mentally I vowed vengeance on Mrs. Keith, for after all, it was her theory which had misled me.

We heard her step at the door, and I devoutly hoped she too would make a similar blunder. Fortune favoured her, or rather Mr. Munro profited by my mistake, which he attributed to his own shortcomings, and he distinctly presented the tall stranger as "My nephew, Malcolm." Why should Mrs. Keith have looked so triumphantly at me? *I* had never said the relative would be a lady, but she certainly glanced victoriously towards my place, and greeted her new guest with the utmost cordiality.

I am not the only person in the world to whom beauty is a passport and a certificate, so I need not apologize for having taken a great fancy to Malcolm Munro at first sight. Not that I ever connected him in my own mind with Elspeth or that lowly cottage roof tree, for it seemed ridiculous to fancy such a giant having ever been a yellow-haired laddie playing at its threshold. I set him down at once in my own mind as a soldier, though in this I was signally wrong ; but his firm step, upright bearing, and even the turn of his head, gave one that idea. Dear me, how good-looking he was ! very brown of course, but it suited his style exactly, and although he was evidently not a young man, he was none the worse for that.

We all went into the dining-room presently, and in the middle of the meal, during one of those silent pauses which will occur in the liveliest parties, Mr. Keith said to his wife,—

"I went over to Glenthorne to-day, and settled with Marjory and the laird that they are to come here to-morrow for a day or two. Mrs. Fraser is much better now, and Madge looks pale and ill after having been shut up so long. She has not really been able to go about as she used to do with her dogs and her father (we all bullied Mr. Keith for putting the laird last, but that was just what he said), and she is not in beauty at all, so I declared she must come over here to be nursed and petted by mother."

I was very glad to hear that Madge was coming, for I had not met her since my arrival; but I felt it quite a personal grievance that she should not be in her best looks when a stranger might possibly see her. It was too bad that she, our pride and boast, could not be always in full bloom and beauty. Just as when one takes a visitor to see a lovely view, and lo! it is all clouded, and misty, and veiled.

I solemnly declare it was not of malice afore-thought that I glanced at Mr. Malcolm whilst our host was speaking of Marjory. In fact, as I am quite an old woman, I may perhaps confess that I looked at him very often during dinner, and the more I looked the more I liked the nice, good, clever face, with its regular features, self-contained expression, and rich bronzed colouring. But upon this occasion my opposite neighbour did not preserve the im-passibility which I, being very impulsive, so much admire. He actually coloured—yes, there was no mistaking the deep crimson flush which mounted up to his hair; and then the next moment he turned pale, till his lips showed white, even under the great, tawny moustache.

" Good gracious," I thought to myself, " he is going to faint, it must be the effects of bad climate—no, he is only nervous, his hand is shaking, and he has actually plunged into a conversation with little Polly, who hardly dares to answer such a big creature."

Mr. Malcolm rather fell off in my good opinion,

when I thought it possible he could be shy, for what but shyness at the prospect of meeting a strange lady the following day could put him in such a state? And yet he did not seem to wish to avoid the trial, for when his uncle hesitated about returning to Strathmore, the nephew expressed so much willingness to remain that Mr. Keith could not but invite him to do so.

It was for no reasons connected with the outdoor sport that Mr. Malcolm lingered at Lough Shellach, it must have been for the pleasure of our society. He loitered about the house and garden all the beautiful autumn day after his uncle had set off homewards; yet with more than the ordinary perversity of his sex (I don't see why only women should be called perverse, they are not more so than men), the moment he heard the barking of dogs, and the chorus of the family voices, crying, "Here they come!" he bolted into the drawing-room, and rushing to the window, wrapped himself up in the ample curtain like a Brobdignagian child playing at hide and seek.

The room was full of nooks and corners, and in one of these I had been settled for some time past with a book; there was no reason why Mr. Malcolm should not have seen me if he had looked around him, but he did not do so: as I have said, he rushed to the window, and hid himself, whilst he gazed as eagerly at the new comers as though he had never seen human beings before. If I had thought him nervous at dinner the preceding day, he was tenfold more nervous now; his face worked as if he were going into a fit, and I could hear his breath coming in short, gasping sobs.

My first instinct was to get up and go towards him, but fortunately a second and wiser thought suggested that I should slip out of the room as softly as possible, and join the noisy, merry group in the hall; and among a small crowd of clamorous welcomers I made my way to Marjory Fraser. It was easy to see that, although so far as the bloom of health went, she might be a little faded, the higher beauty, which was so largely hers, had not deteriorated. Under ordinary circumstances Marjory led such an out-of-doors life in her father's companionship that she had not much time for reading; but her mother's illness during the last year had greatly changed the character of my favourite's daily habits, and long silent hours of thought or study had deepened and brought out the expression of her face, whilst they had robbed it in a slight degree of its open-air freshness. The rest of the party therefore were loud in their expressions of dismay at the sight of a some-

what pale and thin Marjory, but when it came to my
turn for a great hug and a big kiss—as the little
Keiths phrased it—I felt with my inner sight, rather
than saw with my outer eyes, that Madge was more
beautiful, in a higher spiritual sense, than when I had
last seen her.

The evening of the Frasers' arrival was also that
of the bi-weekly departure of the post-bag, consequently we were all rather late for dinner, and the
heavy cares of answering letters which turn up, like
the consequences of evil deeds, when they are least
expected, had driven everybody else's concerns out
of my head.   When I bustled in therefore to the
library I found it empty, and had barely time to take
my place at the dinner table before grace was over.
Mr. Keith reproached me in a playful but exaspe-
rating manner for dawdling, and I retaliated, so it was
some time before peace was restored and I could look
round the table.

Naturally my glance fell first upon Miss Fraser, and
I was shocked to see how altered she was.   Not only
were her cheeks pale, but her face wore a hard,
distressed expression, very different to its ordinary
sweet composure; and quite unlike the lovely,
thoughtful Madge whom I had so much admired
only a few hours before.   She looked grave and

silent, with a timid, subdued air, which was also new to her. Next to Miss Fraser, at the sociable round table, sat Mr. Malcolm Munro, but they did not find much to say to each other, though the laird talked long and joyously to the stranger.

As dinner went on, I could not help discovering that Malcolm had evidently been acquainted with Mr. Fraser in former times, though when and where they could have met, passed my comprehension. Once I ventured to inquire of Mrs. Keith whether Mr. Fraser had ever been in the West Indies, but she looked much surprised at the question and briefly answered " Never," so I did not pursue that train of conjecture any further.

After dinner, before the gentlemen joined us, Mrs. Keith said to me, " We had quite a theatrical *dé-nouement* in the library after you went upstairs. It seems that long ago before I was married or came here, Mr. Malcolm Munro used to live in this part of the country, and he knew Mr. Fraser very well." She then looked cautiously round, but Marjory had taken a plaid from the hall and we could see her walking very fast up and down outside the windows. " In fact he is Elspeth's son," she continued ; " but I have been quite wrong in giving you the impression that there was any unpleasant story about him   He seems, from what Mr. Fraser says, to have been perfectly steady and good always—only he chose to go away rather suddenly. From what I could make out before dinner, this splendid distinguished looking gentleman was once nothing more or less than a factor, or secretary to Mr. Fraser in the days when he was rich enough to afford such a luxury. The laird seems to have a had high opinion of him; but, dear me! Mr. Munro must have been a mere lad at that time; he does not look forty years old now, and it is ages ago since he lived with the Frasers."

"Where has he been ever since?" I inquired, not unnaturally.

"Well, I thought you could have guessed as you have seen them here together. Of course he has been with his uncle, James Munro, out in Jamaica; and a very good thing they both seem to have made of it, for old Mr. Munro told me yesterday they had done with the horrid place, and you see they are neither of them so very yellow."

"Is he going to live at Strathmore always?" I asked.

Now I know quite well my questions must seem very tiresome, but if no one asked stupid questions, either in real life or in stories, there would be no explanations, and we should never know anything about our neighbours' affairs ; so these apparently dull inquiries of mine must be looked upon as necessary evils, and borne with patiently.

Mrs. Keith was not the most patient of her patient sex, and looked a little provoked as she answered, " Of course he is; don't you know he is James Munro's only near relative? and the old man evidently looks upon him as a son. Why, you must have entirely forgotten us during your absence this time, or you would not want to know about the Munros. I have quite made up my mind that this great, tall Mr. Malcolm is going to be the heir of Strathmore, and we shall have all the young ladies in the neighbourhood pulling caps for him after the next county ball. I only wish that Polly were ten years older, I would enter the lists myself for such a nice son-in-law."

This speech surprised me not a little, for the Keiths were well known to retain rather old-fashioned notions respecting a lang pedigree ; and I could only account for it by supposing that her mother would not have made it, if little red-haired Polly had been less safe in short frocks and a long mane hanging down her back. But still it was in no spirit of matchmaking, for we had all been cured of that long ago, that my eyes travelled to the window, and rested on Marjory's muffled figure rapidly pacing up and down the gravelled walk outside it. I said,—

"How altered Miss Fraser is! she looks dreadfully ill."

"Yes, poor dear, I don't know what has come over her. I saw her the other day, and, though she seemed pale and tired from being up at night so much with her mother, I thought her lovelier than ever. The dark shadows under her eyes made them look so soft and tender, and she had such a sweet patient smile on her lips. When she first arrived to-day she looked in great beauty—the fresh air and the drive with her father had brought back a little colour to her cheeks, and the old bright, happy light to her eyes. She was in capital spirits too; we sat down here for a long time having tea and chatting half in the dark: it was then that Mr. Munro came in and made himself known to Mr. Fraser. The laird vowed he would never have recognized him; no wonder, after twenty years' absence in a hot climate; but there can be nothing wrong about Mr. Malcolm, because the laird asked him half a hundred questions, and we all listened of course to the answers, and I am sure nothing could be more satisfactory than they were. The only subject on which he seemed reserved was his sudden departure, and he told

Mr. Fraser he would tell him all about that, some day perhaps. I assure you it was most interesting, and it was quite like a story, hearing it all by the firelight.

"Was Marjory there?" I asked.

I am aware that I don't come out as a brilliant conversationalist in these dialogues, but you see I am drawing from nature.

"Oh! yes, of course," replied Mrs. Keith; "she did not talk much; she never does you know, and we remained listening to all that the two gentlemen had to say to each other, till it was time to dress. I suppose Marjory must be very tired, because it was not until after you came into dinner that I noticed how changed she looked. She ought not to be out there now in the damp. Madge, my dear, come in."

Miss Fraser came in without a word, threw aside the great heavy maud, and seemed intent for a few minutes on smoothing her sadly disarranged hair.

"You want sleep, Madge," said kind, motherly Mrs. Keith, after scanning the sweet, pale face very attentively; "early to bed and late to rise shall be your rule whilst you are here."

"Oh! no, dear Mrs. Keith," said Marjory, quite eagerly. "I am going out with papa before breakfast to-morrow morning, we made the plan whilst

we were driving here, and you must let me get up;
it will do me more good than anything. Won't
it, papa?" she added, turning to Mr. Fraser, who
came in first from dinner.

"It always does a person good to have their own
way," proclaimed Mr. Fraser, "and as your way
happens to be to come with me, why I think it
must be good for you of course." So I suppose
that was settled; at all events, the father and
daughter had their walk the next morning, from
which Madge returned looking thoroughly knocked
up. After breakfast she was driven to her own
room to rest, and kept a close prisoner till luncheon.
It was a wet afternoon, so we played billiards, but
I cannot say we were a very lively party. Marjory
was so different; she seemed eager to be downstairs with us all, but still she had not a word
to say, and her manner was positively awkward.
Yes, our stately gracious Madge evidently felt ill at
ease and nervous, and when two or even three days
had passed over our heads, she did not seem to
regain her composure.

Mr. Munro lingered until the end of the week,
and then he went back to Strathmore. Before he
left us he walked over to his mother's cottage, and
returned in excellent spirits; but even at his gayest,

he was a quiet, reserved man, whose silence, however, was more intelligent than other people's talk. He watched Miss Fraser a good deal, I fancied, though he did not pay her any particular attention ; and Marjory wore a subdued, timid air if he were near her, which gave me the idea that she was afraid of him, though such a notion seemed too preposterous to be entertained for a moment.

CHAPTER IV.

ALL-HALLOW E'EN.

DURING the uncomfortable days to which I have alluded, Marjory Fraser clung to me a good deal, and this was the more remarkable, because she was not of a clinging nature. I do not mean that she was a strong-minded, self-reliant woman; Heaven forbid! Such females have not Madge's soft velvety eyes in the first place, nor are they so generally beloved as she was. Miss Fraser had always been, from her girlhood up to the present time, perfectly free from gushing sentimentality; she never took a fancy to any one, man or woman, though she was frank and cordial to all.

It was therefore quite new to find Madge following me about the house like a dog. I felt instinctively that she was often on the point of speaking to me about something which was troubling her, and as

often some innate fear or reserve kept her silent.
I did not attempt to hurry or force her confidence,
for I long ago learned the truth of what Adelaide
Proctor expresses in her melodious words, when she
says:—

> " To help and to heal a sorrow
> Love and silence are sometimes best."

The night after Mr. Munro went away, Miss Fraser
came into my room just as we had all betaken
ourselves to our separate apartments. She wore an
air of desperate courage, as if she had screwed herself
up to tell me her affairs. I made her very welcome,
and smoothed the way by professing sudden wakefulness and a burning desire to sit up late, which
was a gigantic fib by the way, for my poor old eyes
found it hard to keep themselves open. Marjory's
shyness was unconquerable however, and she left
me after a few minutes, having asked no more
important question than whether I thought it would
be fine to-morrow. I gave my opinion in favour
of sunshine, and asked why.

"Because we are going away in the afternoon,
and I want you very much to take a walk with
me after breakfast. You have never yet seen
one of the loveliest glimpses about here, and it
is really quite close to you. If it were ten miles

away you would always be making excursions to
look at it, but just because it is so near and so
easy to get at, that view is always neglected, I
think."

I stipulated that my age and infirmities should be
considered, and that, if it were not beyond my small
walking powers, I would consider myself pledged to
go out with her after breakfast.

Marjory seemed brighter and less careworn when
she came down the following morning, and we congratulated each other on the loveliness of the day.
The little Keiths looked very much depressed when
they found that we had judiciously chosen an hour
at which they would be shut up in the schoolroom.
These youngsters were very fond of swarming about
us out of doors, and neither Miss Fraser nor I
wished for their company. It was quite the Madge
of former days who waited for me in the hall as
the clocks were striking eleven—a bright-eyed, smiling
Madge, who seemed to have only known twenty-
eight or thirty summers—not the pale, nervous woman
of the last week.

We could not possibly talk as we slowly toiled up
the narrow path which zig-zagged round the hill,
first for want of breath, and next because we had
to walk in Indian file, and I made Madge go last

that she might not force the pace. At last we turned a corner, or rather shoulder, of the steep brae, and came on a lovely view, so different in character from the country which lay around Lough Shellach that it was difficult to believe we were only half an hour's walk from that place. There was scarcely a breath of air stirring, but nevertheless Marjory would not be contented until we had established ourselves under the lee of a great rock, and there we sat, on the elastic springy heather, crushing its lovely purple bloom into a delicious cushion. The stillness was profound, only broken by the hum of a gnat, or by the drone of bees; these sounds fitted in to the quiet around us perfectly, so far from jarring the silence, they only intensified the dreamy, brooding quiet.

As we sat there silently alone with the great comforter, Nature, Marjory's long-formed habits of reserve and self-control melted away beneath the soft, loving touch of the fair Earth-mother. I fancied that I could watch her without being observed, and I saw that gradually each line and curve of the face I had grown to love so dearly softened and relaxed, a yearning, dewy look dawned in her blue eyes, the painful compression around her sensitive mouth gave way to a quiver of human weakness; and, although we were not speaking to each other, I felt that she must perceive my intense sympathy through some mysterious subtle sense for which we have not yet found a scientific name.

It was therefore no surprise when Marjory turned her head quietly towards me, and, as if in answer to spoken words of mine, said in the simplest and most natural way in the world, "Yes, I can tell you all about it now; sitting here in this way it is made easy; and yet I have never said a word on the subject for twenty years. It will be quite a long story, I am afraid, but I will make it as short as possible; I feel now that I *must* speak."

For my part it was as if a lovely, shy bird had alighted for a moment on my hand, and I dreaded lest the least word or look of mine should scare away the lightly-perched visitant. I fairly held my breath for fear a wrong or an impulsive word, however kindly meant, should close Marjory's lips. Not for my sake was this great dread, for I felt certain that it would be an immense relief to her to tell me what was her trouble. My own voice sounded almost cold and unsympathetic, as I assured her that anything which it might be a comfort to tell, would be of the deepest interest to me to hear, and that if earnest affection could inspire wise counsels my advice must needs be good.

My almost whispered words did not scare away
Marjory's shy confidence, and this was the substance—
the bare, cold facts of the story she told me that
balmy morning as we sat alone among the heather,
with the grand distant view stretching away at our
feet, and, overhead, a quivering haze dancing between
us and the blue, cloudless sky.

It was indeed twenty years since Marjory Fraser,
then a slip of a sixteen-years'-old girl, had taken it
into her head to try and peer into her future fate,
one fine All-Hallow e'en. The idea had been suggested to her by hearing her father talking about
old-world fancies and legends. The laird and a
chance visitor were chatting together over a friendly
pipe, and neither of them noticed how interested
Marjory had become in their conversation. She
looked and felt a mere child, and was, as she
described herself, more of a boy than a girl, having
been always her father's closest companion. In fact,
ever since she had attained the ripe age of five,
Madge trotted about incessantly after the laird. She
rode with him, she fished with him, she toiled over
glen and strath by his side. Indoors, what lessons
she studied were conned at his knee, and she only
learned to work in order to hem and mark some
pocket-handkerchiefs for his birthday.

Of course everybody prophesied the girl would grow up a wild, freckled, rough, unfeminine creature but she did not fulfil any of those predictions. On the contrary, Madge's ways were as gentle, and her voice as soft as if she had studied in the prunes and prisms school all her life. Her skin was fair and stainless as a lily, and her open-air life had secured for her an upright figure and an elastic step, which was the envy and admiration of all beholders, besides a constitution as hardy as that of her own pony.

At this distant date, therefore, full twenty long years before Marjory told me the tale, she was a childish-looking lassie, with tawny hair and merry fearless eyes, of which old neighbouring lairds were wont to say that they would make wild havoc with men's hearts yet. Such words only gratified the girl's ears, insomuch as she understood them to mean that she was worthy of a place—and nothing but a first place would content her—in her father's heart. He represented all men in the world to her, and her visions of conquest began and ended with him. Not but that Miss Madge could be a tiny bit coquettish upon occasion, as Elspeth had seen for herself at the young laird's birthday ball; but she had never dreamed of any human being coming before her father in her fresh young heart.

"Then what put it into your head to try a stupid trick on Hallow-e'en?" I asked, feeling rather provoked.

She did not know; it came into her fancy suddenly as she sat on a low stool by her father's side, with her head resting on his knee. They, the laird and his guest, had no idea she was listening to their conversation, for she was quite silent, as silent as Malcolm Munro, who sat at a table on which stood a shaded lamp, writing business letters for Mr. Fraser. She had heard the servants say a word now and then about the superstition, but had not cared to investigate the subject. Now, however, it was very different. Told by lips whose lightest words were as Delphic oracles to her loving ears, the old-time tale became a mystic rite full of horrible fascination.

She heard that if youth or maiden sought to know their future destiny, they must, on that very night, after performing certain incongruous incantations, such as curtseying to the moon, throwing salt over their left shoulder, and various other ceremonies, which differ in different places; steal barefooted, white-clad and alone, out into the farm-yard and pace slowly three times round the last-carted wheat-stack. Then they were to make the best of their way towards the house again, and before they reached its shelter, their fate would be revealed to them. If they met or even saw the phantom appearance of any one (it generally happened that the seekers saw, or declared they saw, the shadowy likeness they hoped to meet), that person would be their fate in marriage; if they met a cat—not an unlikely occurrence—they would be old maids or bachelors all their lives; if a mouse ran out of its hole they would be rich; if a dog howled they would die young; and more fancies than Marjory could remember.

Of course the two gentlemen talked a great deal of nonsense, but we cannot be always wise, and they never remembered that young ears were listening, and a young heart throbbing wildly, as they capped each other's stories of a foreshadowed future. At last the laird rose and knocked the ashes out of his pipe with an exclamation of horror at the lateness of the hour for the sake of his precious Marjory's roses. He must have had a latent misgiving of the pernicious nonsense he had been so gravely discussing, for he said lightly, turning away and taking his bedroom candle from his little daughter's hand—

" Upon my word, Herries, you and I are a couple of old fools. Look what o'clock it is! To think that we have been sitting here all this time and have not found anything better to do than to tell each other old women's stories. You ought to be ashamed of yourself. I know I am!"

So they all separated, but Marjory told me she felt as if she were possessed by an irresistible impulse to find out if she should ever marry anybody. " I declare," Miss Fraser said, at this part of her story, " I had no idea that I should see any one. My dreams for the future all pointed to the perpetual companionship of my father—you don't know how I loved him. I thought that if I met the cat or a mouse what fun it would be to tell him ; and if I shuddered at the idea of hearing old Sharp howl, it was for papa's sake, not my own."

When Marjory had said this, she paused so long that I thought my bird had flown away, but she turned a little more towards me. I was quite shocked to see how deathly pale, with a horrible waxen pallor she became, as she went on to tell me that to her mind the most shocking part of the story, the part which had haunted her all her life, was, that in her girlish, high-wrought enthusiasm she actually knelt down by the open window and prayed devoutly that she might really and truly be shown her coming fate. She told me she even implored with streaming eyes, that if it were written her days should be few, the gracious heavenly Father would deign to specially comfort and help the bereaved earthly parent. That was what she dreaded; it appeared an impossibility that she should see either the reality or semblance of a lover, for no such being existed in her ideal world, and either the cat or the mouse would have been most welcome to her eyes.

She was still so childish that the bare idea of encountering these two last personages of the drama restored her to a sense of the amusing part of the superstition, and, as it was very near the mystic hour, she hastily made her preparations according to the letter of the tradition, and she had barely thrown the last pinch of salt over her shoulder, when it was time to hurry out to the farm-yard.

Any less healthy damsel would have had misgivings about catching cold, but the hardy Highland maiden never dreamed of such an undramatic catastrophe, and she made the best of her way to the proper place, took off her slippers, dropped the dark maud in which she had wrapped herself, and paced slowly three times round the wheat-stack, with her long hair hanging over her white wrapper, and her feet bare.

In walking, she softly chanted the appointed

doggrel rhyme; then, her last line and her last step having been brought to a conclusion together, a great dread seized her lest Sharp should howl: she caught up her plaid and her slippers, without stopping to put on either, and sped swiftly and silently towards the farm-yard gate.

As she passed another wheaten stack, a figure emerged from its shadow, into whose extended arms she rushed, for her speed was so great that she could not stop herself in time. Marjory's eyes had become used to the imperfect light, and when, a second or two later, she recovered her presence of mind sufficiently to draw back from the warm, strong arms which were clasping her to a wildly throbbing heart, the cold faint starlight shone down upon Malcolm Munro's pale, passionate face and eager, hungry eyes.

For a moment each must have thought the other a vision; but whilst it was an unexpected, undreamed-of phantom to Marjory, to poor Malcolm it was a heaven-sent ray of hope and joy. He did not even look surprised; it seemed just what he expected,— to have been permitted for one brief, flying instant to hold that fair, girlish form in his young and loving arms. If it were a phantom, then moon-cast shadows were far sweeter and fairer than any garish realities.

But these wild dreams passed like a flash of summer lightning, opening a glimpse of heaven to make the darkness of the gathering clouds more intense. As soon as Marjory realized that it was Malcolm Munro who stood there—Malcolm in the body, albeit he was as still and silent as any spirit, —she looked at him with a steady, long gaze of mingled contempt and scorn, which must have gone far to break the poor sensitive boy's heart. She did not attempt to run away or scream or faint, or do anything but stand motionless with this dreadful withering expression on her face.

" I hated him," she said; " I could have killed him as he stood there. I despised myself too, most heartily; but oh how I detested that boy! I did not feel afraid, only madly angry with him and myself. I suppose my feelings could be plainly seen, for it was not long before his eyes drooped, and he looked down, but even then he must have perceived what I felt, for presently he covered his face with his hands. This movement appeared to break the spell which had kept my feet fixed to the earth. I remember quite well that the moment his face was hidden, the power of movement came back to me; until then all my life and will seemed absorbed into my eyes, for only through them could I express my rage and scorn. But as soon as his were hidden, I darted off to the house without meeting cat or mouse or any living thing by the way.

"When I found myself safe in my own room again, I sat down on the bed and cried as if my heart would break. Any one would have done the same, and the tears were such a comfort and relief that I am sure they saved me from a brain fever. Up to that time I don't think I had really been conscious of any feeling except anger, and it was not until I looked at the window, with the faint, wintry light coming through it, making a broad square patch on the carpet, that I recollected my prayers an hour before, and my solemn vows that I would abide by whatever fate was shown to me, if only I might be allowed to lift the curtain before my future."

Poor Marjory! Old woman as I was, sitting there beside her on the heathery hill-side, twenty years after that All-Hallow E'en, I could put myself in her place. I could feel the full force of the torrent of shame and remorse which swept over the girl as she remembered her secret pledge (as she called it), and that by her own foolish act and deed she fancied herself bound in honour to consider her hand troth-plighted to a servant in her father's house. She took no comfort to herself from the thought that the lad was really much superior to his station ; that after all his services had not been menial ones ; that the alteration of first arrangements justified him in considering himself Mr. Fraser's secretary or factor, more than his domestic: Malcolm's real beauty of face or figure did not weigh with her in the least. Had he been deformed and hideous to behold, she could not have felt one jot more ashamed or indignant.

Perhaps it is not every girl of even sweet, silly sixteen who would have made herself thus miserable about the unexpected consequences of a ridiculous prank. The young ladies of the present time are born women of the world, and would probably have known exactly how to deal with this difficulty. Their fair cheeks might redden in their own room at the remembrance of such a midnight adventure, but they would show no emotion beyond its threshold ; if the occasional sight of their unexpected and un-wished-for partner annoyed them, they would take the first opportunity of obtaining his dismissal, and so the whole thing would be brought to a natural and speedy conclusion.

But poor Marjory was a simple, enthusiastic, country girl, with high flown and chivalrous notions, caught from reading her favourite Border tales and

poems, where a knight, who thinks nothing of
stealing his neighbour's cattle and sheep, would
not, for the wealth of the whole world, break even
an ˙imaginary pledge. They used certainly to
strain at moral gnats in those days. She, poor
child, felt herself as firmly bound to a suitor from
whom her whole nature revolted, as if the betrothal
had taken place before﹐the eyes of all her family
and friends. The first person she thought of, after
herself, was her father; she seemed to have understood at once that no sophistry about Malcolm's
improved position or even his own good qualities,
which Mr. Fraser so thoroughly appreciated, would
reconcile the laird to such a misfortune; and every
instinct of her mind warned her to conceal the
adventure from her father.

She knew absolutely nothing of Malcolm Munro's
feelings either about her or on any other subject.
Would he persecute her with his clandestine
addresses, or would he claim her openly from Mr.
Fraser? Whose advice could she seek, or to whom
could she turn for protection? Mr. Fraser, as she
well knew, was a passionate man, and prone to
execute his own vengeance himself.

If, she were to tell her mother this dreadful,
shameful story, Mrs. Fraser, who never kept a

secret, or gave a counsel in her whole life, would go straight to the laird, and then take refuge in hysterics within the seclusion of her own apartment. Upon Marjory would fall the full fury of her father's rage, and she thought with dismay that he might possibly not understand at first that her indignation and disgust equalled his own, and might even give her credit for wishing him to see the affair with different eyes. Then, as her imagination built rapidly up an edifice of probabilities, she beheld her father with uplifted arms rushing on young Munro, and here she acknowledged frankly to me that it would have been a satisfaction to her if Mr. Fraser could, without risk to himself, have put the unfortunate youth out of the way. But she was obliged to confess to herself that in the existing state of things this could not be done.

She walked up and down her room till daylight, alternately shivering with horror, and burning with indignation, until she had fairly worked herself into a fever. If the child had felt that there was any human being near her, upon whose tact and judgment she could rely and to whom she could confide the difficulty, all would have been very different. A little common sense and a maturer judgment would have soon reduced the affair to more reasonable proportions ; but the longer Marjory thought on the subject the more it grew, until at last she threw herself on her bed and fairly sobbed and cried herself asleep, to wake up an hour or two later, with a sore throat and a racking headache.

" No wonder ! " I cried, at this part of Miss Fraser's story. " No wonder, after running about a farmyard without shoes or stockings in the middle of a November night, and then parading your room for hours in only your nightgown, I daresay ! Ugh ! it makes me shudder to think of it. I am only surprised you did not go into a consumption and die. Never have I heard of such wicked folly ! "

Poor dear Madge had called herself hard names too often to mind my abusive epithets : she only smiled a sad, weary smile, as she went on to tell me how all her fevered fancies showed her Malcolm Munro appearing to claim her as his bride. She raved against him, she deprecated her father's anger, or besought her mother's compassion ; but how many of her wild words were said aloud, or how many could only be heard by the mythical ears of her little bedroom walls, Marjory never knew. She only guessed that even in her delirium she managed to conceal the real cause of her anxiety ; for from the first moments of her convalescence, when she strained all her weak faculties to discover whether there was any difference in her father's manner, she was unable to detect the least change in the laird's devoted affection to his favourite child.

"Papa could not have kept a secret from me all these years," she added, "though I have been obliged to conceal mine from him; but Heaven knows how willingly I would have told him, only that I feared to add even a feather's weight to his own troubles, poor darling father. As soon as I could think or reason, I cautiously asked Papa about the odious young man, and I actually fainted away from the relief and joy it was to hear he had gone quite away, as the children say. Of course that made matters much easier for me, and I have managed pretty well ever since, though at times the whole horror of that night comes back to me."

"Now we will go down to the house, dear," Miss Fraser continued; "it looks very much as if I had only dragged you up here to listen to my long story, doesn't it? I have often wanted to tell it you, but the right moment never came. Don't ask me any questions now, please: some other time I will tell you whatever you want to know, but I am not very strong, and I don't feel that I can say another word about it."

I got up obediently, with the help of Marjory's
pretty little firm hand, and I did not consider that it
was an infringement of her request to say, with quite
a deep sigh for such an old lady to have left at the
bottom of her heart—

"Poor Mr. Munro, I don't see that he was in the
least to blame : I like him so much, and I am very
sorry for him."

Miss Fraser turned exceedingly red, and I rather
quaked at the probable consequences of my partisan-
ship ; but no, this contradictory young woman (for I
maintain that thirty-six is still youth in some women)
looked actually pleased; charming little dimples
came about the corners of her mouth, and a shy,
happy look dawned in her eyes.

Now, as the immortal Miss Nipper would say,
without being a perfect Argus I am still far from
considering myself a bat or a mole ; so, whilst I
followed Madge down hill, for she went first on our
return, I built up theories, and made mental notes of
future questions to be asked respecting the existing
state of the old vendetta.   Alas ! they were all driven
out of my head by the sight of an ominous rhubarb-
coloured envelope on the hall table at Lough Shellach,
which, being opened, was found to contain a telegram
summoning me South, as soon as might be.

Marjory and her affairs went out of my head, and a horrible anxiety and dread came into my heart instead, as I set off homewards, fast as car and boat and rail could carry me ; and that was not very fast as far as the two former were concerned : but God was merciful, and only smiles and happy tears met me at the end of my hurried journey.

CHAPTER V.

"A MAN'S A MAN FOR A' THAT."

YOU must positively come back and finish your visit to Lough Shellach," wrote kind Mrs. Keith a month or two later. "You want change of scene and mountain breezes more than ever after your fright and anxiety. Now that everything at home is right again, why not come North for two or three weeks? November is lovely with us, and it is quite worth while taking the trouble of the long journey for a month of Highland air. Come. Marjory Fraser wants to see you very much, she is looking so well and so happy."

Now if Mrs. Keith had only put that sentence about Miss Fraser first instead of last, I would not even have waited to finish her note, but would have packed up my boxes and started by the Night Mail for the North directly; as it was, I fancied the

letter was all in the same kind hospitable strain, and
I did not turn over the page, but put it aside to be
answered later. When its turn came in a few days
and I read it carefully through, great was my dismay at having dawdled, and I hastily wrote a cordial
acceptance of her invitation, and followed my letter
the very next day.

It is worth the pain and sorrow of going away
from a beloved place to feel the great joy of
returning. Let us hope that this merciful and
blessed rule may be carried out in a higher, better
state of existence; and that in proportion to the
anguish of farewells Here, will be the bliss of greetings There.

In spite of darkening days and colder nights I found
an inner brightness, a heart-warmth at Lough Shellach, which made those chill October skies seem
glowing and beautiful as the August ones had been.
There were richer tints, too, on moor and hill, and
the deep orange purples of the sunset sky were not
less lovely than the fainter opal tints of summer.
Outside the house, great Nature had mellowed the
beauty of earth and sky: inside, she had asserted
the sovereign right she claims over human hearts,
however they may be fenced in by a hedge of
conventionalities.

What but a touch from that power which poets call Love, and philosophers Nature, had brought the light of youth back to Marjory Fraser's sweet fresh face, or made Mr. Munro so pleasant to all beholders?

At first it was all a confusion of happy gabble. The very youngest of the Keith children had some little story to tell on a subject which they did not however dare to allude to before Miss Fraser's radiant eyes. I could hardly believe the evidence of my senses, especially of my ears, when they conveyed to my bewildered brain the intelligence that Malcolm Munro was going to marry Marjory Fraser, and that shortly.

In my heart I felt it was happy news, and yet—I am almost ashamed to confess it—old prejudices and the force of educational habits made a parting struggle to be heard before they vanished; swept away, I trust for ever, by the great strong wave of nobler convictions. The little whisper said, " She is a lady and he is *not* a gentleman." Even at that moment I laughed, "Malcolm Munro not a gentleman; who then is one? Does a cultivated mind, chivalrous feelings, a reverence for all that is true and good not constitute a gentleman ? "

Fortunately my little mental battle had been

fought and won before Marjory came to claim my congratulations, and I was able to give them with my whole heart. As soon as this rather formal part of the proceedings was over, I settled myself, woman-wise, comfortably down for a good chat and demanded to be told all about it; then, with the least possible touch of malice, I added, "You know, Marjory, the last time we talked about this you were hating him a good deal. Don't you remember?"

"Oh no, I was not hating him at all when I told you that long story. I was afraid you thought so, but I did not quite see my way to undeceiving you just then. I couldn't, you know, because—well because I thought it was he who was hating me.

"He must be a very amiable man not to detest you, Miss Fraser," I replied, "for by your own showing you have been extremely disagreeable to him; but I do not want to exchange desultory remarks with you on the subject. It seems to have come all right now, which is a good deal more than you deserve, and I want to know exactly what happened next after you got well."

It must be a very youthful and inexperienced person who does not perceive that Marjory was likely to love me all the better for my seeming harshness to her. So long as you don't abuse the absent lover, you may say anything personally unkind to the lady of his affections, for humility always goes with true love ; but no hen will be more daring in defence of a solitary chicken than is a woman, when fighting the battles of the man she loves. Through evil report and good report he is sure to have one faithful champion, and no one but himself can ever teach her to see his defects.

Marjory Fraser only considered my acid remarks to mean, that I thought better of Malcolm Munro than I did of her ; this she believed to be owing to a rare and just power of penetration on my part, for which she was not likely to quarrel with me ; so, instead of the least cloud flitting across her clear eyes, they smiled their happiest smile on me as she answered,

" I suppose I have never really disliked him since the evening when papa told me of his sudden disappearance. You cannot understand the relief that news was, unless I could explain to you the state of terror and anguish into which I had worked myself. Of course it was partly owing to the fever, but that did not make the suffering less real ; and I had been such a child up to that time that I had all sorts of ridiculous fancies. If any one had told me, that in consequence of my coming upon poor Malcolm in that sudden way, I was pledged to marry him in defiance of all opposition, I should have believed them, though I hated the idea of doing so. You must try to imagine therefore what dread and terror I held him in, before you can realize the blessedness of the news that he had left the country altogether. In spite of my fainting fit I got better from that very hour, and I also date my gradual change of feeling towards him from that same time."

"Oh! then you left off hating him directly, did you, Marjory? No wonder all this has come to pass so quickly in that case. I thought you disliked poor Mr. Munro up to quite lately."

"Don't be tiresome, dear;" answered Miss Fraser, "I was much too young and ignorant to have any such absurd ideas. I so far left off hating him, that I recognized his innocence of blame. After all no one was in fault except myself; he could not tell that I was going to be such a little fool as to test the charm; and as for catching me in his arms, he could not help himself, for I ran right into them."

"Well, there is just one thing I want to know, and you must answer me truly. Did you make all these excuses for the young man at the time, or have you tried him within the last three or four weeks at a higher court and acquitted him, with a recommendation to mercy?"

"I hardly know when and how I began to think more leniently of him. One cannot remember exactly every phase and turn of one's mind during the last twenty years. I only recollect the joy and thankfulness of hearing of his departure, though I never could quite shake off the feeling of being bound to him. I believe the real truth was that I did not wish to leave papa, and I never chanced to see any one who could tempt me to do so. No doubt if such a hero had come across my path I should have broken my imaginary fetters, but now I feel as if I had really and truly been waiting for Malcolm all these years."

"So you were, evidently," I said, sententiously; "but did you know that he was alive and well? I think Mrs. Keith and many other neighbours fancied he had died abroad, and he certainly was quite forgotten."

"I did not forget him," quoth Marjory, proudly; "I always thought it very noble of him to take himself off out of my way as he did. And papa never forgot him either. At first I disliked hearing his constant regrets for Malcolm Munro, but by degrees, as I came across books with his marks

and notes, and various evidences of what an uncommon mind and nature he possessed, I grew to
wonder if that look in his eyes had meant what
was called love. I did not expect to see him again,
though I heard through papa that his mother had
constant news of him. Once I ventured to go and
see Elspeth after we came home from some visits;
poor dear father had been immensely pleased and
flattered at my having excited a little notice and
attention; and in the pride and joy of the dear
old thing's heart he said to Elspeth on that
occasion, "I suppose we shall be losing this young
lady some day, Mrs. Munro, we can't expect her
to remain always with her old father." Elspeth
looked at me very intently, and said quietly, "You'll
not lose her just yet, laird—fate is fate." That speech
did not do Malcolm any good, for I was getting
too old to be frightened into anything, and my
instinct was to assert my independence at once. But
the feeling passed off, and I saw very little of Mrs.
Munro. Then when her brother James came home,
I heard that Malcolm was to come and live
with him and be to the old man as a son; but yet
I never expected to see him at Lough Shellach,
and that conversation he held with my father by
firelight upset me dreadfully."

"May I inquire respectfully what Mr. Malcolm Munro's feelings were all this time?" I asked. "Of course he has told you, and I consider that you are bound to tell me. When did he leave off hating you for looking at him in that horrid way?"

"Well, I asked him that," confessed Madge, laughing, and blushing a little, "and he said he—he liked me all the better for *glowering* at him. He knew perfectly well that I had no idea of what he had felt for me almost ever since he had been a child, and nothing was further from his thoughts than to betray himself. In his way he was quite as proud as I, and sooner than give me cause to think that he could take the least advantage of a mere accident, he betook himself to the other end of the world. He knew nothing at all about my illness until I told him the other day, but we are both so unsentimental in consequence of our mature age, that we attribute it to exposure to the weather, not at all to over-wrought nerves."

Marjory and I talked a very long time about her affairs, and the conversation left no doubt on my mind, first that my favourite was extremely happy and next that in spite of the original disparity of position—there was none now—she was a very lucky woman. Certainly I never saw two people so much in love with each other, and the laird and even Mrs. Keith were satisfied.

The latter asked Mr. Munro one day why he had never married out in the West Indies. It was a mere random shot on her part, for the story of All-Hallow E'en was a secret even from the laird ; Marjory declaring she was too much ashamed of her part in it to venture to tell her father.

Mr. Munro kept his countenance perfectly, and only replied that he had never been tempted to take any such step. He could not understand why we laughed, when he added with perfect simplicity, and good faith, " You see, I cannot bring myself to admire dark women, and they are all dark there."

" Now that is not true, Mr. Munro, as I happen to know from my own personal experience," proclaimed Mrs. Keith. " However, I am very glad you did not bring us home a stranger, and I should prefer to think you had been waiting for Marjory, for I like to believe that 'fate is fate.'"

IV.

A MAN'S STORY.

IV.

A MAN'S STORY.

CHAPTER I.

A FOOL IN HIS FOLLY.

I WAS so sad and so lonely. That is the only excuse I can make for myself. I am not one of those daring, dashing dragoons who swagger up and down Mr. Mudie's bookshelves, and march triumphantly through several editions of their history.

I may, in fact, be briefly described as the very antithesis to these gay *militaires*. I am not particularly brave nor beautiful. I am neither audacious nor successful. I am not a gambler nor a duellist. My battles have been fought against myself, and I have suffered defeats. I have staked my life's happiness on one card—oh! my darling Queen of Hearts—and I have lost it.

For all this unpromising beginning, I would fain hope that some gentle eyes may rest for a few moments on these pages; when the short story has been read, may they feel that the people in it have lived and suffered, have really, even with all their imperfections, existed, and are not inconsistent, faultless improbabilities, conjured up by golden spells from imagination's vast caverns.

Though mine hath not been, alas! "a life heroic," I yet have found a "new acquist of true experience," and look forward, as Heaven's highest gift, to a future of "calm of mind, all passion spent."

Most men must feel at twenty-five as if life with all its glow and all its glamour was still full of possibilities for them; possibilities of fame, glory, or wealth; possibilities of triumph in that whereon their hopes are fixed. I have no hopes now, except to do my duty; and yet at no former moment of my life has the comprehension or the approbation of my family and friends attended any action of mine. Both are given to me now in the highest degree, just when I am feeling, with all the intensity of my nature, that the act and deed of to-day has shut me out from individual happiness for ever.

I had the misfortune to possess what is called independent means; on a small scale, it is true, but just sufficient to prevent any great necessity for a profession or work. Looking back, I can see that it is far better for a young man to set out on life's journey with health and hope, a fairly good, useful education, and without a sixpence in the world except what he can earn himself. It is not so pleasant, either for the youth or his friends, but it is much better for him.

I know it seems a hard, cold thing to say, but I fear it is true, nevertheless, that misfortunes, as we call them, are, ninety-nine times out of a hundred, simply the consequences of indolence or impulsiveness, or of a want of common sense. Misfortune is a prettier word than consequence; so we use it. I will be as hard upon myself as I am upon others, and acknowledge that every sorrow of my life has been the bitter fruit of a seed of folly, dropped by my own hands into the consequence-bearing soil of existence.

To begin with : I was as unlike my parents and the rest of my brothers and sisters as though I had been chosen at random from a Foundling Hospital; as unlike in appearance as I was in tastes, habits, and character. They were all amiable, worthy people; but I might as well have talked Sanscrit to my father and mother as have attempted to make them understand how deeply a poem, fine music, or grand scenery stirred my whole being. Yet they were wonderfully kind and patient with me ; and when I returned home for good after the educational process was supposed to be finished, they suggested that, instead of deciding at once what I was to do, and following Solomon's advice—doing it with all my might—I was to remain at home and look about me. That was exactly what I did *not* do, however; I only looked into myself, gazed obstinately within, and never once glanced around to see what the world was like. The education which comes from contact with our fellow-creatures has never been mine, and I know nothing, and no one, but myself.

We lived by the sea-side, and I soon learned that there was no companion like the ocean; my moods varied with its changing waves, and neither dulness nor solitude existed for me so long as I could get down to the shore. I was, I am afraid, a dreamer of dreams, and all such visionaries are as fond of blue water as any Jack-tar in the world.

In spite of our minds being so dissimilar, I loved my mother with the deepest and most romantic affection ; and it was probably this devotion on my part which blinded her eyes to the way I was letting all the best years of my life slip away from me. Although the gentle creature could not comprehend her son's dark, stormy moods, she flattered me by a timid reverence for what was a mystery to her in my nature. My father did not interfere with my solitary tastes, he possessed them himself in some degree, and, as I was neither extravagant nor vicious, he simply let me alone.

As for society, I hated and dreaded it. Only those who shine in the company of others like mixing with their fellow-creatures ; whenever I hear any one say he dislikes society, I feel very sure that society dislikes him. At first, I used to be invited to parties for the sake of my parents, and also because, so far as looks go, I was tolerably presentable, though my friends soon grew tired of filling a place at their tables with such a useless guest as I was. Young ladies wearied of trying to find out a reason for my gloomy looks ; the pretty sympathetic little butterflies longed to console me for my imaginary sorrow, and fluttered away in deep disgust, when it was made plain to them that I was dissatisfied with no one and nothing but myself ; that I had neither trouble nor grievance in the world ; that I was merely shy and awkward, with an utter incapability for small talk or flirtation. Yet I wrote poems filled with ravings of ideal loveliness ; my spirit-loves were all fair and stately to behold, and the prettiest woman of my acquaintance fell far short of my requirements in beauty.

If there was one social ordinance which was more odious to me than another, it was that of paying an afternoon visit. I can see now that selfishness is really at the bottom of what is called bad manners : an ill-bred person is ill-bred, because he cannot forget himself completely, and attempt to please others.

One particular afternoon, when I was calling on Mrs. Ashley, I was more awkward and trying than usual, for my thoughts were running on a fine passage in the " Samson Agonistes," which had been haunting me all the morning. I even lacked energy or courage to get up from my chair and convey myself out of the room. My unfortunate hostess had been driven in desperation to take up some work, and we were both silent; I, as did the Laird of Dumbiedykes, "glowering like a wull cat" into empty space, whilst pretty Mrs. Ashley was intent on her embroidery. Nothing could be more unsentimental, more prosaic than my situation that spring afternoon, and yet the knock at the door announced my fate.

Footsteps were heard on the stairs—I grasped my hat and prepared to fly, but it was too late. " Mrs. Carruthers," said the servant, and through the drooping bright curtains of the doorway came, with swift, easy motion, a tall, slight figure in simple black draperies ; a figure as unlike my wild visions of beauty as can well be imagined, but which was yet to be the love of my whole life.

I did not admire or criticise Adelaide Carruthers; I simply loved her, loved her on the spot, as if I had known her always. In my dreams of what love would be when I should feel it, I had pictured an ecstatic state of rapture, a delicious madness, a frantic worship of the most perfectly, faultlessly beautiful woman.

As Mrs. Carruthers finished her greeting to Mrs. Ashley, and, turning to me, laid her slender hand in mine—pitying the embarrassment which a solitary bow cost me—I felt at once, " here is my fate, she is not beautiful, she may be neither witty nor wise, but she is the one human being who suits me thoroughly." The tone of her voice, every movement of her hand, every trick and turn of her head gave me a delightful, *comfortable* feeling all over. Instead of arriving in a tempest of passion, Love had floated calmly in ; instead of clouds, he had brought sunshine. I forgot myself and thought only of her, consequently I was less shy than at first. Half-a-dozen words will sketch Mrs. Carruthers's portrait, so far as words can describe the sympathetic charm which had won her a pet name out of one of Wilkie Collins's prettiest books.

Behold her then as she sat in Mrs. Ashley's shaded drawing-room ; her soft black silk dress making a contrast to the bright chintzes and gay books and flowers with which that little lady loved to surround herself. No garment of Mrs. Carruthers ever crackled or rustled. I have often thought since how exactly her movements answered the description which old Ben Jonson gives us of such a woman :

> " Her treading would not bend a blade of grass,
> Nor shake the downy blow-ball from its stalk,
> But like the south-west wind she mov'd along ;
> And where she went the flowers took thickest root,
> As she had sowed them with her od'rous foot."

I dwell on this air of repose too long perhaps, but I do it because it was one of her greatest fascinations. Quiet without a tinge of dulness or insipidity, that was her chiefest charm. Next came her voice, such a rare beauty, alas! partly, I think, because so few women use their natural tones; they speak in a conventional or affected way, as often rough and harsh, as lisping and indistinct. Adelaide Carruthers's voice caressed your ear, with its clear, rather low tones and its exquisite modulations.

For the rest, imagine a slight, graceful figure, harmonious in outline, but far from perfect in detail and a face whose expression made you forget to judge it by any standard or canon of beauty. Speaking of her afterwards some one said, " I never get beyond her eyes," and that was exactly the case with me. They were not those beautiful orbs which beam out on us from pictures and poems; they were rather deep set, almond-shaped, dark eyes, with somewhat full lids, but, oh! the beauty of the soul which looked forth from those clear windows. It was not a fixed beautiful expression, for it changed and varied with each passing thought; sometimes soft and dreamy, making the pupils like brown velvet, and revealing unfathomable depths of poetry and love. Then, again, they would sparkle like a child's, overbrimming with laughter and frolic ; and when her whole nature was stirred, as I have seen it stirred, by a heroic poem, or still more, by a tale of cruelty and oppression, then woe to that wight upon whom their lurid—yes, positively *red*—glances would dart like little tongues of flame.

Masses of hair, " gold upon a ground of black," waved away from her low forehead, and rested naturally on her soft, dark neck; for indeed she was a brunette of brunettes; or as she described herself, brown as a berry. The dear face was brown, too, and somewhat thin, and its features were irregular, but every line spoke of sense and good temper; whilst the even white teeth and healthy red lips lighted it up and made it pleasant to look upon.

That was my love as I saw her that day, five years ago, as I have seen her often and often since, only she seemed more beautiful to me every time we met, and as I shall never see her again.

CHAPTER II.

ON THE BRINK.

POOR Mrs. Ashley's heart must have died within her when a few days later I called at the house, and, finding admittance, seated myself once more in her drawing-room. My mind was no longer filled by visions of the strong man bound, or of "the sumptuous Dalila, that fallacious bride." My tongue was no longer fettered by self-consciousness, it was not of myself I wanted to speak, but of my new-found enchantress.

Good little Mrs. Ashley was a pearl among wives and mothers, and yet the veriest coquette who ever beguiled men into ephemeral follies; for these same women who cannot for the life of them keep their bright eyes and bewitching smiles from picking and stealing at their neighbours' sons, brothers, or husbands, are often the most charming at home. It does not at all follow that because a woman be ugly she is the more likely to fulfil her domestic duties. Some of the most thorough rakes at heart are singularly unattractive in appearance; whilst on the other hand a fascinating little coquette is pretty sure to be a pleasant sight at home as well as abroad.

Just such a one was Marion Ashley, as innocent and fresh as a daisy; yet if she were alone for ten minutes with any man, varying between the ages of five and of fifty, she would be perfectly certain to try to flirt with him.   It was her nature to, and it made her uncommonly agreeable.   Mr. Ashley took the utmost pride in his wife's conquests, and used to declare that she brought all the hearts she broke and laid them down, retriever-fashion, at his feet; but this accusation the little lady denied with flashing eyes.

She had long ago given me up as a hopeless subject, and was not far from the truth when she declared me to be in love only with myself.   That is to say I was too much occupied with my own psychical condition to have eyes or ears for women or their wiles.

> " Sweetest lips that ever were kissed,
> Brightest eyes that ever have shone,
> May sigh and whisper, and he not list,
> Or look away, and never be missed "

had hitherto been literally true of me.

But now this was all changed. I had found the other half of myself, the human being who suited every fibre of my nature, who understood me without explanations, whose very silence was more full of companionship than the conversation of others.

I had met Mrs. Carruthers once or twice at dinner parties, since our first introduction to each other in Mrs. Ashley's pretty morning room, and now, as I knew there was no chance of soon seeing her again, I had brought myself and my new-born feelings to the spot where they first saw the light.

No one has ever loved as I did, who cannot understand without being told how sacred the place becomes where a great revelation is first made to us; and here, amid these frivolous outer surroundings, had Love, with, as I thought, its highest aspirations and its most unselfish meanings been taught unto me.

Mrs. Ashley did not take up her work this time, and whilst I was thinking—not, as usual, how to introduce the subject of all subjects, but how to keep it a prisoner for a short space longer, deep down in my heart—she opened the golden gates of silence and let sweet, silver speech through, asking me point-blank "what I thought of her greatest friend, dear Adelaide Carruthers?"

Oh, those women, those women—how transparent
our hearts are to their bright eyes! It was of no use
trying to deceive such a proficient in the Art of Love
as my smiling hostess ; on the contrary, my newly
sharpened wits warned me to try to enlist her on my
side without delay as counsel for the prisoner, so I
answered bluntly,

"I simply think her the most thoroughly charming
woman I ever met, and I have not seen any one so
beautiful in my life."

"Poor Mr. Somerset! you are indeed far gone
if you call Adelaide beautiful. She *is* charming,
you are right there, very charming; but beautiful!
no."

" Well then it must be something in her face better
than beauty which misleads me," I answered ; "but I
want you to be so very good as to tell me a little
about her; who is she ? "

Mrs. Ashley affected to be surprised at this
question, and replied drily,

" She is Mrs. Carruthers."

"Don't be too hard upon me," I begged, humbly;
"you know quite well what I mean ; who is *he* I
ought to say perhaps?"

"Ah! that is more to the purpose," answered my
tormentress ; " I have much pleasure in informing you

then, that Admiral Carruthers is not only a gallant
sailor, but he is everything that is most delightful,
and we are all very fond of him."

"Where is he?" I continued, sturdily.

"He is at this moment, I believe, on the North
American Station, but he is expected back in a few
months. Is there anything else you wish to hear,
sir? Perhaps you would like to know that they have
two sweet little girls, one fair as a lily, and the other
a small brownie, like Adelaide."

I am going to confess here that I made a fool of
myself. We all do sometimes, only I am more candid
than most autobiographers; I who hate scenes, who
affect an iron cynicism, behaved, on this occasion,
like the hot-headed idiot which I am. Instead of
retaining the slight advantage gained by my
previous reputation for coldness and indifference
towards the fairer descendants of Mr. Darwin's Asci-
dians, I threw up the game, and like a craven who
fears death—and worse than death to me hung on
her words—I flung myself at Mrs. Ashley's feet,
crying—

"Oh, do not speak in that way! Surely you must
have some idea what agony you are causing me! Don't
you understand my feeling for Mrs. Carruthers is one
which I did not know it was in me to feel for any

woman? You need not say it is hopeless, of course
it is; but do not torture me in this way!"

Now Mrs. Ashley saw nothing ridiculous in men
kneeling in the very selfsame spot, and uttering
similar rhapsodies about her own charms; but when
these follies referred to another woman, that was
quite a different story, and not nearly so agreeable
in the telling. It was therefore with an air of wisdom
beyond her years that she said firmly,

"Get up directly, Mr. Somerset, and don't be
absurd. Can you expect me to be anything but
very angry at hearing you talk such nonsense?
Adelaide Carruthers is a good woman, much better
than most of us, and she would be greatly displeased
if she dreamed of any man speaking such words
about her."

"Good! I know she is good, but still I am as
certain as that I am sitting here, (for by this time I
had returned to the realms of commonplace and of
chairs,) that she knows how much I adore her; I can
tell it by a hundred signs."

"Indeed!" replied Mrs. Ashley; "since when have
you become learned in such matters? Is it not just
possible you may be a little mistaken in some of
these signs?"

"How can you be so cruel!" I almost sobbed; "I

thought you were so fond of her, and I could not help coming to you and telling you that I love her better than my life."

"I am not cruel, you foolish boy, I am kind. Listen to me. Is it not Solomon who says that 'the beginning of Strife is as when one letteth out water'? Well, you may believe me when I tell you that the beginning of Love is fifty times worse, and I only want to try and stop the flood in time. Of course you won't let me; no one ever will. You have been dissatisfied and to a certain degree unhappy all your life; yet I assure you the worst state of mind you have ever known hitherto, is bliss compared to what is before you if you do not try to be wise before it be too late."

"I cannot—oh, I cannot! Don't ask me," I moaned.

" I do ask you ; I do more than ask you, I require you to save Adelaide from a remorse and a misery which will embitter her whole life. Don't misunderstand me," she continued, holding up her hand for silence as I looked an indignant denial. "Of course you are at this moment brave and strong. You only want her to know that you love her with the deepest and purest and truest passion which ever man felt; you only want to hear her say that she loves you as such love deserves to be met ; and then you will both

go your separate ways and no harm will come of it.
You will be great friends. How can you be such a
fool? Do you think any man and woman ever yet,
since the days of Lancelot and Guinevere, said to
each other, fully meaning what they said, ' I love you,'
and stopped at saying it once? Ah, Mr. Somerset, it is
too sweet a phrase to hear or to say, not to be longed
for again. To many women it is nothing more than
an idle compliment, a high-flown way of saying,
' How pretty you are ;' but to Adelaide Carruthers
it would mean something very different."

"But I don't want her to love me," I pleaded; "that
is to say I do not wish her to be unhappy about
it. I only want to tell her what a new life and
new world she has opened up to me."

"That is all the purest nonsense," said Mrs.
Ashley. "It is worse than nonsense, it is sophistry.
You know very well nothing short of an avowal of
love equal to your own would ever content you ;
and then when it is made where are you, or rather
where is Adelaide's peace of mind? Can you not
understand that to such a woman, as I believe her
to be, such words, though heard by no mortal ear
but your own, would be a life-long remorse? Believe
me, I know what I am talking about. Do as
better men before you have done. Run away. It

will not be cowardice in this case, it will be the truest
courage, and Adelaide will bless you for it all your
life."

Ah! if Mrs. Ashley had only stopped before she
uttered those last nine or ten words! But she did
not, and that little phrase changed everything, for
it hinted to me, ever so darkly, that it depended
on my forbearance whether the "charmèd silence"
between Mrs. Carruthers and myself were broken or
not, and with all a man's selfishness I decided on
the spot that I would *not* be wise, and that I would
be miserable. If one could only be miserable
alone! but one cannot. Ever since the days of Eden,
wrong doing has entailed suffering and sorrow on
those we love best.

All that I gathered from Mrs. Ashley's words,
which were many more in number than those recorded
here, was a delicious suspicion, that she, who knew
Mrs. Carruthers well, imagined there might be danger
in my love for her, and implored my forbearance.
With this thought thrilling through every vein
in my body, intoxicating me like new wine, I took
my leave and sped away to one of my old solitary
haunts by the shore.

"A stranger doth not intermeddle" with the heart's
deep joy we are told, and even my mother was a

stranger to me at this moment. I needed to be
alone, and in my solitude I built airy castles, or
rather cottages, in which Adelaide and I dwelt.
Ours was to be "a noble friendship"—I don't know
where I got the silly phrase—and yet if all the
details of my ideal *ménage* had been reduced to a
working plan, the friendly part could have hardly
seemed more impracticable than the rest of it.

Up to the time of my visit to Mrs. Ashley, I had
never imagined that the swift current of my love
could do more than flow to the feet of my Queen
and lave them in all humility, but now everything
was changed; and I question if the new and delicious
.sense of mastery was not fully as exquisite as the
dawning consciousness of my strong affection. I
have read somewhere that those who best love to
rule are always the least fitted to do so, and this
was thoroughly true in my case. And yet I made
haste to rush in and grasp Love's sceptre, when I
should have waited in his lowliest antechamber and
learned how kings are served—on the heart's bended
knee.

Opportunity stood my friend, or, should I say more
truly, my enemy?

A relative of ours, who happened also to be a
friend of Mrs. Carruthers, wrote to my mother,

mentioning Adelaide's name, saying that she was in our neighbourhood and asking my parents to extend their well-known hospitality to her and her children, as it was disagreeable for her to be in lodgings. There were no good hotels, and the sea-air was necessary to the little girls' health.

I must tell you here that, previous to the arrival of this letter, I had left home, feeling thoroughly restless and miserable. It had often been my custom to start suddenly on long, solitary rambles through the adjacent counties; no one, therefore, was surprised at my announcement of a similar resolution one fine morning in the late spring-time, and it did not take an hour to carry out my hastily formed plans.

But, alas! it was no longer in the power of sweet, holy nature to soothe me. Mountains and lakes were but heaps of earth and pools of water in my eyes. Of course I was a love-sick fool, I know that, but it does not make a disease easier to bear when all the doctors in Christendom are agreed upon its right name. And I was sick indeed; my head as well as my heart was sick. Conscience even became weak, and let the traitor Reason lift up its voice and cry, " Why torture yourself thus ? take the good the gods provide, go back and amuse yourself with a pleasant companion, it is all right, and only what others do."

I know now, what I felt then, that I should have gone further and further a-field, that I should have put continents and oceans, if need were, between me and temptation, but I did none of these things. I lingered at a wretched country inn in a Welsh valley, where I was given vile food to eat, and where a harper harped upon his harp continually.

All these trifles helped to send me back to my own home and to my own people. I had not received any tidings of the arrival of our new guest, and when I lifted the latch of the pretty rustic garden gate and entered the shrubbery, I paused with surprise at the merry shouts and peals of childish laughter which I heard.

Our domain was not so large, but that a few steps brought me within sight of a clump of beech trees, which we always called my mother's summer palace. Truly their grand sweeping branches, so noble in outline, so delicately lovely in detail, feathering down to the very ground, formed a royal home for fairy queen; and there, on the soft green moss, which was flecked by the quivering sunbeams with a thousand dancing spots of light, lay my Titania.

Nor were elves and sprites wanting for the picture; her own little girls in their holland pinafores and bright sleeve ribbons, looked like tiny goddesses of night and morning. They were joining with a splendid big dog in keeping their sweet mother prisoner on the ground, and all this laughter which I had heard was the shout of battle.

At first they did not see me, and I stood for a happy moment watching the sunshine come and go on Adelaide's disordered locks, turning each hair which it touched into a golden thread.

If it had not been for seeing my own dear mother seated on one of the uncomfortable sofas made of crooked sticks, which constituted our outdoor furniture, I should have thought that I was in fairy land. No, I am not sure I should have thought that; for I well remember I was hungry and tired, weary and foot-sore, and none of those material disagreeables exist in dream-countries.

My mother was the first to see me.

"What, Paul, is that you?" she asked, in the usual absurd phraseology which we adopt towards unexpected visitors.

I answered, following the stereotyped formula, "Yes, it is me, back again you see."

Mrs. Carruthers sprang to her feet at my mother's

first words, and now turned towards her instead of
me, saying, almost fiercely,

"I did not know you expected your son home,
Mrs. Somerset; you told me only to-day that he
would probably not return for a month."

"So I did, my dear," answered the elder lady;
"certainly I had no idea of seeing him this evening.
What has brought you back so soon, Paul?" she continued, smiling a warmer welcome than her words
convey.

"I will tell you presently, mother," I replied; then,
with my newly acquired boldness, I moved a step
nearer to Mrs. Carruthers and whispered,

"You!"

She looked displeased at my impertinence and
turned away, calling the children to come to her.
The little creatures had danced off towards the
grass slope, and were busily engaged in harnessing
the patient St. Bernard to a garden roller with their
tiny pocket-handkerchiefs.

I followed her, and said earnestly,

"It is quite true that you brought me back, and
yet I did not know that I should find you in this
spot."

"We have been staying here, but our visit comes
to an end to-morrow," she said drily; "I hope the

children's noise will not disturb you much during these few remaining hours."

"Good heavens! Mrs. Carruthers, why should you fancy I dislike such happy sounds and sights as those?" I asked, pointing to the bright, joyous triad on the lawn. "I will go away directly if my presence be disagreeable to you; but although it is true that I did not expect to find you in this house, (we were not in a house as it happened,) it was nevertheless a strong craving to see you which brought me back."

Mrs. Carruthers looked grave, but there was just the least touch of entreaty in her glance, which revived all my old masterful feelings with full force.

I continued, "Do not make me think I am driving you away; indeed I will not let you leave the house as I enter it; you must remain just as if I were not here."

And so it was settled by her silence, a silence which gave consent to our both shutting our eyes, and hand in hand walking to the very brink of a flower-hidden precipice.

We have many fellow-travellers, and it is to warn those who are not yet absolutely blinded by specious arguments with themselves in favour of the attainment of their hearts' desire, that I write this record of two lives made miserable. by that journey.

CHAPTER III.

TEMPTATION.

AND so, as I have said before, we journeyed on, with "a gentle ecstasie"; blind and deaf to all the smothered, struggling cries of Conscience. Poor Conscience! Passion had her by the throat, and would fain have stifled her with kisses; but the fair white creature, strong with the strength of right, was not to be thus subdued, and she spoke loudly and sternly to me, at all times, but chiefly in the silent night-watches. We each know what she says to us, and her words are better than mine; I will, therefore, hasten on with the record of that halcyon time, so pleasant and so wrong.

Turning over the pages of memory, I find few distinct pictures. They are mostly blurred and imperfect sketches, but perhaps that is because mine eyes are holden, I cannot see. There is always one figure in the foreground, a tall, gentle lady, with a slightly drooping air ; that is new to her ; she feels and she knows, disguise it as she may, that, with this growing love for me in her heart, her moral nature is not fearless and erect; therefore she bends her head, and walks slowly.

For me it was a new heaven and a new earth in which I lived, and yet I had little to boast of. Mrs. Carruthers certainly avoided me, but such avoidance was infinitely more flattering than the most eagerly sought companionship. Hours had ticked themselves on into days, days had dawned and set into weeks, and still Adelaide Carruthers lingered in my home.

All its inmates loved her ; who could help it, oh my bonny Queen of Hearts? I have never met your equal for tact ; and yet it was probably something higher than tact which taught you how to avoid all discords, and to bring your life into harmony with the lives around. Yours was, I am sure,

> " A heart at leisure from itself
> To soothe and sympathize."

There is one picture I must try to reproduce. It is as clear and sharp before me this day as if it had been photographed for ever on my heart and brain.

See, then ! It is a wild, stormy evening, one of those early Summer evenings when she seems playing hide and seek with us, and has concealed herself behind her blustering sister, Spring.

Adelaide had often said she liked a high wind, and I availed myself of this as an excuse to tempt her to climb a hill a little way off, on whose summit stood a few fir-trees. Even in still, true summer weather, you could always hear a breezy whisper if you stood beneath their fragrant branches; and on such a windy afternoon as this, I promised Mrs. Carruthers that she should have a fine prospect and a slight gale if she would only brave the easy ascent. The original programme of the walk had included other people, but, for some forgotten reason, they had dropped away from us, and we stood alone, my love and I, under the great, gaunt Conifers.

Presently she moved round to a more sheltered side of the hill, and made as though she intended to begin its descent. Up to this time we had been almost silent, but suddenly I felt that I could speak; for, as Matthew Arnold so truly says in his most beautiful "Buried Life," it is not always that—

> " A bolt is shot back somewhere in our breast,
> And a lost pulse of feeling stirs again.
> And what we mean we say, and what we would we know."

I touched her arm to stop her, and said, beseechingly, " Don't go."

Mrs. Carruthers stood still as if she had been made of marble; turning her head slowly towards me, she raised those lovely, soft eyes to my face, and said, in a timid voice,

" I am so very tired."

No need was there for her to explain to me that it was not bodily fatigue which ailed her. I knew well she spoke of weariness of soul, of the ceaseless struggle between love and duty. There are moments when the stoutest soldier feels cuirass and helm a heavy weight, when he aches with the tire of keeping constant watch and ward. What would be thought of the fellow-warrior who advised him, when he complained of these things, to lay them aside, to turn away from his post and seek his ease under yonder flowering branches? Yet I was that craven knight. Instead of helping my love in the hottest hours of life's daily battle, I drew near to her and whispered of rest and peace; rest from the struggle, before it was over, peace in wrong doing. Has any one ever yet found them in either one or the other?

I could not repeat, if I would, all that I urged, all the arguments which came so readily to my tongue as we sat together under the lee of the hill. The ground around us was strewn with fragrant, slender fir-needles; above us roared and thundered the wild wind among the lofty branches of the old trees. But there was a wilder war going on in my own heart; and now, at all events, I did not deceive myself as to what the issue of that battle would be.

Adelaide was so simply free from all affectations that she could not dissemble if she wished to do so. With her there was no pretence of misunderstanding me, no proffer of friendship, no sophisms about a pure, holy love. None knew better than she how high and holy love could be, but that between us was not so, for she was another man's wife. She was no coquette either, to whom lovers' vows were as oft-told tales, for she acknowledged naïvely that she had never listened to such words before.

"This is my first temptation, and, at all events, it teaches me the depth of my weakness. I am not strong, you know, Paul, but I have always fancied that it would be so easy to be brave and good if ever I were tried; and see here, how feeble and how wicked I am!"

"We cannot be always strong, my darling," 1 said. "How can you help my loving you? I have loved you from the first moment I saw you."

"If I had perceived that, then, perhaps I might

have been wise enough just at first to run away; but yet," she continued, musingly, "I don't know; it seems to me now as if I must have loved you always."

In spite of such words as these, which should have been as music to a lover's ear, I felt an uneasy impression that this frankness was fatal to my hopes, to my wild visions of future meetings, of hearing again, and yet again, the sweetest words which are ever uttered on earth. Adelaide spoke to me as the dying speak; at that solemn moment when all Shams are brushed away, like the cobwebs they are, and the great Reality stands before us.

We sat and talked there for a long time; gradually the wind dropped and died away in fitful gusts. We spoke of many things which I have neither heart nor time to set down here. Adelaide mentioned her husband; she told me how good and true a friend he had always been to her.

" I was a mere child when I married him," she said, " a mere tiresome child. I have often wondered what could have induced him to choose me; and I sometimes think it must have been that he always considered my mother to be the best woman in the world, and hoped that her daughter might hereafter resemble her."

"And so you do, my sweetest one, you resemble goodness itself; but, oh! why, why were you in such a hurry to decide your future fate? You might have known that you were capable of feeling some stronger emotion than the love you gave your husband on your marriage day."

"No, indeed, Paul," she answered, simply, "I firmly believed that the feeling I had then for him, a feeling made up of respect, admiration, and gratitude, a feeling which each year of my married life has only intensified, was the blessed substitute, in my case, for that stormy, unreasoning love of which I had read and heard. Ah! I know better now;" and she hid her face in her hands, but not to conceal either tears or blushes, for her sorrow and her remorse were alike pale, dry-eyed spectres.

"I love him still with the deepest reverence," she continued; "I can never forget all these years of patient goodness towards me on his part. Much older than I am, often obliged to be away from me and his children, he has always treated me with the most generous confidence. I know I can trust safely to his forbearance and kindness. Like the prodigal of old, I will arise and go to him and confess the wickedness of my heart."

"Adelaide, you will not be so cruel to me, you are

not thinking of going away; no, you cannot mean that you dream of leaving me here, alone and miserable. I will not allow it."

"It is our only chance of safety, Paul," she replied; "I know exactly how far I can trust myself. I must be brave for both; ah! help me if you love me, help me to decide on the one thing which remains to be done—confession to the only human ears entitled to hear it, and then a life of expiation and repentance."

"I will not help you to any romantic folly of the kind," I cried, roughly; "I only know that you love me as I love you, and no earthly power shall separate us now."

"It is not an earthly power which will do it," she said, sweetly and gravely; and then she rose, and with firm steps walked down the zig-zagged path of the hill-side.

I followed her, pouring forth reproaches, entreaties, yes, even threats, so base and selfish had this "pure and elevated" love made me already.

Mrs. Carruthers did not leave her room that evening. Her absence was a relief to me, for I felt the need of collecting my thoughts and marshalling those reasons, which had appeared so substantial a few short hours ago, and now, when I most needed their assistance, were crumbling away into dust and ashes.

I spent a miserable night, walking about my room during most of its long, dark hours. Sometimes I felt triumphant. " She loves me, she loves me," was the refrain of my pæan; then came the next moment a voice monotonously repeating the dirge-like burden, " She will leave you, she will leave you." I alternated in rapid vibrations between hope and despair, joy and desolation. With all my morbid views of life, my forced and false sentiment, I had never been weak or puling in my unreal griefs. Now I flung myself on the floor and cried like a child. I don't know to this day which was the greater agony—the suffering which wrung the tears from my eyes, or those scorching drops themselves. Truly I have wondered since to hear such showers called refreshing; they burned my face as they fell. From time to time I felt a savage joy, a hope that Mrs. Carruthers would taste the full bitterness of this draught of self-denial and duty which she held to my lips; then again I softened, and prayed that my love might be calmly sleeping, and that on me and me only might fall the suffering.

I am well aware that to many people this sketch must appear over-coloured and exaggerated, but it

depicts very faintly the anguish and misery of that
night. I had not frittered away my affections in a
thousand and one little love affairs, I had never
before looked upon mortal woman to covet her for
my very own. I was young, ardent, and an unpractical visionary. All my strongest feelings had
been garnered up till now, and lo! my love would
have none of the heart's deep wealth which I was
so ready to pour at her feet.

At last the morning dawned, and so soon as it
was daylight I hastened down to the sea and plunged
again and again into the delicious, bright, sparkling
waves. The excitement of struggling with them, and
the shock of the cold water restored some degree of
common-sense and calmness to my excited brain, and
made me a little more reasonable when I returned to
the house later. I went as straight to the Beechen-par-
lour out of doors as if I had made an appointment with
Mrs. Carruthers, and found her seated there, alone, with
a small table before her, and some hot coffee and bread
on it. Unpoetical as it must sound, I was very thankful to accept her offer of the refreshment, and, after
we had finished, she was the first to speak to me on
the subject of our wild words of the evening before.

I suppose the reaction had set in, and I was
exhausted after a sleepless night; I only know that

I felt quite unable to argue with her; all that she said seemed the hardest, coldest truth in the world, and, as such, not to be gainsayed. The shafts of the rising sunbeams had been even as Ithuriel's spear to my visions of the evening before; at their touch my beautiful forms and fancies had shrunk to bare, naked facts, with ugly names. I listened therefore with comparative patience, feeling in my heart the wisdom of her words, when Mrs. Carruthers said :

"I have made all the necessary arrangements, and I am going away from this at once, going in fact to London. There is no need to tell you that I have had a great struggle with myself, but I have been taught what is best—the highest best—for both of us."

"It is so easy to talk like that," I answered savagely. "You cannot love me as I thought you did, if you can believe in any 'highest best' away from me."

She quietly put this oft-repeated argument behind her, as it were, and continued :

"It has been on my mind for some time past that I ought to go out to Halifax and remain there with the little girls whilst my husband is on that station. I cannot quite decide yet, but I have an instinct which tells me that will be the best thing to do."

"You do not appear to think what will be good for *me*," I observed, as she paused for a moment; "all your endeavour seems to be to get away to new scenes and leave disagreeable memories behind you."

"They would not be left behind, if I wished it, Paul," she said, ever so gently, compassionating my great anguish; "and, in spite of my remorse, they are only too sweet and precious to me."

"Remorse," I answered, roughly, "I don't see what you have to be remorseful about. You could not help my loving you, nor my telling you that I did so."

"We need not go back to that part of the story, dear, let us try to see what is right now, and when we see it, to act upon it. You must feel that it is like a desecration of your home my remaining in it, and the only place to which I can go and know that I shall be safe is my husband's house. Thank God, I can still dare to return there, and I will try to atone for my wavering duty towards him."

What need is there to go over and over again the well-trodden ground? The only difference between my Adelaide and other women who, like her, have found too late that they are married to the wrong person, is that she honestly and really wished to be kept from temptation. She looked her fault—

though Heaven knows it was an involuntary error of the heart—boldly in the face; she saw its smirched present, its blackened future; she unwrapped it from its pretty fanciful coverings of sentiment and poetry, and then when she beheld it standing before her in its true, ugly form, she turned and fled from it.

Yes, fled from her love "who loved her so," and never stopped her headlong flight until she had crossed the ocean, and stood travel-stained and weary, but pure and spotless, in her husband's house.

As for me, I was well-nigh mad with rage and grief; and I verily believe that I should have died if I had not taken this great sorrow of my manhood— even as I used to take my childish troubles—to my mother's knee. The dear good soul comforted me to the utmost of her power, but she would have been false to her own instincts if she had not condemned Mrs. Carruthers very strongly. I said one day to her,

"How hard you are, mother, you don't understand it in the least. How can you blame us for loving each other? You might as well scold us for suffering heat or cold. Heaven knows we are miserable enough!"

"I understand it so far, Paul," answered she, "that I know the moment you felt all these high-flown, ridiculous sentiments which you have been describing to me for the last hour, you ought to have turned your back upon the temptation and gone away.

"So Mrs. Ashley said, weeks ago," I pettishly rejoined ; "but it was not so easy to do."

" Easier than you imagine, my son ; there are many things besides hills which look large at a distance, and diminish when you get close to them."

"You may blame me as much as you like, mother, for I have been wrong from first to last, but I won't hear a word against her. Why, she is as good as gold. I don't believe there is another woman in the world who would have acted in the same way."

" I hope so," replied my mother gravely; " I believe and trust that a great deal of the behaviour we see around us, even in this quiet little place, is only on the surface. It is undignified and silly enough, but I cannot bring myself to think it is worse than that."

" Well, why should not Adelaide and I have been silly and undignified and exquisitely happy? We only wanted to be friends."

" Now, Paul, that is nonsense, and you know it. Worse than nonsense ; it is false. In some cases it may be possible for grown-up children to play with fire and escape unhurt, but you and—— " I remem-

ber so well how she paused and pronounced the
beloved name with difficulty — " Adelaide have
already, by your own account, singed your wings. In
spite of the unhappiness to both of you, I am glad
her nature is not shallow enough to permit her to
amuse herself with impunity."

Harsh though my mother's words look, even to my
eyes, as I write them down, there was no harshness
in her voice or tender touch. " I should not be a
faithful friend to you, dearest," she said to me one
day, "if I cried, ' Peace, peace, when there is no
peace.' "

CHAPTER IV.

DISAPPOINTMENT.

MRS. CARRUTHERS left us early in the summer; the days were shortening and the leaves falling, when the great cable beneath the Atlantic waters flashed home tidings from the North American squadron, which set every pulse in my body leaping and thrilling as if it would burst.

The words were necessarily few and brief, but they told of disaster and shipwreck. The fleet had been overtaken by a hurricane, all the ships suffered more or less, and the flag-ship had foundered with all hands on board. Admiral Carruthers went down with his splendid vessel, and was lying in a sailor's grave, in too profound a depth of quiet ever to feel storm or tempest again.

Selfish and brutal as I seem even to myself when I read these pages, I was not so utterly without feeling as to be incapable of joining the nation's lamentation over so great a loss and so sad a story. That is to say, I grieved with the surface, as it were, of my heart; but, beneath its thin outer crust, the volcanic fires of my love burned fiercer and clearer.

"She is free," said every beat of my pulse ; "she is free," said all things animate and inanimate.

I tried to conceal this growing, triumphant happiness from my mother's eyes with but indifferent success. To her it was positively disgusting that so dreadful a catastrophe should make one, and oh! shameful thought! perhaps two human hearts to sing for joy.

Small cause was there for exultation however, if I had known Mrs. Carruthers's nature. I thought I knew it, but I did not—not in the least.

The impatience which, like a fiend of old, possessed me, drove my steps one day towards the house of the friend who had formerly written to beg my mother's hospitality for Adelaide. The lady was not at home, but I saw her husband, a blunt, outspoken man, who made no secret of his surprise at Mrs. Carruthers's sudden departure from England.

"And it was all for nothing," he said, "the poor admiral was away when she arrived ; he had been cruising towards the tropics, and was on his way back to Halifax when they were caught in that gale She has written once to my wife, and I never read anything so heartbroken as her expressions of grief. The worst part of the sorrow seems to be that she had not seen him for—let me see— three or four years. She keeps harping on the string, 'If I could have only spoken to him once. 'Pon my word I think better of her, I do indeed. A charming young woman like her to make such a fuss about a man thirty years older than herself!"

I let him run on in a mingled strain of commendation and surprise and regret, for I was thinking deeply; the extra sense which lovers possess, warned me of rocks ahead.

Which of our perceptive faculties is it, I wonder, that so quickly grasps a danger, yea, even a risk, for any one we love very much? Do not we all know, all who have loved I mean, how, when a plan is proposed or a suggestion made touching the welfare of our heart's treasure, a sudden thought flits, lightning-winged through us, " It is not for their good?" We may laugh at, or reason the warning away, but has not that fleeting impression often and often proved itself a very Cassandra ? So it was with me.

I returned home slowly, shapeless forms of dread and terror dragging at my heart.

I reasoned within myself that it was but natural Adelaide should feel shocked and grieved at the sudden and violent death of the kind old man to whom she owed so much. I thought, "I will make her so happy in the long bright years before us, that she shall confess her greatest bliss has, after all, arisen from what is now an affliction to her."

It was in vain; the more I thought on the subject, the stronger grew the conviction which had sprung into existence during that talkative man's discursive sentences.

" Of what am I afraid ? " I asked.

" Of nothing," answered I.

" Yes, you are, you are afraid of Adelaide herself," whispered the dreadful not-to-be-silenced voice within me.

Was it well or ill-done that, with this burning impatience for tidings of my love, I wrote, after vainly endeavouring to persuade my mother to do so, to Mrs. Carruthers, who still remained at Halifax, dreading the winter voyage for her children ?

I wrote as calmly and coldly as I could, I spoke of our sympathy for her (I dared not say *mine*, so I made it plural), our hope that her health was good

I reminded her of the happiness to be found in her children, and, as I ventured timidly to add, in her friends. I know not if my letter was really so guarded as I tried to make it, for surely it is hard to write or to speak grave, friendly words when your heart is clamorously demanding a warmer expression of its deepest feelings.

There is not a phase or characteristic of the heart-sickness springing from deferred hope, which I did not learn, with a horrible aptitude, that winter. I watched and waited for the answer which never came to my letter. I sought information of Mrs. Carruthers's movements from her acquaintances. No one could tell me a word about her. Our beloved Queen of Hearts had laid down her sceptre and deserted her kingdom completely.

At last I grew desperate ; news I must have, and so I wrote again, far less guardedly.

I fancy those written words must have seemed both rough and masterful to my gentle love. I demanded, as a right, that she should tell me of her welfare; I claimed control over her future plans. I even dared to assume, as a matter of course, that when the conventional time of mourning should have expired—and it was more than half over—our lives should be joined, and that we should agree to forget in a radiant, blissful future all of disagreeable or unpleasant in the past.

This time there was no delay in the arrival of a reply. " Unreasonable creature that I am!" cried I, standing with the unopened letter in my hand, " I tell her to write quickly, she answers me instantly, and yet I dare not break the seal. I know there is something wrong."

That letter lies open before me now. I am looking at it for the last time to-night, for I shall destroy in an hour or two with my own hands all the written chronicles of the past.

As I touch the senseless paper I feel again the thrill of horror which ran through me as I first read it. I experience once more the old incapability of belief that such a disappointment could be in store for me—and yet it was looking out on me from those pages.

Adelaide wrote, as she always spoke, quite simply and frankly, but in words that conveyed an utter hopelessness to my heart, which I can never make you feel.

She entirely and utterly repudiated the notion of my influencing her future life. She told me, what I had known before, that the opportunity had been denied to her of seeing her husband once more or earth, and telling him with her own lips that she loved another man, and entreating his forgiveness for her involuntary fault.

"If I had been able thus to ease my heart," she wrote, "it might, perhaps, have been different with me now; I do not know. I can only deal with the case as it stands before me, and I assure you that it has become as impossible to me to think of you with my former feelings as if I were altogether a different person. I cannot, in a letter, tell you all I have gone through of remorse and suffering, I do not even say I am right in having reached this conclusion; all I wish to convey distinctly and decidedly is that I could not be more completely lost to you as a wife in this world, if I had gone down last autumn in the Thunderer."

She spoke briefly and firmly of her future plans, in which she seemed to consider nothing but her children's welfare; and she absolutely and entirely forbade me to seek or hold any communication with her by word or deed.

It is not necessary to describe here my disappointment, my indignation, and my deep despair. I felt, as we do of all great sorrows, that it was *impossible* so dreadful a thing could be true. I wonder the experience of the whole human race, which certainly goes to prove that it is quite possible we can be desperately miserable, did not occur to me. My instincts warned me to hide myself, like a wounded animal, during the first days of my hurt; but there came a time when speech was relief, and my mother's sympathy was the first I sought. I told her, as briefly as I could, of the substance of the two letters I had sent, and then, without a word, I put Adelaide's cold, cruel letter into her hands.

I thought I had passed through so fierce a furnace that I had absolutely no feelings left; but oh! the rush and sweep with which all my love came back upon me, like a great tidal wave, when my mother, wiping her eyes, handed me back the letter, and in a low, reverential whisper, said, "She is a better woman than I took her for, Paul; I can thoroughly understand how she feels about it. Poor soul! what she must have suffered."

"You do not think her right, mother!" I exclaimed ; "you cannot believe her to be justified in wrecking my happiness for some ridiculous scruples of her own! Good Heavens! is it possible all women can be the same? We give them ardent love, and they tender us a cool, calm reasonable sentiment in exchange !"

"If you ask me, Paul, what I think, I must say

I consider that you are both wrong. Still, as a woman, I can understand what Mrs. Carruthers feels better than you do. I can quite imagine a true, good, pure woman as she is, never being able to get over her remorse and her self-accusing memories, and being utterly unable to accept the freedom her heart longed for, when it comes to her in this sudden and dreadful way."

"Then my ruined life does not weigh with you?" I asked, indignantly; "you, of whose love and sympathy I felt so secure—you can calmly approve of these cold words!" and I flung the letter down on the floor before her.

"My darling, your sorrow is my sorrow; you know that, don't you? But still I feel with every womanly instinct, not with any cold, reasoning power, that I approve and endorse each word in that letter. I would give my very life, Paul, to make you really happy, but there is no happiness here;" and she gently picked up and smoothed the despised, crumpled sheets of paper.

"Perhaps I have been too hasty. Do you think that the lapse of time may soften and alter her mind on the subject?" I asked, with a desperate craving for the least crumb of hope.

My mother shook her head. "I do not believe

it will ever be different, dear; and if it were, you would still be disappointed. The Adelaide Carruthers, who may hereafter emerge from this fiery trial, will not be the same fresh, unscathed woman you loved. Fire makes gold more precious; but it hardens it, remember."

The great, wonderful mother-love had taught this dear woman wisdom. She was thoroughly right. At first I could not believe her, and would not, if I could. It seemed so impossible that any personal calamity or affliction could have done aught but intensify my love for Adelaide.

"Why should she shrink from me, if she be ever so unhappy?" I argued to Mrs. Ashley, who spoke to me once, and only once, about it. "I cannot understand the love which does not grow and strengthen in the dark hours."

"There is love and love, sir," replied that little lady, sententiously; "don't you see that she shrinks from you because you remind her of suffering? It is just a natural instinct which she obeys in avoiding you, as she would anybody or anything which reminded her of a desperate illness."

The moment Mrs. Ashley was unable to refrain from reminding me of her counsel and advice, that moment I turned and fled. I could not stand

it. Of course the bitterness of the draught lay in
the fact that it was of my own mixing; no aloes
and quassia could equal that reflection.

These two women— my dear, quiet mother and
bright, gay, little Mrs. Ashley, so different in their
characters—agreed then thoroughly in approving
Mrs. Carruthers's treatment of me. I wonder if
others would do the same? It is to me incomprehensible how she could have acted thus; but, alas!
it is not a fiction I relate, but a fact, which has
saddened and darkened my whole life.

Yet as I write a great gush of tenderness comes
over me, and I lay down my pen, and pray that
my love has found rest and peace; that she is
forgiven for the errors of her heart, and that she
does not know the blank desolation which has settled
on my life like a pall.

CHAPTER V.

MRS. HAVILAND.

AND yet I am jotting down this rough sketch of the past on my marriage-day. My fair girl-wife took leave of me an hour or two since; she has gone, under my mother's care, to the old home by the sea, where I first saw and loved Mrs. Carruthers, five years ago.

I shall never see that low, rambling house, nor those lovely, drooping beech trees again. When a few years have come and gone, my mother's plan is to bring Ethel to join me in some of the quiet Swiss valleys; and I have promised that I will then try to take up the life which hangs so wearily on my hands now, and see whether happiness may not be found growing, as doth a wild flower, on Duty's steep path. May Heaven forgive me for feeling, with a thrill of joy, that perhaps before that time arrives, I may have gone Home—home to the Eternal Forgiveness—home to where Adelaide Carruthers rests.

Yes, she has been safe in those All-embracing Arms for a long time now. They say it was the cold Northern winter which killed her. I know better. She broke down under the strain of the load with which her life was burthened. I helped to murder her by my impatience, and violent protests against the promptings of her sensitive, pure nature. Would I have had her feel her fault—our fault—less, though it was but a sin of our hearts? No—not now.

And yet I have married to-day, married a fair young wife, with half an English county for her dower.

Before you fling aside my poor story as the hypocritical cant of a sordid worldling, before you take back again the momentary sympathy which I would fain hope has been given to me, and which is infinitely more precious in my eyes than all my wife's gold pieces, read on for a few pages, and then condemn me if you will.

I have not dwelt longer on my entreaties, my anguish, and my great despair, partly because I dare not revive too vividly the remembrance of those days— yea, those nights, of anguish and of alternating

hopes and fears. Nor dare I venture to touch the un-
healed wound which the news of my love's early death
in that icy, distant land dealt to my bare and bleeding
soul.

It had always been my mother's great desire to
find a wife for me, more especially since the summer-
days under the beech-trees. Until then she fancied,
good, simple soul, that I was wedded to my books.
She did not dream that it was chiefly from their
pages I had drawn my conception of a lovely and
beloved woman, and that I found it very difficult
to realize my ideal. So difficult, that I am obliged
to confess that in many points at first, I was fain to
idealize the real, as it appeared in Mrs. Carruthers.

But having done so once, and failed when success
seemed nearest, I would not try again. I returned
to my old, silent friends with intensified loyalty, and
I would have been, at all events, content in their
society.

Suddenly all the quiet of my life was upset by an
unexpected visit from that dear anxious mother.
Have I told you that I was living by myself, among
the bleak moor-lands and purple fells under the
shadow of the northern ranges ? There, into this
gloomy solitude, my mother penetrated. She knew
it would have been useless to ask me to come to her

on any plea but that of sickness, so she set forth, at
her advancing age, and in bleak, unseasonable weather,
to seek her melancholy son.

After the first anxious inquiry on my part whether
disease or disaster had sent me so unexpected, but
so welcome a visitor, I said, half-laughingly, and
without the faintest shadow of an idea how near the
truth my haphazard words struck:

"You have not brought me a wife, have you,
mother? I know your great ambition is to see me
married, but I am much too busy just now to think
of such trifles."

The dear old lady blushed a most guilty blush, and
answered, with some confusion,

"I have had a very extraordinary letter, Paul, which
I have brought to show you myself:" and she held out
an old-fashioned big sheet of square letter-paper, on
which the penny stamp looked quite out of place. It
was folded and addressed as in the old days of franks;
and, as I say, the stamp had an altogether incongruous and pert appearance.

"Have you received this epistle lately, mother?"
I asked, fancying it might refer to some family affair
of bygone date.

"Yes, only two days since; but won't you take it
and see what Mrs. Haviland says?"

"Certainly I will, if you wish it," I replied; "yet I cannot imagine what she can have to say to you concerning me."

"Read it, and you will know," was the obvious answer. So I read, with an amazement which increased at every word, an earnest entreaty on the part of old Mrs. Haviland to my mother for her consent to a scheme which she had formed for marrying her granddaughter, a little girl of fifteen years old, to me.

Beyond knowing that such a person as Mrs. Haviland existed in some remote and splendid home, none of our mother's children had any acquaintance with this eccentric old lady. In former years her only daughter had been a school friend of our mother's, and she was often invited to spend her holidays at their beautiful place in the country. Miss Haviland married young, and, as it turned out, most unhappily. Our mother had been her bridesmaid, and after the wedding Mrs. Haviland, who was herself a widow, took immense pleasure in the society of her absent daughter's favourite companion.

For some years, in spite of the disparity of age between them, old Mrs. Haviland and our mother kept up the closest and most affectionate intimacy, and we, as children, delighted to hear tales of these old times. Indeed I could boast of having been taken, when a

two-years-old babe, to the stately abode of the last of
the Havilands.

As Time went on, it brought cares and engrossing
interests to both the old and the younger lady. To
the picturesque Chatelaine of Haviland Hall it brought
a widowed, heart-broken woman to die in her arms, in
place of the bright and bonny bride who had left her a
few years previously. Before this last crowning sorrow
happened, many grandchildren had been born to Mrs.
Haviland, but they all died young, and she was left
the sole guardian of a puny, sickly baby, who had
now struggled with difficulty, and many lets and
hindrances, from measles, scarlatina, &c., up to the
age of early girlhood.

Our mother's more sheltered life had been free from
these trials; her cares were chiefly connected with out-
grown little wardrobes and shoemakers' bills of inter-
minable length. Without any diminution of affection
on either side, the intercourse between the friends had
gradually dropped down to an annual letter from each
household.

Great, then, was her amazement at receiving such
an appeal as the one I held in my hands; and,
obeying her first instincts, dreading to lose time, and
unwilling to wound her old friend by a curt refusal,
she had brought the letter straight to me.

Before I tell you how we regarded it, I ought perhaps to say a few words about the letter itself.

It was necessarily lengthy, for it had to recapitulate the circumstances which had induced Mrs. Haviland to take so strange a step. Its language was simple and pathetic, and told of a life of disappointment, ending in a fixed distrust of everybody around the writer. There had been attempted treachery, deceit, and fraud enough to poison the mind of a less susceptible person than Mrs. Haviland. She was now on what she knew and felt to be her death-bed. All the enormous wealth of the family would then centre on the little frail grandchild Ethel, whom she loved tenderly.

"I am frightened to think how rich she will be, poor child," wrote Mrs. Haviland. "Money has been the curse of mine and her mother's lives. We were both married for it, though we chose for ourselves, and fondly hoped we were beloved. But it was not so. I cannot bear to think of Ethel's fate being so unutterably sad as ours has been, and I am going to try the bold experiment of choosing for her."

The letter dwelt on the former intimacy, referred to the jesting arrangement between the school-girls, that if ever they married and had children, "your son shall

marry my daughter ;" and finally entreated my mother
to ease a dying woman's last moments by permitting
her to see the welfare and happiness of her last
descendant made secure.

" Believe me, I know what I am about," Mrs. Haviland urged in her concluding lines, "I have caused
inquiries to be made in your neighbourhood ; I need
hardly say in no spirit of vulgar curiosity, but to
satisfy myself. I am aware of your son's great unhappiness, but I feel certain nevertheless that he will make
Ethel a good husband, and, above all, I cannot die
content unless I leave her in *your* care. No other
arrangement than the one I propose, namely, an immediate marriage, will relieve you of the responsibili-
ties of guardianship to the richest heiress, alas! in the
three kingdoms, and prevent my Snow-drop from
falling into the sordid hands of a fortune-hunter."

I had read on with interest and sympathy until my
eyes met these last words ; then I put the letter down,
and, with somewhat ungracious abruptness, said,

" That is exactly what I cannot hear. If the poor
child were penniless, and the shelter of our home
and name would stand between her and a life of
misery, it would be just possible for me to sacrifice
myself to do her good ; but how can you ask me,
dear mother, to play so odious a part, as to prevent

Y

her from marrying hereafter some one whom she may really care for ?

" I am not asking you to do anything of the sort, Paul," answered my mother ; " I see, as plainly as you do, how unjust it would be to the girl. I confess that I do not know what to advise. Mrs. Haviland seems quite bent upon it, and the only thing I fancied you might agree to, would be to come with me, as she wishes, to the Hall at once.

"Do not think me selfish or unkind, darling mother, if I say that it seems to me better you should go there alone."

My mother looked wistfully at me without speaking a word. If women only knew how much more persuasive such sweet, gentle eloquence is than their most passionate entreaties, they would oftener have recourse to it. Her silence gave me leisure to consider that I was old enough to refuse to be married against my will, and that I should be wanting in respect and affection if I objected to accompany her on her long, uncomfortable journey. So, after a brief pause, I said, "Do you wish me to come with you and take care of you, mother ?"

" Yes I do, dear ; it is so sweet to me to be taken care of by my son," added she, apologetically.

"Very well then, we will start as early as you like

to-morrow. I shall begin my care-taking at once by positively forbidding you to travel any more to-night; you look quite worn out and fit for nothing but supper and bed. It is of no use thinking of going a step further to-night. I won't allow it."

"Poor Mrs. Haviland!" said my mother, with a wistful sigh. "I am very happy and comfortable here with you, my boy; (I was twenty-five, you remember!) but it is dreadful to fancy her lying wearying and watching for my arrival."

I remained firm, however, and the journey was not resumed until the next morning. The night also had brought counsel, or rather I had taken counsel with myself during its solemn, silent hours.

If I were composing an imaginary record, my sense of the Unities would probably urge me to represent myself as arising in the morning with the same fixed determination to oppose Mrs. Haviland's project. But it was not so. During the darkness a higher and nobler spirit had come to me. It had swept aside by a touch all the narrow, selfish fences with which I had enclosed and protected my daily life. It had taught me, hardest task of all, to disregard the probable risk of ungenerous suspicions. I perceived that if my own conscience were clear, as it certainly was, from the faintest accusation of seeking to secure the child-bride for the sake of her wealth, I could afford to dispense with the dread of the judgment of others. It seemed made plain to me that all men, if they were incapable of sordid reasoning, would feel as I did, that the girl's wealth made a barrier between her and a happy sheltered home, and that therefore she would be thrown into grasping hands. In short, I determined to wait until an opportunity arrived of showing Mrs. Haviland my whole heart about the matter, and then, if she still wished for the realization of her strange plan, I would see if it were not possible for me to sacrifice my tastes and habits for this poor friendless child's welfare.

When my mother and I had fairly started on our journeyings, after a hurried and early breakfast, I told her a little of my changed feelings. She showed no exultation, rather surprise I fancied, and a dread lest I should mistake a fit of enthusiasm for an impulse of the heart.

"You know, Paul, I wish you above all to be happy," she said. "When I urge you to marry, it is because your father and I have been so happy all these years it is only natural we should wish you to secure a nice, good wife. But we do not desire you to sell yourself, dear, or to sacrifice your own choice and taste for all the heiresses in the world."

" Dear mother, who could suspect you of mercenary ideas? We both know, don't we, that there is a happiness which money cannot buy? It is evident that poor Mrs. Haviland has found this out also, or she would not be so anxious to force Ethel and her wealth upon our acceptance."

We hurried on as fast as the nature of the country would allow us, but it was dark and cold before we reached the Hall. To our surprise, instead of finding its windows closed and dark, they were streaming with light, blazing forth a welcome to us from every carved stone, lintel, and doorway. My mother smiled, and said, " That is just like Mrs. Haviland; depend upon it she has ordered this to be done to show that she is anxious to receive us cordially."

If such were the case, the intention had certainly been carried out in every detail. I had pictured to myself our arrival at a gloomy, shrouded house, with the Great Silence already brooding over it, and hushing the voices and steps within to the faintest whispers. Instead of this, here were lights and flowers and warmth and perfume, all the glow of refined beauty, of artistic instincts, and liberal Life.

I felt as if I were in a dream, and said in a low voice, " It must be all a mistake; Mrs. Haviland cannot be very ill if she takes pleasure still in these surroundings. I suppose that letter to you was but a mad woman's whim ; what fools we shall look to have come on such an errand;" and I had already turned back, as if to leave the house.

But my mother, usually so yielding, took the initiative now; she laid her hand on my arm, and said, " It may seem strange to you because you don't know her, but this is exactly like the Mrs. Haviland I remember. Things will go on precisely in the same way so long as she is alive."

We were received and welcomed as if we had been royal guests by a Steward of the Household, a Groom of the Chambers, and divers other stately functionaries. An exquisite dinner was served to us, and after it had been cleared away, an elegant, middle-aged lady, who was announced as the housekeeper, introduced herself to my mother, and offered to show her the way to where Mrs. Haviland awaited her.

As for me, no sooner was I left alone, than an intense dread and hatred of the whole affair took possession of me. Never had my untidy den at home, with its litter of books and papers, its common shelves and print-hung walls, seemed half so attractive in my eyes. I felt that it would be impossible to change my life, with its simple, Spartan freedom, for this splendid slavery. I was ill at ease and awkward ; so far from coveting the magnificence around me, it appeared quite impossible that I could even endure an existence which would need to be thus guarded and waited upon. During this unfavourable state of mind I had hardly noticed that an hour or more had slipped by, and it seemed still like an oppressive morning dream, when I was summoned to join my mother in Mrs. Haviland's own room.

Still more perplexing was the change when, having reached a certain heavy swing-door, the tall footman who strutted before me, opened it, and suddenly found his "occupation gone," his mission superseded, by a neat parlour-maid, who received me on the other side of the baize portal. She evidently felt no awe of the splendid male creature, though she was but the smallest of her sex, and attired in only a light print gown. His demeanour changed, he "lowered his flag," as it were, and absolutely sneaked off again to his gorgeous domain.

My brisk little guide led me through a corridor where grey felt took the place of velvet-pile carpets, prints and photographs in simple frames, of suits of armour and full-length portraits. She threw open a somewhat low door, and announced my name. The dim, shaded lamps cast a grateful gloom over the simple apartment, at whose threshold I paused for an instant. What light there was, fell upon a sofa drawn near the fireplace, on which lay a motionless figure, whose whole life seemed absorbed into the great gleaming eyes; on my mother who sat in a low chair facing Mrs. Haviland, with a little tea-table between them, and on a slight, pale girl, who was half lying on the hearth-rug, which she shared with a big dog.

Instead of conducting myself like a hero, or, at least, like a grown-up man, I felt as if by some magic I had slipped back again to my school-boy days, and this awkwardness was increased by Mrs. Haviland saying, as if she were surprised, "Dear me, how tall he has grown !"

Now, I was not particularly tall, but as my hostess had not seen me since I was two years old, it was hardly to be wondered at that there was more of me now than there had been then. Every word of the English language went out of my head. To the activity of my brain during the last twenty-four hours, succeeded an absolute torpor. It was there-fore in the most perfect silence that I advanced to greet my mother's oldest friend, the woman for whose sake I had once thought, an immense time ago it seemed, of bartering my precious liberty.

"He is very quiet, but I like him," said Mrs. Haviland, as if I were deaf as well as dumb. "He has your eyes, Mary; I hope he has your heart."

My mother looked at me wistfully, with all her tender soul brimming up to her eyes, as she answered, simply, "He is not a bit like me; you know I was never clever."

"If he is clever enough to be good and true I shall be satisfied; so many talented people stop short of those qualities," observed Mrs. Haviland, bitterly.

I suddenly found my tongue and my courage, and said bluntly, "Truth is not often agreeable, though people are always calling out for it, Mrs. Haviland. I very seldom feel in the least good, but you must excuse my giving a specimen of my sincerity when I say that I hope you understand I only came in obedience to my mother's wish that I should escort her hither."

The fair, curly-headed child, who had hardly moved from her easy attitude on the rug, now scrambled up on her feet, shook her simple frock into order, and came up to me with an outstretched hand, which she placed in my somewhat reluctant one.

"How do you do?" she asked; "you are Mrs. Somerset's son, are you not? I rather like you, only you look a little cross. You must not be cross to grandmamma, though," she added, decidedly, "because she is going to die very soon, and we ought all to do exactly what she wishes; oughtn't we, Juno?" And she turned to the great black retriever, with an air at once wise and childish.

"Well, then, you must run away to bed at once," said Mrs. Haviland, calmly; "that is what I wish now. Good-night, little one; kiss Mrs. Somerset and go."

"And Mr. Somerset, too, if he is going to be nice and kind to you, grandmamma," said the girl, putting up her little pallid face to receive my unwilling kiss as she left the room.

"I cannot learn to call you Mr. Somerset, Paul," said Mrs. Haviland, "and it is not worth while to take any trouble about names for these few hours of life, is it? You will have the night to think over my plan. Your mother has wisely prepared your mind and so saved my strength; I am very near the end of it."

Her voice was unlike the voice of a dying person, but I believed every word she spoke. Still, it was not possible for me to reply. Mrs. Haviland looked at my mother, who went on with the sentence which her old friend lacked energy to finish.

"We wish you to think the whole subject well over,

Paul. Do nothing which your conscience disapproves ; but if it be possible for you to help that dear child to bear the burthen of all this splendour, tell us in the morning that you will do so. I can trust to my son's sense of honour, but I must entreat him not to sacrifice anything to a morbid sensitiveness or a weak dread of censure. Now, I am going to treat you, for all your size and age, exactly as Mrs. Haviland treated Ethel just now. Kiss me, Paul, and go to bed."

I obeyed her, and then bent over the wasted, transparent hand which the strange mistress of the house held forth to me.

Then I departed, to find a simple, comfortable room prepared for me, and no sooner had I lain down in bed than a deep sleep fell upon me, and the late morning light was shining in at the windows before I awoke—awoke to remember all that had to be weighed and thought of, and possibly settled, before night.

CHAPTER VI.

MY CHILD-WIFE.

THE time left to us for thought and decision was even shorter than we imagined.

Scarcely had I finished dressing when my mother's maid summoned me to the morning room where I had been introduced to Mrs. Haviland last night. I am far away from that spot now, and yet it is barely midnight.

My mother came to me there almost instantly. She looked pale and deeply agitated, and said,

" The end is very near. She knows it herself, and the doctor does not contradict her. Her mind is as clear and strong as when I first knew her, nearly thirty years ago ; and the most earnest desire of her few remaining hours on earth is to see you married at once, before mid-day in fact, to little Ethel."

" It is utter madness as well as wickedness," I answered. " Why should the poor child's life be made miserable to gratify an obstinate old woman's whim ?"

"Oh, Paul! how can you speak in such a way? How can you call it a whim? It has been Mrs. Haviland's fixed idea for years, by what she tells me; do you expect me to think that your marriage with Ethel would ensure the girl a wretched future?"

"It is impossible!" I cried, "quite impossible; she is but a child. How could you expect me to travel about with a nurse and governess for my wife? And then there is all this horrible wealth. It stifles me; I could not endure it."

"Do not trouble your head about those points; there is no time. Mrs. Haviland has had two sets of legal documents prepared, which are complete, even to her signature. As soon as you decide, 'yes,' or 'no' (that is all you have to say) one of these sets will be burned. The other will take effect after her death. Supposing you consent, and oh! if it be possible, Paul, pray make a dying woman happy, I am to take Ethel to live with me for five years. At the end of that time you may claim her if you will, but not before. A large sum, amply sufficient for everything, is set aside in the hands of trustees for Ethel's education and maintenance. There are certain charities named which Mrs Haviland wishes you to endow, if you choose, out of a portion of the remainder, but everything else is absolutely and entirely in your own power. Did you ever hear of such wonderful trust and confidence ? There is not even a suggestion about a change of name, such as was made when Ethel's mother married. I mentioned it, but, poor old lady, she said, ' It has not been a lucky or a happy name for the women of the family. Let the spell be broken in this generation, and the next can return to it if they like.' "

I was obliged, in spite of pressing time, to beg my mother to repeat the substance of what I have set down above.

" There is positively no time for debating," said she " I must go back with your answer immediately, and if you can gratify her, for Heaven's sake do so."

" If I were to die before the five years expired, would Ethel suffer—in a pecuniary point of view ? " I asked.

" No, I fancy not. You could, however make any arrangements you choose out of the enormous balance of her fortune. She is to be my ward and remain under my care until she be twenty-one, unless, as I have told you, you claim her five years hence."

" She is such a baby," I urged ; " even for her age I never saw so simple a creature."

" So much the better, Paul." She has a charming disposition, and will, I firmly believe, grow into a lovely and loveable woman."

" The money — it is possible to have too much

of a good thing, mother. It would be a regular nightmare to me."

"Reduce it to a moderate fortune then. Mrs. Haviland would be very glad if you were to do so. Have you not noticed how simply she lives among all this splendour? You could do the same. Ethel's tastes are as primitive as if she were a pauper; for Mrs. Haviland has brought her up with a perfect horror of wealth. I need make no changes for her at home; our quiet life will just suit her. Ah! Paul, give me the happiness of bringing up my son's wife!"

I am suffering at this moment from the reaction of the day's excitement, so that I can scarcely tell now whether I did right or wrong in yielding to my mother's desire. It seems to me, sitting alone in the quiet night-hours that I have been cruel and wicked towards Ethel, but I will try to shield and guard her interest and her life as far as may be.

You see I yielded. The moment I had said "Yes," my mother left me, returning again instantly to bid me go and have some breakfast, and be sure to come the moment I was summoned.

Two hours later I was sent for. There was but scant time for greetings or for explanations. To my inexperienced eyes no very material outward change had taken place, but my mother whispered to me to make no unnecessary delay. Heaven knows I was

in no hurry to take upon myself this overwelming
responsibility of a rich wife. I signified my assent
in reply to the intense questioning look in the
dying woman's eyes, and only added a word or two
about my intention of carrying out any schemes
I might find prepared, for diverting some of Ethel's
fortune to charitable channels.

Mrs. Haviland listened attentively and said distinctly, "Good." She then made a sign to my
mother, who went to the door and led in Ethel
wearing her everyday simple frock, with her colourless
hair curling around her pale face. The child looked
frightened, but I am glad to think now that she
showed no aversion to me; on the contrary, she
rather clung to my hand, and said quite frankly,

"I don't mind marrying you, Mr. Somerset, not
a bit, but I wish you could make grandmamma
well."

I said nothing except a brief assurance that I
would do my best to take care of her (Ethel), and
then the clergyman opened his book, and in a few
moments Ethel was my wife. I ought perhaps to
have mentioned before, that Mrs. Haviland had
taken care to have proper witnesses in attendance.
She herself gave the child-bride away, signifying
her assent to the marriage in a wonderfully clear
voice, and desiring every one present to remember

that it only took place at her especial request and
earnest desire.

I can distinctly recollect the doctor's look of
amazed admiration at the strong will thus triumphing
over the weak body, for these distinct words were
nearly the last she spoke.

I kissed the withered hand that had bestowed so
freely and so nobly upon me that wealth for which
men have been known to barter willingly life and
honour, yea, even their very souls. Then I bowed to
the assembled group of strangers and left the room,
feeling as if I were in a fevered dream ; all was
at once so real and so unreal. Instead of grasping
the principal points of the scene, I idly wondered
from whence some common flowers came which stood
in a little glass on a table near me. I remember
that I finally decided they must have grown in a
cottager's garden, and it was a relief to me to settle
this point even whilst the clergyman's voice was
sounding in my ears.

Thank God ! For He mercifully kept Adelaide
Carruthers's eyes and voice from recurring to my
memory. They are before me now, as plainly and
distinctly as if I had just parted from her ; but I
must hurry on with my story, it is nearly finished.

The weather was still too cold and wet for me
to care to leave the house. I found my way into

a long gallery, and paced up and down its immense length, undisturbed.

But not for very long; that is to say not long to me. The desolate, cheerless day was waning towards its grey afternoon when my mother joined me. She advanced with outstretched hands to meet me, and cried—

"Oh, Paul, I am so thankful you were enabled to give her such rest! It has all been perfect peace, and her last whisper was a blessing on you."

Poor, dear mother! Her quiet life had known so little emotion, so few scenes, that last night and this morning's excitement had quite broken down her ordinary sweet composure, and she clung to me, trembling and sobbing with grief and excitement.

"It is all over, then?" I asked, reverently. There was no need for an answer, and my mother's tears were sufficient reply.

"Where is Ethel, poor child?" I next inquired.

"I must go back to her directly. She is in great grief, but I will take her away immediately; we are to start in two hours' time. We can only get as far as —— to-night, but any change will help her. Everything is ready for your journey too, dear Paul," she added.

"But surely there is something horrible in our all rushing out of the house directly!" I exclaimed.

"It is what she wished," said my mother, with a fresh burst of sobs. "You had better see the Vicar, he will tell you how minutely she has arranged everything."

We went together into one of the least showy and splendid of the anterooms, and there I spoke to the Vicar. He confirmed my mother's statements in every particular; but added that I was to return if I thought fit, in a week's time, for the funeral.

Mrs. Haviland wished me to have that space for the consideration of my future plans. I should then meet her men of business and receive from them the dreaded bequest. By that time I should also have been able to mature her schemes for the various endowments and charities which she contemplated.

As the Vicar made this last suggestion I could easily perceive that he very much doubted my being inclined to give up any portion of the large capital now at my disposal. He had probably lived long enough to discover that our generous intentions are apt to undergo a marvellous change after the cash has been lodged at our banker's. Up to that time many a hospital and school-house and church are built in the air and endowed with Aladdin's dream-wealth, but I fear that their number and proportions decrease sadly after the legacy duty has been paid.

All the money in the world would not buy me back one hour of those summer days, past and gone five years ago, so I need not hoard it ; and the good old Vicar's pet projects are nearer their realization than he dreams of.

Now I am going to close this record and put it away. Like a silly school-girl, I have found comfort and relief in writing about my emotions; like her I have attempted to be impartial; but I am, at all events, more candid than autobiographers or diarists in general. So candid in fact, that I am convinced, were I to look at these pages a year hence, I should throw them into the fire, and thus save myself from falling into the hands of those who may judge me harshly. Unpractical and sentimental,—words, especially the latter, which need not be terms of reproach,—I may be, but at the same time I try to be true and sincere.

Pity me for the suffering I have brought into my life ; and believe me when I declare, that if I live I will attempt to make Ethel and my mother content and happy in the coming years.

LONDON : R. CLAY, SONS, AND TAYLOR, PRINTERS.

BEDFORD STREET, COVENT GARDEN, LONDON.

April, 1871.

MACMILLAN & CO.'S GENERAL CATALOGUE of Works in the Departments of History, Biography, Travels, Poetry, and Belles Lettres. With some short Account or Critical Notice concerning each Book.

SECTION I.

HISTORY, BIOGRAPHY, and TRAVELS.

Baker (Sir Samuel W.).—THE NILE TRIBUTARIES OF ABYSSINIA, and the Sword Hunters of the Hamran Arabs. By SIR SAMUEL W. BAKER, M.A., F.R.G.S. With Maps and Illustrations. Fourth and Cheaper Edition. Crown 8vo. 6s.

Sir Samuel Baker here describes twelve months' exploration, during which he examined the rivers that are tributary to the Nile from Abyssinia, including the Atbara, Settite, Royan, Salaam, Angrab, Rahad, Dinder, and the Blue Nile. The interest attached to these portions of Africa differs entirely from that of the White Nile regions, as the whole of Upper Egypt and Abyssinia is capable of development, and is inhabited by races having some degree of civilization; while Central Africa is peopled by a race of savages, whose future is more problematical.

THE ALBERT N'YANZA Great Basin of the Nile, and Exploration of the Nile Sources. New and Cheaper Edition, with Portraits, Maps, and Illustrations. Two vols. crown 8vo. 16s.

" Bruce won the source of the Blue Nile; Speke and Grant won the Victoria source of the great White Nile; and I have been permitted to

A. 2.   **A**

10.000.4.71.

Baker (Sir Samuel W.) *(continued)*—

succeed in completing the Nile Sources by the discovery of the great reservoir of the equatorial waters, the Albert N'yanza, from which the river issues as the entire White Nile."—PREFACE.

NEW AND CHEAP EDITION OF THE ALBERT N'YANZA. I vol. crown 8vo. With Maps and Illustrations. 7s. 6d.

Barker (Lady).—STATION LIFE IN NEW ZEALAND.
By LADY BARKER. Second and Cheaper Edition. Globe 8vo. 3s. 6d.

" *These letters are the exact account of a lady's experience of the brighter and less practical side of colonization. They record the expeditions, adventures, and emergencies diversifying the daily life of the wife of a New Zealand sheep-farmer ; and, as each was written while the novelty and excitement of the scenes it describes were fresh upon her, they may succeed in giving here in England an adequate impression of the delight and freedom of an existence so far removed from our own highly-wrought civilization."*—PREFACE.

" *We have never read a more truthful or a pleasanter little book.*"
ATHENÆUM.

Baxter (R. Dudley, M.A.).—THE TAXATION OF THE
UNITED KINGDOM. By R. DUDLEY BAXTER, M.A. 8vo. cloth, 4s. 6d.

The First Part of this work, originally read before the Statistical Society of London, deals with the Amount of Taxation ; the Second Part, which now constitutes the main portion of the work, is almost entirely new, and embraces the important questions of Rating, of the relative Taxation of Land, Personalty, and Industry, and of the direct effect of Taxes upon Prices. The author trusts that the body of facts here collected may be of permanent value as a record of the past progress and present condition of the population of the United Kingdom, independently of the transitory circumstances of its present Taxation.

NATIONAL INCOME. With Coloured Diagrams. 8vo. 3s. 6d.

PART I.—*Classification of the Population, Upper, Middle, and Labour Classes.* II.—*Income of the United Kingdom.*

A painstaking and certainly most interesting inquiry."—PALL MALL GAZETTE.

Bernard.—FOUR LECTURES ON SUBJECTS CONNECTED WITH DIPLOMACY. By MOUNTAGUE BERNARD, M.A., Chichele Professor of International Law and Diplomacy, Oxford. 8vo. 9s.

Four Lectures, dealing with (1) The Congress of Westphalia; (2) Systems of Policy; (3) Diplomacy, Past and Present; (4) The Obligations of Treaties.

Blake.—THE LIFE OF WILLIAM BLAKE, THE ARTIST. By ALEXANDER GILCHRIST. With numerous Illustrations from Blake's designs, and Fac-similes of his studies of the "Book of Job." Medium 8vo. half morocco, 18s.

These volumes contain a Life of Blake; Selections from his Writings, including Poems; Letters; Annotated Catalogue of Pictures and Drawings, List, with occasional notes, of Blake's Engravings and Writings. There are appended Engraved Designs by Blake; (1) The Book of Job, twenty-one photo-lithographs from the originals; (2) Songs of Innocence and Experience, sixteen of the original Plates.

Blanford (W. T.).—GEOLOGY AND ZOOLOGY OF ABYSSINIA. By W. T. BLANFORD. 8vo. 21s.

This work contains an account of the Geological and Zoological Observations made by the Author in Abyssinia, when accompanying the British Army on its march to Magdala and back in 1868, and during a short journey in Northern Abyssinia, after the departure of the troops. Part I. Personal Narrative; Part II. Geology; Part III. Zoology. With Coloured Illustrations and Geological Map.

Bright (John, M.P.).—SPEECHES ON QUESTIONS OF PUBLIC POLICY. By the Right Hon. JOHN BRIGHT, M.P. Edited by Professor THOROLD ROGERS. Two vols. 8vo. 25s. Second Edition, with Portrait.

"I have divided the Speeches contained in these volumes into groups. The materials for selection are so abundant, that I have been constrained to omit many a speech which is worthy of careful perusal. I have naturally given prominence to those subjects with which Mr. Bright has been especially identified, as, for example, India, America, Ireland, and Parliamentary Reform. But nearly every topic of great public interest on which Mr. Bright has spoken is represented in these volumes."

EDITOR'S PREFACE.

Bright (John, M.P.) *(continued)*—

AUTHOR'S POPULAR EDITION. Extra fcap. 8vo. cloth. Second Edition. 3*s.* 6*d.*

Bryce.—THE HOLY ROMAN EMPIRE. By JAMES BRYCE, B.C.L., Regius Professor of Civil Law, Oxford. New and Revised Edition. Crown 8vo. 7*s.* 6*d.*

CHATTERTON : A Biographical Study. BY DANIEL WILSON, LL.D., Professor of History and English Literature in University College, Toronto. Crown 8vo. 6*s.* 6*d.*

The Author here regards Chatterton as a Poet, not as a mere " resetter and defacer of stolen literary treasures." Reviewed in this light, he has found much in the old materials capable of being turned to new account; and to these materials research in various directions has enabled him to make some additions.

Clay.—THE PRISON CHAPLAIN. A Memoir of the Rev. JOHN CLAY, B.D., late Chaplain of the Preston Gaol. With Selections from his Reports and Correspondence, and a Sketch of Prison Discipline in England. By his Son, the Rev. W. L. CLAY, M.A. 8vo. 15*s.*

*"Few books have appeared of late years better entitled to an attentive perusal. . . . It presents a complete narrative of all that has been done and attempted by various philanthropists for the amelioration of the condition and the improvement of the morals of the criminal classes in the British dominions."—*LONDON REVIEW.

Cobden.—SPEECHES ON QUESTIONS OF PUBLIC POLICY. By RICHARD COBDEN. Edited by the Right Hon. JOHN BRIGHT, M.P., and Professor ROGERS. Two vols. 8vo. With Portrait. (Uniform with BRIGHT'S SPEECHES.)

The Speeches contained in these two volumes have been selected and edited at the instance of the Cobden Club. They form an important part of that collective contribution to political science which has conferred on their author so vast a reputation.

Cooper.—ATHENÆ CANTABRIGIENSES. By CHARLES HENRY COOPER, F.S.A., and THOMPSON COOPER, F.S.A. Vol. I. 8vo., 1500—85, 18*s.* ; Vol. II., 1586—1609, 18*s.*

This elaborate work, which is dedicated by permission to Lord Macaulay, contains lives of the eminent men sent forth by Cambridge, after the fashion of Anthony à Wood, in his famous " Athenæ Oxonienses."

Cox (G. V., M.A.).—RECOLLECTIONS OF OXFORD.
By G. V. Cox, M.A., New College, Late Esquire Bedel and Coroner in the University of Oxford. *Second Edition.* Crown 8vo. 10s. 6d.

"*An amusing* farrago *of anecdote, and will pleasantly recall in many a country parsonage the memory of youthful days.*"—TIMES.

"Daily News."—THE WAR CORRESPONDENCE OF
THE *DAILY NEWS*, 1870. Edited, with Notes and Comments, forming a Continuous Narrative of the War between Germany and France. With Maps. *Third Edition, revised.* Crown 8vo. 7s. 6d.

This volume brings before the public in a convenient and portable form the record of the momentous events which have marked the last six months of 1870.

The special value of letters from camps and battle-fields consists in the vividness with which they reproduce the life and spirit of the scenes and transactions in the midst of which they are written. In the letters which have appeared in the DAILY NEWS *since the Franco-Prussian War, the public has recognized this quality as present in an eminent degree.*

*The book begins with a chronology of the war from July 4th, when the French government called out the army reserves, to December 4th; the detailes of the campaign are illustrated by four maps representing—*1. The *battles of Weissenburg and Wörth.* 2. *The battles of Saarbrücken and Speiecheren.* 3. *The battle-field before Sedan.* 4. *A plan of Metz and its vicinity.*

THE WAR CORRESPONDENCE OF THE *DAILY NEWS*
continued to the Peace. Edited, with Notes and Comments. Second Edition, Crown 8vo. with Map, 7s. 6d.

Dicey (Edward).—THE MORNING LAND. By EDWARD
DICEY. Two vols. crown 8vo. 16s.

"*An invitation to be present at the opening of the Suez Canal was the immediate cause of my journey. But I made it my object also to see as much of the Morning Land, of whose marvels the canal across the Isthmus is only the least and latest, as time and opportunity would permit. The result of my observations was communicated to the journal I then represented, in a series of letters, which I now give to the public in a collected form.*"—Extract from AUTHOR'S PREFACE.

Dilke.—GREATER BRITAIN. A Record of Travel in English-speaking Countries during 1866-7. (America, Australia, India.) By Sir CHARLES WENTWORTH DILKE, M.P. Fifth and Cheap Edition. Crown 8vo. 6*s.*

" *Mr. Dilke has written a book which is probably as well worth reading as any book of the same aims and character that ever was written. Its merits are that it is written in a lively and agreeable style, that it implies a great deal of physical pluck, that no page of it fails to show an acute and highly intelligent observer, that it stimulates the imagination as well as the judgment of the reader, and that it is on perhaps the most interesting subject that can attract an Englishman who cares about his country.*"

SATURDAY REVIEW.

Dürer (Albrecht).—HISTORY OF THE LIFE OF AL-BRECHT DÜRER, of Nürnberg. With a Translation of his Letters and Journal, and some account of his works. By Mrs. CHARLES HEATON. Royal 8vo. bevelled boards, extra gilt. 31*s.* 6*d.*

This work contains about Thirty Illustrations, ten of which are productions by the Autotype (carbon) process, and are printed in permanent tints by Messrs. Cundall and Fleming, under license from the Autotype Company, Limited ; the rest are Photographs and Woodcuts.

EARLY EGYPTIAN HISTORY FOR THE YOUNG. *See* "JUVENILE SECTION."

Elliott.—LIFE OF HENRY VENN ELLIOTT, of Brighton. By JOSIAH BATEMAN, M.A., Author of "Life of Daniel Wilson, Bishop of Calcutta," &c. With Portrait, engraved by JEENS ; and an Appendix containing a short sketch of the life of the Rev. Julius Elliott (who met with accidental death while ascending the Schreckhorn in July, 1869.) Crown 8vo. 8*s.* 6*d.* Second Edition, with Appendix.

"*A very charming piece of religious biography; no one can read it without both pleasure and profit.*"—BRITISH QUARTERLY REVIEW.

EUROPEAN HISTORY, narrated in a Series of Historical Selections from the best Authorities. Edited and arranged by E. M. SEWELL and C. M. YONGE. First Series, crown 8vo. 6*s.* ; Second Series, 1088-1228, crown 8vo. 6*s.*

When young children have acquired the outlines of history from abridg-ments and catechisms, and it becomes desirable to give a more enlarged view of the subject, in order to render it really useful and interesting, a difficulty often arises as to the choice of books. Two courses are open, either to take a general and consequently dry history of facts, such as Russell's Modern Europe, or to choose some work treating of a particular period or subject, such as the works of Macaulay and Froude. The former course usually renders history uninteresting ; the latter is unsatisfactory, because it is not sufficiently comprehensive. To remedy this difficulty, selections, continuous and chronological, have in the present volume been taken from the larger works of Freeman, Milman, Palgrave, and others, which may serve as distinct landmarks of historical reading. "We know of scarcely anything," says the Guardian, *of this volume, "which is so likely to raise to a higher level the average standard of English education."*

Fairfax.—A LIFE OF THE GREAT LORD FAIRFAX, Commander-in-Chief of the Army of the Parliament of England. By CLEMENTS R. MARKHAM, F.S.A. With Portraits, Maps, Plans, and Illustrations. Demy 8vo. 16s.

No full Life of the great Parliamentary Commander has appeared ; and it is here sought to produce one—based upon careful research in con-temporary records and upon family and other documents.

*" Highly useful to the careful student of the History of the Civil War. . . Probably as a military chronicle Mr. Markham's book is one of the most full and accurate that we possess about the Civil War."—*FORTNIGHTLY REVIEW.

Forbes.—LIFE OF PROFESSOR EDWARD FORBES, F.R.S. By GEORGE WILSON, M.D., F.R.S.E., and ARCHIBALD GEIKIE, F.R.S. 8vo. with Portrait, 14s.

*" From the first page to the last the book claims careful reading, as being a full but not overcrowded rehearsal of a most instructive life, and the true picture of a mind that was rare in strength and beauty."—*EXAMINER.

Freeman.—HISTORY OF FEDERAL GOVERNMENT, from the Foundation of the Achaian League to the Disruption of the United States. By EDWARD A. FREEMAN, M.A. Vol. I. General Introduction. History of the Greek Federations. 8vo. 21s.

" The task Mr. Freeman has undertaken is one of great magnitude and importance. It is also a task of an almost entirely novel character. No

other work professing to give the history of a political principle occurs to us, except the slight contributions to the history of representative government that is contained in a course of M. Guizot's lectures . . . . The history of the development of a principle is at least as important as the history of a dynasty, or of a race." —SATURDAY REVIEW.

OLD ENGLISH HISTORY. By EDWARD A. FREEMAN, M.A., late Fellow of Trinity College, Oxford. With *Five Coloured Maps.* Second Edition extra. Fcap. 8vo., half-bound. 6s.

" Its object is to show that clear, accurate, and scientific views of history, or indeed of any subject, may be easily given to children from the very first. . . I have, I hope, shown that it is perfectly easy to teach children, from the very first, to distinguish true history alike from legend and from wilful invention, and also to understand the nature of historical authorities, and to weigh one statement against another. . . . . I have throughout striven to connect the history of England with the general history of civilized Europe, and I have especially tried to make the book serve as an incentive to a more accurate study of historical geography."—PREFACE.

HISTORY OF THE CATHEDRAL CHURCH OF WELLS, as illustrating the History of the Cathedral Churches of the Old Foundation. By EDWARD A. FREEMAN, D.C.L., formerly Fellow of Trinity College, Oxford. Crown 8vo. 3s. 6d.

" I have here tried to treat the history of the Church of Wells as a contribution to the general history of the Church and Kingdom of England, and specially to the history of Cathedral Churches of the Old Foundation. . . . I wish to point out the general principles of the original founders as the model to which the Old Foundations should be brought back, and the New Foundations reformed after their pattern."—PREFACE.

French (George Russell). — SHAKSPEAREANA GENEALOGICA. 8vo. cloth extra, 15s. Uniform with the "Cambridge Shakespeare."

Part I.—Identification of the dramatis personæ in the historical plays, from King John to King Henry VIII. ; Notes on Characters in Macbeth and Hamlet ; Persons and Places belonging to Warwickshire alluded to. Part II.—The Shakspeare and Arden families and their connexions, with Tables of descent. The present is the first attempt to give a detailed description, in consecutive order, of each of the dramatis personæ in Shakspeare's immortal chronicle-histories, and some of the characters have been, it is believed, herein identified for the first time A clue is furnished which, followed up with ordinary diligence, may enable any one, with a taste for the pursuit, to trace a distinguished Shakspearean worthy to his lineal representative in the present day.

Galileo.—THE PRIVATE LIFE OF GALILEO. Compiled principally from his Correspondence and that of his eldest daughter, Sister Maria Celeste, Nun in the Franciscan Convent of S. Matthew in Arcetri. With Portrait. Crown 8vo. 7s. 6d.

It has been the endeavour of the compiler to place before the reader a plain, ungarbled statement of facts; and as a means to this end, to allow Galileo, his friends, and his judges to speak for themselves as far as possible.

Gladstone (Right Hon. W. E., M.P.).—JUVENTUS MUNDI. The Gods and Men of the Heroic Age. Crown 8vo. cloth extra. With Map. 10s. 6d. Second Edition.

This new work of Mr. Gladstone deals especially with the historic element in Homer, expounding that element and furnishing by its aid a full account of the Homeric men and the Homeric religion. It starts, after the introductory chapter, with a discussion of the several races then existing in Hellas, including the influence of the Phœnicians and Egyptians. It contains chapters on the Olympian system, with its several deities; on the Ethics and the Polity of the Heroic age; on the geography of Homer; on the characters of the Poems; presenting, in fine, a view of primitive life and primitive society as found in the poems of Homer. To this New Edition various additions have been made.

"CLOBE" ATLAS OF EUROPE. Uniform in size with Macmillan's Globe Series, containing 45 Coloured Maps, on a uniform scale and projection; with Plans of London and Paris, and a copious Index. Strongly bound in half-morocco, with flexible back, 9s.

This Atlas includes all the countries of Europe in a series of 48 Maps, drawn on the same scale, with an Alphabetical Index to the situation of more than ten thousand places, and the relation of the various maps and countries to each other is defined in a general Key-map. All the maps being on a uniform scale facilitates the comparison of extent and distance, and conveys a just impression of the relative magnitude of different countries. The size suffices to show the provincial divisions, the railways and main roads, the principal rivers and mountain ranges. "This atlas," writes the

British Quarterly, "*will be an invaluable boon for the school, the desk, or the traveller's portmanteau.*"

Godkin (James).—THE LAND WAR IN IRELAND. A History for the Times. By JAMES GODKIN, Author of "Ireland and her Churches," late Irish Correspondent of the *Times.* 8vo. 12s.

A History of the Irish Land Question.

Guizot.—(Author of "JOHN HALIFAX, GENTLEMAN.")—M. DE BARANTE, a Memoir, Biographical and Autobiographical. By M. GUIZOT. Translated by the Author of "JOHN HALIFAX, GENTLEMAN." Crown 8vo. 6s. 6d.

" *The highest purposes of both history and biography are answered by a memoir so lifelike, so faithful, and so philosophical.*"
BRITISH QUARTERLY REVIEW.

Hole.—A GENEALOGICAL STEMMA OF THE KINGS OF ENGLAND AND FRANCE. By the Rev. C. HOLE, M.A., Trinity College, Cambridge. On Sheet, 1s.

The different families are printed in distinguishing colours, thus facilitating reference.

A BRIEF BIOGRAPHICAL DICTIONARY. Compiled and Arranged by the Rev. CHARLES HOLE, M.A. Second Edition. 18mo. neatly and strongly bound in cloth. 4s. 6d.

One of the most comprehensive and accurate Biographical Dictionaries in the world, containing more than 18,000 *persons of all countries, with dates of birth and death, and what they were distinguished for. Extreme care has been bestowed on the verification of the dates ; and thus numerous errors, current in previous works, have been corrected. Its size adapts it for the desk, portmanteau, or pocket.*

" *An invaluable addition to our manuals of reference, and, from its moderate price, cannot fail to become as popular as it is useful.*"—TIMES.

Hozier.—THE SEVEN WEEKS' WAR ; Its Antecedents and its Incidents. By H. M. HOZIER. With Maps and Plans. Two vols. 8vo. 28s.

This work is based upon letters reprinted by permission from "The Times." *For the most part it is a product of a personal eye-witness of some of the most interesting incidents of a war which, for rapidity and decisive results, may claim an almost unrivalled position in history.*

THE BRITISH EXPEDITION TO ABYSSINIA. Compiled from Authentic Documents. By CAPTAIN HENRY M. HOZIER, late Assistant Military Secretary to Lord Napier of Magdala. 8vo. 9s.

"Several accounts of the British Expedition have been published. .... They have, however, been written by those who have not had access to those authentic documents, which cannot be collected directly after the termination of a campaign. .... The endeavour of the author of this sketch has been to present to readers a succinct and impartial account of an enterprise which has rarely been equalled in the annals of war."—PREFACE.

Irving.—THE ANNALS OF OUR TIME. A Diurnal of Events, Social and Political, which have happened in or had relation to the Kingdom of Great Britain, from the Accession of Queen Victoria to the Opening of the present Parliament. By JOSEPH IRVING. Second Edition, continued to the present time. 8vo. half-bound. 18s. [*Immediately.*

" We have before us a trusty and ready guide to the events of the past thirty years, available equally for the statesman, the politician, the public writer, and the general reader. If Mr. Irving's object has been to bring before the reader all the most noteworthy occurrences which have happened since the beginning of Her Majesty's reign, he may justly claim the credit of having done so most briefly, succinctly, and simply, and in such a manner, too, as to furnish him with the details necessary in each case to comprehend the event of which he is in search in an intelligent manner. Reflection will serve to show the great value of such a work as this to the journalist and statesman, and indeed to every one who feels an interest in the progress of the age; and we may add that its value is considerably increased by the addition of that most important of all appendices, an accurate and instructive index."—TIMES.

Kingsley (Canon).—ON THE ANCIEN REGIME as it existed on the Continent before the FRENCH REVOLUTION. Three Lectures delivered at the Royal Institution. By the Rev. C. KINGSLEY, M.A., formerly Professor of Modern History in the University of Cambridge. Crown 8vo. 6s.

These three lectures discuss severally (1) Caste, (2) Centralization, (3) The Explosive Forces by which the Revolution was superinduced. The Preface deals at some length with certain political questions of the present day.

THE ROMAN AND THE TEUTON. A Series of Lectures delivered before the University of Cambridge. By Rev. C. KINGSLEY, M.A. 8vo. 12s.

CONTENTS :—*Inaugural Lecture ; The Forest Children ; The Dying Empire ; The Human Deluge ; The Gothic Civilizer; Dietrich's End; The Nemesis of the Goths ; Paulus Diaconus ; The Clergy and the Heathen ; The Monk a Civilizer ; The Lombard Laws ; The Popes and the Lombards ; The Strategy of Providence.*

Kingsley (Henry, F.R.G.S.).—TALES OF OLD TRAVEL. Re-narrated by HENRY KINGSLEY, F.R.G.S. With *Eight Illustrations* by HUARD. Third Edition. Crown 8vo. 6s.

CONTENTS :—*Marco Polo; The Shipwreck of Pelsart; The Wonderful Adventures of Andrew Battel; The Wanderings of a Capuchin; Peter Carder; The Preservation of the "Terra Nova;" Spitzbergen; D'Erme-nonville's Acclimatization Adventure; The Old Slave Trade; Miles Philips; The Sufferings of Robert Everard; John Fox; Alvaro Nunez; The Foundation of an Empire.*

Latham.—BLACK AND WHITE: A Journal of a Three Months' Tour in the United States. By HENRY LATHAM, M.A., Barrister-at-Law. 8vo. 10s. 6d.

" *The spirit in which Mr. Latham has written about our brethren in America is commendable in high degree.*"—ATHENÆUM.

Law.—THE ALPS OF HANNIBAL. By WILLIAM JOHN LAW, M.A., formerly Student of Christ Church, Oxford. Two vols. 8vo. 21s.

" *No one can read the work and not acquire a conviction that, in addition to a thorough grasp of a particular topic, its writer has at command a large store of reading and thought upon many cognate points of ancient history and geography.*"—QUARTERLY REVIEW.

Liverpool.—THE LIFE AND ADMINISTRATION OF ROBERT BANKS, SECOND EARL OF LIVERPOOL, K.G. Compiled from Original Family Documents by CHARLES DUKE YONGE, Regius Professor of History and English Literature in Queen's College, Belfast ; and Author of " The History of the British Navy," " The History of France under the Bourbons," etc. Three vols. 8vo. 42s.

Since the time of Lord Burleigh no one, except the second Pitt, ever enjoyed so long a tenure of power; with the same exception, no one ever held office at so critical a time . . . . Lord Liverpool is the very last minister who has been able fully to carry out his own political views; who has been so strong that in matters of general policy the Opposition could extort no concessions from him which were not sanctioned by his own deliberate judgment. The present work is founded almost entirely on the correspondence left behind him by Lord Liverpool, and now in the possession of Colonel and Lady Catherine Harcourt.

" Full of information and instruction."—FORTNIGHTLY REVIEW.

Macmillan (Rev. Hugh).—HOLIDAYS ON HIGH

LANDS ; or, Rambles and Incidents in search of Alpine Plants. By the Rev. HUGH MACMILLAN, Author of "Bible Teachings in Nature," etc. Crown 8vo. cloth. 6s.

" Botanical knowledge is blended with a love of nature, a pious enthusiasm, and a rich felicity of diction not to be met with in any works of kindred ·character, if we except those of Hugh Miller."—DAILY TELEGRAPH.

FOOT-NOTES FROM THE PAGE OF NATURE. With numerous Illustrations. Fcap. 8vo. 5s.

" Those who have derived pleasure and profit from the study of flowers and ferns—subjects, it is pleasing to find, now everywhere popular—by descending lower into the arcana of the vegetable kingdom, will find a still more interesting and delightful field of research in the objects brought under review in the following pages."—PREFACE.

BIBLE TEACHINGS IN NATURE. Fifth Edition. Fcap. 8vo. 6s.

Martin (Frederick).—THE STATESMAN'S YEAR-BOOK :

A Statistical and Historical Account of the States of the Civilized World. Manual for Politicians and Merchants for the year 1871. BY FREDERICK MARTIN. *Eighth Annual Publication.* Crown 8vo. 10s. 6d.

The new issue has been entirely re-written, revised, and corrected, on the basis of official reports received direct from the heads of the leading Governments of the World, in reply to letters sent to them by the Editor.

Martin (Frederick).—*(continued)*—

"*Everybody who knows this work is aware that it is a book that is indispensable to writers, financiers, politicians, statesmen, and all who are directly or indirectly interested in the political, social, industrial, commercial, and financial condition of their fellow-creatures at home and abroad. Mr. Martin deserves warm commendation for the care he takes in making ' The Statesman's Year Book' complete and correct.*"

STANDARD.

HANDBOOK OF CONTEMPORARY BIOGRAPHY. By FREDERICK MARTIN, Author of "The Statesman's Year-Book." Extra fcap. 8vo. 6s.

This volume is an attempt to produce a book of reference, furnishing in a condensed form some biographical particulars of notable living men. The leading idea has been to give only facts, and those in the briefest form, and to exclude opinions.

Martineau.—BIOGRAPHICAL SKETCHES, 1852—1868. By HARRIET MARTINEAU. Third and cheaper Edition, with New Preface. Crown 8vo. 6s.

A Collection of Memoirs under these several sections:—(1) *Royal,* (2) *Politicians,* (3) *Professional,* (4) *Scientific,* (5) *Social,* (6) *Literary. These Memoirs appeared originally in the columns of the* "Daily News."

Milton.—LIFE OF JOHN MILTON. Narrated in connexion with the Political, Ecclesiastical, and Literary History of his Time. By DAVID MASSON, M.A., LL.D., Professor of Rhetoric at Edinburgh. Vol. I. with Portraits. 8vo. 18s. Vol. II. in a few days.—Vol. III. in the Press.

It is intended to exhibit Milton's life in its connexions with all the more notable phenomena of the period of British history in which it was cast— its state politics, its ecclesiastical variations, its literature and speculative thought. Commencing in 1608, the Life of Milton proceeds through the last sixteen years of the reign of James I., includes the whole of the reign of Charles I. and the subsequent years of the Commonwealth and the Protectorate, and then, passing the Restoration, extends itself to 1674, or through fourteen years of the new state of things under Charles II. The first volume deals with the life of Milton as extending from 1608 to 1640, which was the period of his education and of his minor poems.

Mitford (A. B).—TALES OF OLD JAPAN. By A. B. MITFORD, Second Secretary to the British Legation in Japan. With upwards of 30 Illustrations, drawn and cut on Wood by Japanese Artists. Two vols. crown 8vo. 21s.

This work is an attempt to do for Japan what Sir J. Davis, Dr. Legge, and M. Stanislas Julien, have done for China. Under the influence of more enlightened ideas and of a liberal system of policy, the old Japanese civilization is fast disappearing, and will, in a few years, be completely extinct. It was important, therefore, to preserve as far as possible trustworthy records of a state of society which although venerable from its antiquity, has for Europeans the dawn of novelty ; hence the series of narratives and legends translated by Mr. Mitford, and in which the Japanese are very judiciously left to tell their own tale. The two volumes comprise not only stories and episodes illustrative of Asiatic superstitions, but also three sermons. The preface, appendices, and notes explain a number of local peculiarities ; the thirty-one woodcuts are the genuine work of a native artist, who, unconsciously of course, has adopted the process first introduced by the early German masters.

Morley (John).—EDMUND BURKE, a Historical Study By JOHN MORLEY, B.A. Oxon. Crown 8vo. 7s. 6d.

" The style is terse and incisive, and brilliant with epigram and point. It contains pithy aphoristic sentences which Burke himself would not have?

Morison.—THE LIFE AND TIMES OF SAINT BERNARD, Abbot of Clairvaux. By JAMES COTTER MORISON, M.A. New Edition, revised. Crown 8vo. 7s. 6d.

" One of the best contributions in our literature towards a vivid, intelligent, and worthy knowledge of European interests and thoughts and feelings during the twelfth century. A delightful and instructive volume, and one of the best products of the modern historic spirit."
PALL MALL GAZETTE.

disowned. But these are not its best features: its sustained power of reasoning, its wide sweep of observation and reflection, its elevated ethical and social tone, stamp it as a work of high excellence, and as such we cordially recommend it to our readers."—SATURDAY REVIEW.

Mullinger.—CAMBRIDGE CHARACTERISTICS IN THE SEVENTEENTH CENTURY. By J. B. MULLINGER, B.A. Crown 8vo. 4s. 6d.

| *"It is a very entertaining and readable book."*—SATURDAY REVIEW.

"The chapters on the Cartesian Philosophy and the Cambridge Platonists are admirable."—ATHENÆUM.

Palgrave.—HISTORY OF NORMANDY AND OF ENG-LAND. By Sir FRANCIS PALGRAVE, Deputy Keeper of Her Majesty's Public Records. Completing the History to the Death of William Rufus. Four vols. 8vo. £4 4s.

Volume I. General Relations of Mediæval Europe—The Carlovingian Empire—The Danish Expeditions in the Gauls—And the Establishment of Rollo. Volume II. The Three First Dukes of Normandy; Rollo, Guillaume Longue-Épée, and Richard Sans-Peur—The Carlovingian line supplanted by the Capets. Volume III. Richard Sans-Peur— Richard Le-Bon—Richard III.—Robert Le Diable—William the Conqueror. Volume IV. William Rufus—Accession of Henry Beauclerc.

Palgrave (W. G.).—A NARRATIVE OF A YEAR'S JOURNEY THROUGH CENTRAL AND EASTERN ARABIA, 1862-3. By WILLIAM GIFFORD PALGRAVE, late of the Eighth Regiment Bombay N. I. Fifth and cheaper Edition. With Maps, Plans, and Portrait of Author, engraved on steel by Jeens. Crown 8vo. 6s.

"Considering the extent of our previous ignorance, the amount of his achievements, and the importance of his contributions to our knowledge, we cannot say less of him than was once said of a far greater discoverer. Mr. Palgrave has indeed given a new world to Europe."

| PALL MALL GAZETTE.

Parkes (Henry).—AUSTRALIAN VIEWS OF ENGLAND. By HENRY PARKES. Crown 8vo. cloth. 3s. 6d.

" *The following letters were written during a residence in England, in the years* 1861 *and* 1862, *and were published in the* "Sydney Morning Herald" *on the arrival of the monthly mails* . . . . *On re-perusal, these letters appear to contain views of English life and impressions of English notabilities which, as the views and impressions of an Englishman on his return to his native country after an absence of twenty years, may not be without interest to the English reader. The writer had opportunities of mixing with different classes of the British people, and of hearing opinions on passing events from opposite standpoints of observation.*"—AUTHOR'S PREFACE.

Prichard.—THE ADMINISTRATION OF INDIA. From 1859 to 1868. The First Ten Years of Administration under the Crown. By ILTUDUS THOMAS PRICHARD, Barrister-at-Law. Two vols. Demy 8vo. With Map. 21s.

In these volumes the author has aimed to supply a full, impartial, and independent account of British India between 1859 *and* 1868—*which is in many respects the most important epoch in the history of that country which the present century has seen.*

Ralegh.—THE LIFE OF SIR WALTER RALEGH, based upon Contemporary Documents. By EDWARD EDWARDS. Together with Ralegh's Letters, now first collected. With Portrait. Two vols. 8vo. 32s.

" *Mr. Edwards has certainly written the Life of Ralegh from fuller information than any previous biographer. He is intelligent, industrious, sympathetic: and the world has in his two volumes larger means afforded it of knowing Ralegh than it ever possessed before. The new letters and the newly-edited old letters are in themselves a boon.*"—PALL MALL GAZETTE.

Robinson (Crabb).—DIARY, REMINISCENCES, AND CORRESPONDENCE OF HENRY CRABB ROBINSON. Selected and Edited by Dr. SADLER. With Portrait. Second Edition. Three vols. 8vo. cloth. 36s.

Mr. Crabb Robinson's Diary extends over the greater part of three-quarters of a century. It contains personal reminiscences of some of the most distinguished characters of that period, including Goethe, Wieland, De Quincey, Wordsworth (with whom Mr. Crabb Robinson was on terms of great intimacy), Madame de Staël, Lafayette, Coleridge, Lamb, Milman, &c. &c.: and includes a vast variety of subjects, political, literary, ecclesiastical, and miscellaneous.

Rogers (James E. Thorold).—HISTORICAL GLEANINGS : A Series of Sketches. Montague, Walpole, Adam Smith, Cobbett. By Professor ROGERS. Crown 8vo. 4s. 6d.

Professor Rogers's object in the following sketches is to present a set of historical facts, grouped round a principal figure. The essays are in the form of lectures.

HISTORICAL GLEANINGS. Second Series. Crown 8vo. 6s.

A companion volume to the First Series recently published. It contains papers on Wiklif, Laud, Wilkes, Horne Tooke. In these lectures the author has aimed to state the social facts of the time in which the individual whose history is handled took part in public business.

Smith (Professor Goldwin).— THREE ENGLISH STATESMEN : PYM, CROMWELL, PITT. A Course of Lectures on the Political History of England. By GOLDWIN SMITH, M.A. Extra fcap. 8vo. New and Cheaper Edition. 5s.

"A work which neither historian nor politician can safely afford to neglect."—SATURDAY REVIEW.

SYSTEMS OF LAND TENURE IN VARIOUS COUNTRIES. A Series of Essays published under the sanction of the COBDEN CLUB. Demy 8vo. Second Edition. 12s.

The subjects treated are:—1. Tenure of Land in Ireland; 2. Land Laws of England; 3. Tenure of Land in India; 4. Land System of Belgium and Holland; 5. Agrarian Legislation of Prussia during the Present Century; 6. Land System of France; 7. Russian Agrarian Legislation of 1861; 8. Farm Land and Land Laws of the United States.

Tacitus.—THE HISTORY OF TACITUS, translated into English. By A. J. CHURCH, M.A. and W. J. BRODRIBB, M.A. With a Map and Notes. 8vo. 10s. 6d.

The translators have endeavoured to adhere as closely to the original as was thought consistent with a proper observance of English idiom. At the same time it has been their aim to reproduce the precise expressions of the author. This work is characterised by the Spectator *as " a scholarly and faithful translation."*

THE AGRICOLA AND GERMANIA. Translated into English by A. J. CHURCH, M.A. and W. J. BRODRIBB, M.A. With Maps and Notes. Extra fcap. 8vo. 2s. 6d.

The translators have sought to produce such a version as may satisfy scholars who demand a faithful rendering of the original, and English readers who are offended by the baldness and frigidity which commonly disfigure translations. The treatises are accompanied by introductions, notes, maps, and a chronological summary. The Athenæum *says of this work that it is " a version at once readable and exact, which may be perused with pleasure by all, and consulted with advantage by the classical student."*

Taylor (Rev. Isaac).—WORDS AND PLACES; or Etymological Illustrations of History, Etymology, and Geography. By the Rev. ISAAC TAYLOR. Second Edition. Crown 8vo. 12s. 6d.

" Mr. Taylor has produced a really useful book, and one which stands alone in our language."—SATURDAY REVIEW.

Trench (Archbishop).—GUSTAVUS ADOLPHUS : Social Aspects of the Thirty Years' War. By R. CHENEVIX TRENCH, D.D., Archbishop of Dublin. Fcap. 8vo. 2s. 6d.

" Clear and lucid in style, these lectures will be a treasure to many to whom the subject is unfamiliar."—DUBLIN EVENING MAIL.

Trench (Mrs. R.).—Remains of the late MRS. RICHARD TRENCH. Being Selections from her Journals, Letters, ar d other Papers. Edited by ARCHBISHOP TRENCH. New and Cheaper Issue, with Portrait, 8vo. 6s.

Contains notices and anecdotes illustrating the social life of the period —extending over a quarter of a century (1799—1827). It includes also poems and other miscellaneous pieces by Mrs. Trench.

Trench (Capt. F., F.R.G.S.).—THE RUSSO-INDIAN

QUESTION, Historically, Strategically, and Politically considered. By Capt. TRENCH, F.R.G.S. With a Sketch of Central Asiatic Politics and Map of Central Asia. Crown 8vo. 7s. 6d.

" *The Russo-Indian, or Central Asian question has for several obvious reasons been attracting much public attention in England, in Russia, and also on the Continent, within the last year or two. . . . I have thought that the present volume, giving a short sketch of the history of this question from its earliest origin, and condensing much of the most recent and interesting information on the subject, and on its collateral phases, might perhaps be acceptable to those who take an interest in it.*"—AUTHOR'S PREFACE.

Trevelyan (G.O., M.P.).—CAWNPORE. Illustrated with

Plan. By G. O. TREVELYAN, M.P., Author of " The Competition Wallah." Second Edition. Crown 8vo. 6s.

" *In this book we are not spared one fact of the sad story; but our feelings are not harrowed by the recital of imaginary outrages. It is good for us at home that we have one who tells his tale so well as does Mr. Trevelyan.*"—PALL MALL GAZETTE.

THE COMPETITION WALLAH. New Edition. Crown 8vo. 6s.

" *The earlier letters are especially interesting for their racy descriptions of European life in India. . . . . Those that follow are of more serious import, seeking to tell the truth about the Hindoo character and English influences, good and bad, upon it, as well as to suggest some better course of treatment than that hitherto adopted.*"—EXAMINER.

Vaughan (late Rev. Dr. Robert, of the British

Quarterly).—MEMOIR OF ROBERT A. VAUGHAN.

Author of " Hours with the Mystics." By ROBERT VAUGHAN, D.D. Second Edition, revised and enlarged. Extra fcap. 8vo. 5s.

" *It deserves a place on the same shelf with Stanley's ' Life of Arnold,' and Carlyle's ' Stirling.' Dr. Vaughan has performed his painful but not all unpleasing task with exquisite good taste and feeling.*"—NONCONFORMIST.

Wagner.—MEMOIR OF THE REV. GEORGE WAGNER, M.A., late Incumbent of St. Stephen's Church, Brighton. By the Rev. J. N. SIMPKINSON, M.A. Third and Cheaper Edition, corrected and abridged. 5*s.*

" *A more edifying biography we have rarely met with.*"—LITERARY CHURCHMAN.

Wallace.—THE MALAY ARCHIPELAGO : the Land of the Orang Utan and the Bird of Paradise. A Narrative of Travel with Studies of Man and Nature. By ALFRED RUSSEL WALLACE. With Maps and Illustrations. Second Edition. Two vols. crown 8vo. 24*s.*

" *A carefully and deliberately composed narrative. . . . We advise our readers to do as we have done, read his book through.*"—TIMES.

Ward (Professor).—THE HOUSE OF AUSTRIA IN THE THIRTY YEARS' WAR. Two Lectures, with Notes and Illustrations. By ADOLPHUS W. WARD, M.A., Professor of History in Owens College, Manchester. Extra fcap. 8vo. 2*s.* 6*d.*

" *Very compact and instructive.*"—FORTNIGHTLY REVIEW.

Warren.—AN ESSAY ON GREEK FEDERAL COINAGE. By the Hon. J. LEICESTER WARREN, M.A. 8vo. 2*s.* 6*d.*

" *The present essay is an attempt to illustrate Mr. Freeman's Federal Government by evidence deduced from the coinage of the times and countries therein treated of.*"—PREFACE.

Wedgwood.—JOHN WESLEY AND THE EVANGELICAL REACTION of the Eighteenth Century. By JULIA WEDGWOOD. Crown 8vo. 8*s.* 6*d.*

This book is an attempt to delineate the influence of a particular man upon his age.

Wilson.—A MEMOIR OF GEORGE WILSON, M.D., F.R.S.E., Regius Professor of Technology in the University of Edinburgh. By his SISTER. New Edition. Crown 8vo. 6*s.*

" *An exquisite and touching portrait of a rare and beautiful spirit.*"— GUARDIAN.

Wilson (Daniel, LL.D.).—PREHISTORIC ANNALS OF SCOTLAND. By DANIEL WILSON, LL.D., Professor of History and English Literature in University College, Toronto. New Edition, with numerous Illustrations. Two vols. demy 8vo. 36s.

This elaborate and learned work is divided into four Parts. Part I. deals with The Primeval or Stone Period : Aboriginal Traces, Sepulchral Memorials, Dwellings, and Catacombs, Temples, Weapons, &c. &c. ; Part II., The Bronze Period : The Metallurgic Transition, Primitive Bronze, Personal Ornaments, Religion, Arts, and Domestic Habits, with other topics ; Part III., The Iron Period : The Introduction of Iron, The Roman Invasion, Strongholds, &c. &c.; Part IV., The Christian Period : Historical Data, the Norrie's Law Relics, Primitive and Mediæval Ecclesiology, Ecclesiastical and Miscellaneous Antiquities. The work is furnished with an elaborate Index.

PREHISTORIC MAN. New Edition, revised and partly re-written, with numerous Illustrations. One vol. 8vo. 21s.

This work, which carries out the principle of the preceding one, but with a wider scope, aims to " view Man, as far as possible, unaffected by those modifying influences which accompany the development of nations and the maturity of a true historic period, in order thereby to ascertain the sources from whence such development and maturity proceed." It contains, for example, chapters on the Primeval Transition ; Speech ; Metals ; the Mound-Builders ; Primitive Architecture ; the American Type ; the Red Blood of the West, &c. &c.

CHATTERTON : A Biographical Study. By DANIEL WILSON, LL.D., Professor of History and English Literature in University College, Toronto. Crown 8vo. 6s. 6d.

The Author here regards Chatterton as a Poet, not as a " mere resetter and defacer of stolen literary treasures." Reviewed in this light, he has found much in the old materials capable of being turned to new account ; and to these materials research in various directions has enabled him to make some additions.

Yonge (Charlotte M.)—A PARALLEL HISTORY OF FRANCE AND ENGLAND : consisting of Outlines and Dates. By CHARLOTTE M. YONGE, Author of "The Heir of Redclyffe," "Cameos from English History," &c. &c. Oblong 4to. 3s. 6d.

This tabular history has been drawn up to supply a want felt by many teachers of some means of making their pupils realize what events in the two countries were contemporary. A skeleton narrative has been constructed of the chief transactions in either country, placing a column between for what affected both alike, by which means it is hoped that young people may be assisted in grasping the mutual relation of events.

SECTION II.

POETRY AND BELLES LETTRES.

Allingham.—LAURENCE BLOOMFIELD IN IRELAND
or, the New Landlord. By WILLIAM ALLINGHAM. New and
Cheaper Issue, with a Preface. Fcap. 8vo. cloth, 4s. 6d.

*In the new Preface, the state of Ireland, with special reference to the
Church measure, is discussed.*

*" It is vital with the national character. . . . It has something of Pope's
point and Goldsmith's simplicity, touched to a more modern issue."—*
ATHENÆUM.

Arnold (Matthew).—POEMS. By MATTHEW ARNOLD.
Two vols. Extra fcap. 8vo. cloth. 12s. Also sold separately at 6s.
each.

*Volume I. contains Narrative and Elegiac Poems; Volume II. Dra-
matic and Lyric Poems. The two volumes comprehend the First and
Second Series of the Poems, and the New Poems.*

NEW POEMS. Extra fcap. 8vo. 6s. 6d.

*In this volume will be found "Empedocles on Etna;" " Thyrsis " (written
in commemoration of the late Professor Clough); " Epilogue to Lessing's
Laocoön;" " Heine's Grave ;" " Obermann once more." All these
poems are also included in the Edition (two vols.) above-mentioned.*

ESSAYS IN CRITICISM. New Edition, with Additions. Extra
fcap. 8vo. 6s.

*CONTENTS :—Preface ; The Function of Criticism at the present time ;
The Literary Influence of Academies ; Maurice de Guerin ; Eugenie
de Guerin ; Heinrich Heine ; Pagan and Mediæval Religious Sentiment ;
Joubert ; Spinoza and the Bible ; Marcus Aurelius.*

ASPROMONTE, AND OTHER POEMS. Fcap. 8vo. cloth extra. 4s. 6d.

CONTENTS :—*Poems for Italy; Dramatic Lyrics; Miscellaneous.*

" Uncommon lyrical power and deep poetic feeling."—LITERARY CHURCHMAN.

Barnes (Rev. W.).—POEMS OF RURAL LIFE IN COMMON ENGLISH. By the REV. W. BARNES, Author of " Poems of Rural Life in the Dorset Dialect." Fcap. 8vo. 6s.

" In a high degree pleasant and novel. The book is by no means one which the lovers of descriptive poetry can afford to lose."—ATHENÆUM.

Bell.—ROMANCES AND MINOR POEMS. By HENRY GLASSFORD BELL. Fcap. 8vo. 6s.

" Full of life and genius."—COURT CIRCULAR.

Besant.—STUDIES IN EARLY FRENCH POETRY. By WALTER BESANT, M.A. Crown. 8vo. 8s. 6d.

A sort of impression rests on most minds that French literature begins with the "siècle de Louis Quatorze;" any previous literature being for the most part unknown or ignored. Few know anything of the enormous literary activity that began in the thirteenth century, was carried on by Rutebeuf, Marie de France, Gaston de Foix, Thibault de Champagne, and Lorris; was fostered by Charles of Orleans, by Margaret of Valois, by Francis the First; that gave a crowd of versifiers to France, enriched, strengthened, developed, and fixed the French language, and prepared the way for Corneille and for Racine. The present work aims to afford information and direction touching the early efforts of France in poetical literature.

" In one moderately sized volume he has contrived to introduce us to the very best, if not to all of the early French poets."—ATHENÆUM.

Bradshaw.—AN ATTEMPT TO ASCERTAIN THE STATE OF CHAUCER'S WORKS, AS THEY WERE LEFT AT HIS DEATH. With some Notes of their Subsequent History. By HENRY BRADSHAW, of King's College, and the University Library, Cambridge. *In the Press.*

Brimley.—ESSAYS BY THE LATE GEORGE BRIMLEY, M.A. Edited by the Rev. W. G. CLARK, M.A. With Portrait. Cheaper Edition. Fcap. 8vo. 3*s*. 6*d*.

Essays on literary topics, such as Tennyson's "Poems," Carlyle's "Life of Stirling," "Bleak House," &c., reprinted from Fraser, the Spectator, *and like periodicals.*

Broome.—THE STRANGER OF SERIPHOS. A Dramatic Poem. By FREDERICK NAPIER BROOME. Fcap. 8vo. 5*s*.

Founded on the Greek legend of Danae and Perseus.

"Grace and beauty of expression are Mr. Broome's characteristics; and these qualities are displayed in many passages."—ATHENÆUM.

Church (A. J.).—HORÆ TENNYSONIANÆ, Sive Eclogæ e Tennysono Latine redditæ. Cura A. J. CHURCH, A.M. Extra fcap. 8vo. 6*s*.

Latin versions of Selections from Tennyson. Among the authors are the Editor, the late Professor Conington, Professor Seeley, Dr. Hessey, Mr. Kebbel, and other gentlemen.

Clough (Arthur Hugh).—THE POEMS AND PROSE REMAINS OF ARTHUR HUGH CLOUGH. With a Selection from his Letters and a Memoir. Edited by his Wife. With Portrait. Two vols. crown 8vo. 21*s*. Or Poems separately, as below.

The late Professor Clough is well known as a graceful, tender poet, and as the scholarly translator of Plutarch. The letters possess high interest, not biographical only, but literary—discussing, as they do, the most important questions of the time, always in a genial spirit. The "Remains" include papers on "Retrenchment at Oxford;" on Professor F. W. Newman's book "The Soul;" on Wordsworth; on the Formation of Classical English; on some Modern Poems (Matthew Arnold and the late Alexander Smith), &c. &c.

THE POEMS OF ARTHUR HUGH CLOUGH, sometime Fellow of Oriel College, Oxford. Third Edition. Fcap. 8vo. 6*s*.

"From the higher mind of cultivated, all-questioning, but still conservative England, in this our puzzled generation, we do not know of any utterance in literature so characteristic as the poems of Arthur Hugh Clough."—FRASER'S MAGAZINE.

Dante.—DANTE'S COMEDY, THE HELL. Translated by W. M. ROSSETTI. Fcap. 8vo. cloth. 5s.

" The aim of this translation of Dante may be summed up in one word —Literality. . . . To follow Dante sentence for sentence, line for line, word for word—neither more nor less—has been my strenuous endeavour." —AUTHOR'S PREFACE.

De Vere.—THE INFANT BRIDAL, and other Poems. By AUBREY DE VERE. Fcap. 8vo. 7s. 6d.

"Mr. De Vere has taken his place among the poets of the day. Pure and tender feeling, and that polished restraint of style which is called classical, are the charms of the volume."—SPECTATOR.

Doyle (Sir F. H.).—Works by Sir FRANCIS HASTINGS DOYLE, Professor of Poetry in the University of Oxford :—

THE RETURN OF THE GUARDS, AND OTHER POEMS. Fcap. 8vo. 7s.

" Good wine needs no bush, nor good verse a preface; and Sir Francis Doyle's verses run bright and clear, and smack of a classic vintage. . . . His chief characteristic, as it is his greatest charm, is the simple manliness which gives force to all he writes. It is a characteristic in these days rare enough."—EXAMINER.

LECTURES ON POETRY, delivered before the University of Oxford in 1868. Crown 8vo. 3s. 6d.

THREE LECTURES :—(1) *Inaugural;* (2) *Provincial Poetry;* (3) *Dr. Newman's " Dream of Gerontius."*

"Full of thoughtful discrimination and fine insight: the lecture on ' Provincial Poetry' seems to us singularly true, eloquent, and instructive." —SPECTATOR.

Evans.—BROTHER FABIAN'S MANUSCRIPT, AND OTHER POEMS. By SEBASTIAN EVANS. Fcap. 8vo. cloth. 6s.

" In this volume we have full assurance that he has ' the vision and the faculty divine.' . . . Clever and full of kindly humour."—GLOBE.

Furnivall.—LE MORTE D'ARTHUR. Edited from the *Harleian* M.S. 2252, in the British Museum. By F. J. FURNIVALL. M.A. With Essay by the late HERBERT COLERIDGE. Fcap. 8vo. 7s. 6d.

Looking to the interest shown by so many thousands in Mr. Tennyson's Arthurian poems, the editor and publishers have thought that the old version would possess considerable interest. It is a reprint of the celebrated Harleian copy ; and is accompanied by index and glossary.

Garnett.—IDYLLS AND EPIGRAMS. Chiefly from the Greek Anthology. By RICHARD GARNETT. Fcap. 8vo. 2s. 6d.

" A charming little book. For English readers, Mr. Garnett's translations will open a new world of thought."—WESTMINSTER REVIEW.

GUESSES AT TRUTH. By TWO BROTHERS. With Vignette, Title, and Frontispiece. New Edition, with Memoir. Fcap. 8vo. 6s.

" The following year was memorable for the commencement of the ' Guesses at Truth.' He and his Oxford brother, living as they did in constant and free interchange of thought on questions of philosophy and literature and art ; delighting, each of them, in the epigrammatic terseness which is the charm of the ' Pensées ' of Pascal, and the ' Caractères ' of La Bruyère—agreed to utter themselves in this form, and the book appeared, anonymously, in two volumes, in 1827."—MEMOIR.

Hamerton.—A PAINTER'S CAMP. By PHILIP GILBERT HAMERTON. Second Edition, revised. Extra fcap. 8vo. 6s.

BOOK I. *In England;* BOOK II. *In Scotland;* BOOK III. *In France. This is the story of an Artist's encampments and adventures. The headings of a few chapters may serve to convey a notion of the character of the book: A Walk on the Lancashire Moors ; the Author his own Housekeeper and Cook ; Tents and Boats for the Highlands ; The Author encamps on an uninhabited Island ; A Lake Voyage ; A Gipsy Journey to Glen Coe ; Concerning Moonlight and Old Castles ; A little French City ; A Farm in the Autunois, &c. &c.*

" His pages sparkle with many turns of expression, not a few well-told anecdotes, and many observations which are the fruit of attentive study and wise reflection on the complicated phenomena of human life, as well as of unconscious nature."—WESTMINSTER REVIEW.

ETCHING AND ETCHERS. A Treatise Critical and Practical. By P. G. HAMERTON. With Original Plates by REMBRANDT, CALLOT, DUJARDIN, PAUL POTTER, &c. Royal 8vo. Half morocco. 31s. 6d.

" It is a work of which author, printer, and publisher may alike feel proud. It is a·work, too, of which none but a genuine artist could by possibility have been the author."—SATURDAY REVIEW.

Herschel.—THE ILIAD OF HOMER. Translated into English Hexameters. By Sir JOHN HERSCHEL, Bart. 8vo. 18s.

A version of the Iliad in English Hexameters. The question of Homeric translation is fully discussed in the Preface.

" It is admirable, not only for many intrinsic merits, but as a great man's tribute to Genius."—ILLUSTRATED LONDON NEWS.

HIATUS : the Void in Modern Education. Its Cause and Antidote. By OUTIS. 8vo. 8s. 6d.

The main object of this Essay is to point out how the emotional element which underlies the Fine Arts is disregarded and undeveloped at this time so far as (despite a pretence at filling it up) to constitute an Educational Hiatus.

Huxley (Professor).—LAY SERMONS, ADDRESSES, AND REVIEWS. By T. H. HUXLEY, LL.D., F.R.S. Second and Cheaper Edition, crown 8vo. 7s. 6d.

Fourteen discourses on the following subjects :—On the Advisableness of Improving Natural Knowledge Emancipation—Black and White ; A Liberal Education, ana where to find it ; Scientific Education ; on the Educational Value of the Natural History Sciences ; on the Study of Zoology ; on the Physical Basis of Life ; the Scientific Aspects of Positivism ; on a Piece of Chalk ; Geological Contemporaneity and Persistent Types of Life ; Geological Reform ; the Origin of Species ; Criticisms on the " Origin of Species ;" on Descartes' " Discourse touching the Method of using one's Reason rightly and of seeking Scientific Truth."

ESSAYS SELECTED FROM LAY SERMONS, ADDRESSES, AND REVIEWS. Crown 8vo. Cloth. 2*s.*

Whilst publishing a second edition of his Lay Sermons, Addresses, and Reviews, *Professor Huxley has, at the suggestion of many friends, issued in a cheap and popular form the selection we are now noticing. It includes the following essays:*—(1) *On the Advisableness of Improving Natural Knowledge.* (2) *A Liberal Education, and where to find it.* (3) *Scientific Education, notes of an after-dinner speech.* (4) *On the Physical Basis of Life.* (5) *The Scientific Aspects of Positivism.* (6) *On Descartes'* "*Discourse touching the Method of using one's Reason Rightly and of seeking Scientific Truth.*"

Kennedy.—LEGENDARY FICTIONS OF THE IRISH CELTS. Collected and Narrated by PATRICK KENNEDY. Crown 8vo. With Two Illustrations. 7*s.* 6*d.*

"*A very admirable popular selection of the Irish fairy stories and legends, in which those who are familiar with Mr. Croker's, and other selections of the same kind, will find much that is fresh, and full of the peculiar vivacity and humour, and sometimes even of the ideal beauty, of the true Celtic Legend.*"—SPECTATOR.

Kingsley (Canon).—*See also* "HISTORIC SECTION," "WORKS OF FICTION," *and* "PHILOSOPHY;" *also* "JUVENILE BOOKS," *and* "THEOLOGY."

THE SAINTS' TRAGEDY: or, The True Story of Elizabeth of Hungary: By the Rev. CHARLES KINGSLEY. With a Preface by the Rev. F. D. MAURICE. Third Edition. Fcap. 8vo. 5*s.*

ANDROMEDA, AND OTHER POEMS. Third Edition. Fcap. 8vo. 5*s.*

PHAETHON; or, Loose Thoughts for Loose Thinkers. Third Edition. Crown 8vo. 2*s.*

Lowell (Professor).—AMONG MY BOOKS. Six Essays. By JAMES RUSSELL LOWELL, M.A., Professor of Belles Lettres in Harvar College. Crown 8vo. 7*s.* 6*d.*

Six Essays: Dryden ; Witchcraft ; Shakespeare Once More ; New England Two Centuries ago ; Lessing ; Rousseau and the Sentimentalists.

UNDER THE WILLOWS, AND OTHER POEMS.   By JAMES RUSSELL LOWELL.   Fcap. 8vo.   6s.

"*Under the Willows is one of the most admirable bits of idyllic work, short as it is, or perhaps because it is short, that have been done in our generation.*"—SATURDAY REVIEW.

Masson (Professor).—ESSAYS, BIOGRAPHICAL AND CRITICAL.   Chiefly on the British Poets.   By DAVID MASSON, LL.D., Professor of Rhetoric in the University of Edinburgh.   8vo.   12s. 6d.

"*Distinguished by a remarkable power of analysis, a clear statement of the actual facts on which speculation is based, and an appropriate beauty of language.   These essays should be popular with serious men.*"— ATHENÆUM.

BRITISH NOVELISTS AND THEIR STYLES.   Being a Critical Sketch of the History of British Prose Fiction.   Crown 8vo.   7s. 6d.

"*Valuable for its lucid analysis of fundamental principles, its breadth of view, and sustained animation of style.*"—SPECTATOR.

MRS. JERNINGHAM'S JOURNAL.   Second Edition.   Extra fcap. 8vo.   3s. 6d.   A Poem of the boudoir or domestic class, purporting to be the journal of a newly-married lady.

"*One quality in the piece, sufficient of itself to claim a moment's attention, is that it is unique—original, indeed, is not too strong a word—in the manner of its conception and execution.*"—PALL MALL GAZETTE.

Mistral (F.).—MIRELLE: a Pastoral Epic of Provence.   Translated by H. CRICHTON.   Extra fcap. 8vo.   6s.

"*This is a capital translation of the elegant and richly-coloured pastoral epic poem of M. Mistral which, in 1859, he dedicated in enthusiastic terms to Lamartine. . . . . . It would be hard to overpraise the sweetness and pleasing freshness of this charming epic.*"—ATHENÆUM.

Myers (Ernest).—THE PURITANS. By ERNEST MYERS. Extra fcap. 8vo. cloth. 2*s.* 6*d.*

" It is not too much to call it a really grand poem, stately and dignified, and showing not only a high poetic mind, but also great power over poetic expression."—LITERARY CHURCHMAN.

Myers (F. W. H.).—Poems. By F. W. H. MYERS. Extra fcap. 8vo. 4*s.* 6*d.* Containing "ST. PAUL," "St. JOHN," and other Poems.

" St. Paul stands without a rival as the noblest religious poem which has been written in an age which beyond any other has been prolific in this class of poetry. The sublimest conceptions are expressed in language which for richness, taste, and purity, we have never seen excelled."—JOHN BULL.

Nettleship.—ESSAYS ON ROBERT BROWNING'S POETRY. By JOHN T. NETTLESHIP. Extra fcap. 8vo. 6*s.* 6*d.*

Noel.—BEATRICE, AND OTHER POEMS. By the Hon. RODEN NOEL. Fcap. 8vo. 6*s.*

" Beatrice is in many respects a noble poem; it displays a splendour of landscape painting, a strong definite precision of highly-coloured description, which has not often been surpassed."—PALL MALL GAZETTE.

Norton.—THE LADY OF LA GARAYE. By the HON. MRS. NORTON. With Vignette and Frontispiece. Sixth Edition. Fcap. 8vo. 4*s.* 6*d.*

" There is no lack of vigour, no faltering of power, plenty of passion, much bright description, much musical verse. . . . Full of thoughts well-expressed, and may be classed among her best works."—TIMES.

Orwell.—THE BISHOP'S WALK AND THE BISHOP'S TIMES. Poems on the days of Archbishop Leighton and the Scottish Covenant. By ORWELL. Fcap. 8vo. 5*s.*

" Pure taste and faultless precision of language, the fruits of deep thought, insight into human nature, and lively sympathy."—NONCONFORMIST.

Palgrave (Francis T.).—ESSAYS ON ART. By FRANCIS TURNER PALGRAVE, M.A., late Fellow of Exeter College, Oxford. Extra fcap. 8vo. 6*s.*

Mulready—Dyce—Holman Hunt—Herbert—Poetry, Prose, and Sensationalism in Art—Sculpture in England—The Albert Cross, &c.

SHAKESPEARE'S SONNETS AND SONGS. Edited by F. T. PALGRAVE. Gem Edition. With Vignette Title by JEENS. 3s. 6d.

" For minute elegance no volume could possibly excel the ' Gem Edition.' "—SCOTSMAN.

ORIGINAL HYMNS. By F. T. PALGRAVE. Third Edition, enlarged, 18mo. 1s. 6d.

LYRICAL POEMS. By F. T. PALGRAVE. [*Nearly ready.*

Patmore.—Works by COVENTRY PATMORE :—

THE ANGEL IN THE HOUSE.

BOOK I. *The Betrothal;* BOOK II. *The Espousals;* BOOK III. *Faithful for Ever. With Tamerton Church Tower. Two vols. Fcap. 8vo.* 12s.

*** *A New and Cheap Edition in one vol.* 18mo., *beautifully printed on toned paper, price* 2s. 6d.

THE VICTORIES OF LOVE. Fcap. 8vo. 4s. 6d.

The intrinsic merit of his poem will secure it a permanent place in literature. . . .'. Mr. Patmore has fully earned a place in the catalogue of poets by the finished idealization of domestic life."—SATURDAY REVIEW.

Pember (E. H.).—THE TRAGEDY OF LESBOS. A Dramatic Poem. By E. H PEMBER. Fcap. 8vo. 4s. 6d.

Founded upon the story of Sappho.

Richardson.—THE ILIAD OF THE EAST. A Selection of Legends drawn from Valmiki's Sanskrit Poem "The Ramayana." By FREDERIKA RICHARDSON. Crown 8vo. 7s. 6d.

" A charming volume which at once enmeshes the reader in its snares." —ATHENÆUM.

Rhoades (James).—POEMS. By JAMES RHOADES. Fcap. 8vo. 4s. 6d.

POEMS AND SONNETS. *Contents:—Ode to Harmony; To the Spirit of Unrest; Ode to Winter; The Tunnel; To the Spirit of Beauty; Song of a Leaf; By the Rotha; An Old Orchard; Love and Rest; The Flowers Surprised; On the Death of Artemus Ward; The Two Paths; The Ballad of Little Maisie; Sonnets.*

C

Rossetti.—Works by CHRISTINA ROSSETTI :—

GOBLIN MARKET, AND OTHER POEMS. With two Designs by D. G. ROSSETTI. Second Edition. Fcap. 8vo. 5*s.*

"She handles her little marvel with that rare poetic discrimination which neither exhausts it of its simple wonders by pushing symbolism too far, nor keeps those wonders in the merely fabulous and capricious stage. In fact she has produced a true children's poem, which is far more delightful to the mature than to children, though it would be delightful to all."— SPECTATOR.

THE PRINCE'S PROGRESS, AND OTHER POEMS. With two Designs by D. G. ROSSETTI. Fcap. 8vo. 6*s.*

*" Miss Rossetti's poems are of the kind which recalls Shelley's definition of Poetry as the record of the best and happiest moments of the best and happiest minds. . . . They are like the piping of a bird on the spray in the sunshine, or the quaint singing with which a child amuses itself when it forgets that anybody is listening."—*SATURDAY REVIEW.

Rossetti (W. M.).—DANTE'S HELL. *See* "DANTE."

FINE ART, chiefly Contemporary. By WILLIAM M. ROSSETTI. Crown 8vo. 10*s.* 6*d.*

This volume consists of Criticism on Contemporary Art, reprinted from Fraser, The Saturday Review, The Pall Mall Gazette, *and other publications.*

Roby.—STORY OF A HOUSEHOLD, AND OTHER POEMS. By MARY K. ROBY. Fcap. 8vo. 5*s.*

Seeley (Professor). — LECTURES AND ESSAYS. By J. R. SEELEY, M.A. Professor of Modern History in the University of Cambridge. 8vo. 10*s.* 6*d.*

CONTENTS :—*Roman Imperialism:* 1. *The Great Roman Revolution;* 2. *The Proximate cause of the Fall of the Roman Empire;* 3. *The Later Empire.*—*Milton's Political Opinions*—*Milton's Poetry*—*Elementary Principles in Art*—*Liberal Education in Universities*—*English in Schools*—*The Church as a Teacher of Morality*—*The Teaching of Politics: an Inaugural Lecture delivered at Cambridge.*

Shairp (Principal).—KILMAHOE, a Highland Pastoral, with other Poems. By JOHN CAMPBELL SHAIRP. Fcap. 8vo. 5*s.*

" Kilmahoe is a Highland Pastoral, redolent of the warm soft air of the Western Lochs and Moors, sketched out with remarkable grace and picturesqueness."—SATURDAY REVIEW.

Smith.—Works by ALEXANDER SMITH :—

A LIFE DRAMA, AND OTHER POEMS. Fcap. 8vo. 2*s.* 6*d.*

CITY POEMS. Fcap. 8vo. 5*s.*

EDWIN OF DEIRA. Second Edition. Fcap. 8vo. 5*s.*

" A poem which is marked by the strength, sustained sweetness, and compact texture of real life."—NORTH BRITISH REVIEW.

Smith.—POEMS. By CATHERINE BARNARD SMITH. Fcap. 8vo. 5*s.*

" Wealthy in feeling, meaning, finish, and grace; not without passion, which is suppressed, but the keener for that."—ATHENÆUM.

Smith (Rev. Walter).—HYMNS OF CHRIST AND THE CHRISTIAN LIFE. By the Rev. WALTER C. SMITH, M.A. Fcap. 8vo. 6*s.*

" These are among the sweetest sacred poems we have read for a long time. With no profuse imagery, expressing a range of feeling and expression by no means uncommon, they are true and elevated, and their pathos is profound and simple."—NONCONFORMIST.

Stratford de Redcliffe (Viscount).—SHADOWS OF THE PAST, in Verse. By VISCOUNT STRATFORD DE REDCLIFFE. Crown 8vo. 10*s.* 6*d.*

" The vigorous words of one who has acted vigorously. They combine the fervour of politicians and poet."—GUARDIAN.

Trench.—Works by R. CHENEVIX TRENCH, D.D., Archbishop of Dublin. *See also Sections* "PHILOSOPHY," "THEOLOGY," &c.

POEMS. Collected and arranged anew. Fcap. 8vo. 7s. 6d.

ELEGIAC POEMS. Third Edition. Fcap. 8vo. 2s. 6d.

CALDERON'S LIFE'S A DREAM : The Great Theatre of the World. With an Essay on his Life and Genius. Fcap. 8vo. 4s. 6d.

HOUSEHOLD BOOK OF ENGLISH POETRY. Selected and arranged, with Notes, by R. C. TRENCH, D.D., Archbishop of Dublin. Second Edition. Extra fcap. 8vo. 5s. 6d.

This volume is called a " Household Book," by this name implying that it is a book for all—that there is nothing in it to prevent it from being confidently placed in the hands of every member of the household. Specimens of all classes of poetry are given, including selections from living authors. The Editor has aimed to produce a book "which the emigrant, finding room for little not absolutely necessary, might yet find a room for in his trunk, and the traveller in his knapsack, and that on some narrow shelves where there are few books this might be one."

*" The Archbishop has conferred in this delightful volume an important gift on the whole English-speaking population of the world."—*PALL MALL GAZETTE.

SACRED LATIN POETRY, Chiefly Lyrical. Selected and arranged for Use. Second Edition, Corrected and Improved. Fcap. 8vo. 7s.

*" The aim of the present volume is to offer to members of our English Church a collection of the best sacred Latin poetry, such as they shall be able entirely and heartily to accept and approve—a collection, that is, in which they shall not be evermore liable to be offended, and to have the current of their sympathies checked, by coming upon that which, however beautiful as poetry, out of higher respects they must reject and condemn—in which, too, they shall not fear that snares are being laid for them, to entangle them unawares in admiration for aught which is inconsistent with their faith and fealty to their own spiritual mother."—*PREFACE.

Turner.—SONNETS. By the Rev. CHARLES TENNYSON TURNER. Dedicated to his brother, the Poet Laureate. Fcap. 8vo. 4s. 6d.

"*The Sonnets are dedicated to Mr. Tennyson by his brother, and have, independently of their merits, an interest of association. They both love to write in simple expressive Saxon; both love to touch their imagery in epithets rather than in formal similes; both have a delicate perception of rhythmical movement, and thus Mr. Turner has occasional lines which, for phrase and music, might be ascribed to his brother. . . He knows the haunts of the wild rose, the shady nooks where light quivers through the leaves, the ruralities, in short, of the land of imagination.*"—ATHENÆUM.

SMALL TABLEAUX. Fcap. 8vo. 4s. 6d.

"*These brief poems have not only a peculiar kind of interest for the student of English poetry, but are intrinsically delightful, and will reward a careful and frequent perusal. Full of naïvete, piety, love, and knowledge of natural objects, and each expressing a single and generally a simple subject by means of minute and original pictorial touches, these sonnets have a place of their own.*"—PALL MALL GAZETTE.

Vittoria Colonna.—LIFE AND POEMS. By MRS. HENRY ROSCOE. Crown 8vo. 9s.

The life of Vittoria Colonna, the celebrated Marchesa di Pescara, has received but cursory notice from any English writer, though in every history of Italy her name is mentioned with great honour among the poets of the sixteenth century. "In three hundred and fifty years," says her biographer, Visconti, "there has been no other Italian lady who can be compared to her."

"*It is written with good taste, with quick and intelligent sympathy, occasionally with a real freshness and charm of style.*"—PALL MALL GAZETTE.

Webster.—Works by AUGUSTA WEBSTER :—

"*If Mrs. Webster only remains true to herself, she will assuredly take a higher rank as a poet than any woman has yet done.*"—WESTMINSTER REVIEW.

DRAMATIC STUDIES. Extra fcap. 8vo. 5s.

"*A volume as strongly marked by perfect taste as by poetic power.*"—NONCONFORMIST.

PROMETHEUS BOUND OF ÆSCHYLUS. Literally translated into English Verse. Extra fcap. 8vo. 3s. 6d.

"*Closeness and simplicity combined with literary skill.*"—ATHENÆUM.

" Mrs. Webster's 'Dramatic Studies' and 'Translation of Prometheus' have won for her an honourable place among our female poets. She writes with remarkable vigour and dramatic realization, and bids fair to be the most successful claimant of Mrs. Browning's mantle."—BRITISH QUARTERLY REVIEW.

MEDEA OF EURIPIDES.   Literally translated into English Verse. Extra fcap. 8vo.   3s. 6d.

" Mrs. Webster's translation surpasses our utmost expectations. It is a photograph of the original without any of that harshness which so often accompanies a photograph."—WESTMINSTER REVIEW.

A WOMAN SOLD, AND OTHER POEMS.   Crown 8vo.   7s. 6d.

" Mrs. Webster has shown us that she is able to draw admirably from the life; that she can observe with subtlety, and render her observations with delicacy; that she can impersonate complex conceptions, and venture into which few living writers can follow her."—GUARDIAN.

PORTRAITS.   Second Edition.   Extra fcap. 8vo.   3s. 6d.

" Mrs. Webster's poems exhibit simplicity and tenderness . . . her taste is perfect . . . This simplicity is combined with a subtlety of thought, feeling, and observation which demand that attention which only real lovers of poetry are apt to bestow. . . . If she only remains true to herself she will most assuredly take a higher rank as a poet than any woman has yet done."—WESTMINSTER REVIEW.

" With this volume before us it would be hard to deny her the proud position of the first living English poetess."—EXAMINER.

Woodward (B. B., F.S.A.).—SPECIMENS OF THE DRAWINGS OF TEN MASTERS, from the Royal Collection at Windsor Castle. With Descriptive Text by the late B. B. WOODWARD, B.A., F.S.A., Librarian to the Queen, and Keeper of Prints and Drawings. Illustrated by Twenty Autotypes by EDWARDS and KIDD. In 4to. handsomely bound, price 25s.

This volume contains facsimiles of the works of Michael Angelo, Perugino, Raphael, Julio Romano, Leonardo da Vinci, Giorgione, Paul Veronese, Poussin, Albert Dürer, Holbein, executed by the Autotype (Carbon) process, which may be accepted as, so far, perfect representations of the originals. In most cases some reduction in size was necessary, and then the dimensions of the drawing itself have been given. Brief biographical memoranda of the life of each master are inserted, solely to prevent the need of reference to other works.

Woolner.—MY BEAUTIFUL LADY. By THOMAS WOOLNER. With a Vignette by ARTHUR HUGHES. Third Edition. Fcap. 8vo. 5*s.*

"*It is clearly the product of no idle hour, but a highly-conceived and faithfully-executed task, self-imposed, and prompted by that inward yearning to utter great thoughts, and a wealth of passionate feeling which is poetic genius. No man can read this poem without being struck by the fitness and finish of the workmanship, so to speak, as well as by the chastened and unpretending loftiness of thought which pervades the whole.*"— GLOBE.

WORDS FROM THE POETS. Selected by the Editor of " Rays of Sunlight." With a Vignette and Frontispiece. 18mo. limp., 1*s.*

Wyatt (Sir M. Digby).—FINE ART : a Sketch of its History, Theory, Practice, and application to Industry. A Course of Lectures delivered before the University of Cambridge. By Sir M. DIGBY WYATT, M. A. Slade Professor of Fine Art. 8vo. 10*s. 6d.*

THE GLOBE LIBRARY.

Beautifully printed on toned paper and bound in cloth elegant, price 4s. 6d. each. In plain cloth, 3s. 6d. Also kept in various styles of Morocco and Calf bindings.

THE SATURDAY REVIEW says—" The Globe Editions' are¹ admirable for their scholarly editing, their typographical excellence, their compendious form, and their cheapness."

UNDER the title GLOBE EDITIONS, the Publishers are issuing a uniform Series of Standard English Authors, carefully edited, clearly and elegantly printed on toned paper, strongly bound, and at a small cost. The names of the Editors whom they have been fortunate enough to secure constitute an indisputable guarantee as to the character of the Series. The greatest care has been taken to ensure accuracy of text; adequate notes, elucidating historical, literary, and philological points, have been supplied; and, to the older Authors, glossaries are appended. The series is especially adapted to Students of our national Literature; while the small price places good editions of certain books, hitherto popularly inaccessible, within the reach of all. The *Saturday Review* says: "The Globe Editions of our English Poets are admirable for their scholarly editing, their typographical excellence, their compendious form, and their cheapness."

Shakespeare.—THE COMPLETE WORKS OF WILLIAM SHAKESPEARE. Edited by W. G. CLARK and W. ALDIS WRIGHT.

" *A marvel of beauty, cheapness, and compactness. The whole works— plays, poems, and sonnets—are contained in one small volume: yet the page is perfectly clear and readable. . . . For the busy man, above all for the working student, the Globe Edition is the best of all existing Shakespeare books."*—ATHENÆUM.

Morte D'Arthur.—SIR THOMAS MALORY'S BOOK OF KING ARTHUR AND OF HIS NOBLE KNIGHTS OF THE ROUND TABLE. The Edition of CAXTON, revised for Modern Use. With an Introduction by SIR EDWARD STRACHEY, Bart.

" *It is with the most perfect confidence that we recommend this edition of the old romance to every class of readers."*—PALL MALL GAZETTE.

Scott.—THE POETICAL WORKS OF SIR WALTER SCOTT. With Biographical Essay by F. T. PALGRAVE. New Edition.

" *As a popular edition it leaves nothing to be desired. The want of such an one has long been felt, combining real excellence with cheapness."* —SPECTATOR.

Burns.—THE POETICAL WORKS AND LETTERS OF ROBERT BURNS. Edited, with Life, by ALEXANDER SMITH. New Edition.

" *The works of the bard have never been offered in such a complete form in a single volume."*—GLASGOW DAILY HERALD.

" *Admirable in all respects."*—SPECTATOR.

Robinson Crusoe.—THE ADVENTURES OF ROBINSON CRUSOE. By DEFOE. Edited, from the Original Edition, by J. W. CLARK, M.A., Fellow of Trinity College, Cambridge. With Introduction by HENRY KINGSLEY.

" *The Globe Edition of Robinson Crusoe is a book to have and to keep. It is printed after the original editions, with the quaint old spelling, and is published in admirable style as regards type, paper, and binding. A well-written and genial biographical introduction, by Mr. Henry Kingsley, is likewise an attractive feature of this edition."*—MORNING STAR.

Goldsmith.—GOLDSMITH'S MISCELLANEOUS WORKS.
With Biographical Essay by Professor MASSON.

This edition includes the whole of Goldsmith's Miscellaneous Works— the Vicar of Wakefield, Plays, Poems, &c. Of the memoir the SCOTSMAN *newspaper writes: " Such an admirable compendium of the facts of Goldsmith's life, and so careful and minute a delineation of the mixed traits of his peculiar character, as to be a very model of a literary biography."*

Pope.—THE POETICAL WORKS OF ALEXANDER POPE.
Edited, with Memoir and Notes, by Professor WARD.

" The book is handsome and handy. . . . The notes are many, and the matter of them is rich in interest."—ATHENÆUM.

Spenser. — THE COMPLETE WORKS OF EDMUND
SPENSER. Edited from the Original Editions and Manuscripts, by R. MORRIS, Member of the Council of the Philological Society. With a Memoir by J. W. HALES, M.A., late Fellow of Christ's College, Cambridge, Member of the Council of the Philological Society.

" A complete and clearly printed edition of the whole works of Spenser, carefully collated with the originals," with copious glossary, worthy—and higher praise it needs not—of the beautiful Globe Series. The work is edited with all the care so noble a poet deserves."—DAILY NEWS.

Dryden.—-THE POETICAL WORKS OF JOHN DRYDEN.
Edited, with a Revised Text, Memoir, and Notes, by W. D. CHRISTIE.

" The work of the Editor has been done with much fulness, care, and knowledge ; a well-written and exhaustive memoir is prefixed, and the notes and text together have been so well treated as to make the volume a fitting companion for those which have preceded it—which is saying not a little."—DAILY TELEGRAPH.

Cowper.—THE POETICAL WORKS OF WILLIAM COW-
PER. Edited, with Biographical Introduction and Notes, by W.
BENHAM.

"*Mr. Benham's edition of Cowper is one of permanent value. The
biographical introduction is excellent, full of information, singularly
neat and readable, and modest—too modest, indeed—in its comments.
The notes seem concise and accurate, and the editor has been able to
discover and introduce some hitherto unprinted matter.*"—SATURDAY
REVIEW.

Virgil.—THE WORKS OF VIRGIL RENDERED INTO
ENGLISH PROSE, with Introductions, Running Analysis, and
an Index, by JAMES LONSDALE, M.A., and SAMUEL LEE, M.A.
Globe 8vo.

*The preface of this new volume informs us that " the original has been
faithfully rendered, and paraphrase altogether avoided. At the same time,
the translators have endeavoured to adapt the book to the use of the English
reader. Some amount of rhythm in the structure of the sentence has been
generally maintained; and, when in the Latin the sound of the words is
an echo to the sense (as so frequently happens in Virgil), an attempt has
been made to produce the same result in English.*"

*The general introduction gives us whatever is known of the poet's life,
an estimate of his genius, an account of the principal editions and translations of his works, and a brief view of the influence he has had on
modern poets; special introductory essays are prefixed to the* Eclogues,
Georgics, *and* Æneid. *The text is divided into sections, each of which is
headed by a concise analysis of the subject; the index contains references to
all the characters and events of any importance.*

*** Other Standard Works are in the Press.

. The Volumes of this Series may be had in a variety of morocco
and calf bindings at very moderate prices.

MACMILLAN'S
GOLDEN TREASURY SERIES.

Uniformly printed in 18mo., with Vignette Titles by SIR
NOEL PATON, T. WOOLNER, W. HOLMAN HUNT, J. E.
MILLAIS, ARTHUR HUGHES, &c. Engraved on Steel by
JEENS. Bound in extra cloth, 4s. 6d. each volume. Also
kept in morocco and calf bindings.

"*Messrs. Macmillan have, in their Golden Treasury Series especially,
provided editions of standard works, volumes of selected poetry, and
original compositions, which entitle this series to be called classical.
Nothing can be better than the literary execution, nothing more elegant
than the material workmanship.*"—BRITISH QUARTERLY REVIEW.

THE GOLDEN TREASURY OF THE BEST SONGS AND
LYRICAL POEMS IN THE ENGLISH LANGUAGE.
Selected and arranged, with Notes, by FRANCIS TURNER
PALGRAVE.

"*This delightful little volume, the Golden Treasury, which contains
many of the best original lyrical pieces and songs in our language, grouped
with care and skill, so as to illustrate each other like the pictures in a
well-arranged gallery.*"—QUARTERLY REVIEW.

THE CHILDREN'S GARLAND FROM THE BEST POETS
Selected and arranged by COVENTRY PATMORE.

"*It includes specimens of all the great masters in the art of poetry,
selected with the matured judgment of a man concentrated on obtaining
insight into the feelings and tastes of childhood, and desirous to awaken its
finest impulses, to cultivate its keenest sensibilities.*"—MORNING POST.

THE BOOK OF PRAISE. From the Best English Hymn Writers. Selected and arranged by SIR ROUNDELL PALMER. *A New and Enlarged Edition.*

"*All previous compilations of this kind must undeniably for the present give place to the Book of Praise. . . . The selection has been made throughout with sound judgment and critical taste. The pains involved in this compilation must have been immense, embracing, as it does, every writer of note in this special province of English literature, and ranging over the most widely divergent tracks of religious thought.*"—SATURDAY REVIEW.

THE FAIRY BOOK; the Best Popular Fairy Stories. Selected and rendered anew by the Author of "JOHN HALIFAX, GENTLEMAN."

"*A delightful selection, in a delightful external form; full of the physical splendour and vast opulence of proper fairy tales.*"—SPECTATOR.

THE BALLAD BOOK. A Selection of the Choicest British Ballads. Edited by WILLIAM ALLINGHAM.

"*His taste as a judge of old poetry will be found, by all acquainted with the various readings of old English ballads, true enough to justify his undertaking so critical a task.*"—SATURDAY REVIEW.

THE JEST BOOK. The Choicest Anecdotes and Sayings. Selected and arranged by MARK LEMON.

"*The fullest and best jest book that has yet appeared.*"—SATURDAY REVIEW.

BACON'S ESSAYS AND COLOURS OF GOOD AND EVIL. With Notes and Glossarial Index. By W. ALDIS WRIGHT, M.A.

"*The beautiful little edition of Bacon's Essays, now before us, does credit to the taste and scholarship of Mr. Aldis Wright. . . . It puts the reader in possession of all the essential literary facts and chronology necessary for reading the Essays in connexion with Bacon's life and times.*"—SPECTATOR.

"*By far the most complete as well as the most elegant edition we possess.*"—WESTMINSTER REVIEW.

THE PILGRIM'S PROGRESS from this World to that which is to come. By JOHN BUNYAN.
"*A beautiful and scholarly reprint.*"—SPECTATOR.

THE SUNDAY BOOK OF POETRY FOR THE YOUNG. Selected and arranged by C. F. ALEXANDER.
"*A well-selected volume of Sacred Poetry.*"—SPECTATOR.

A BOOK OF GOLDEN DEEDS of all Times and all Countries. Gathered and narrated anew. By the Author of "THE HEIR OF REDCLYFFE."
"*. . . To the young, for whom it is especially intended, as a most interesting collection of thrilling tales well told; and to their elders, as a useful handbook of reference, and a pleasant one to take up when their wish is to while away a weary half-hour. We have seen no prettier gift-book for a long time.*"—ATHENÆUM.

THE POETICAL WORKS OF ROBERT BURNS. Edited, with Biographical Memoir, Notes and Glossary, by ALEXANDER SMITH. Two Vols.
"*Beyond all question this is the most beautiful edition of Burns yet out.*"—EDINBURGH DAILY REVIEW.

THE ADVENTURES OF ROBINSON CRUSOE. Edited from the Original Edition by J. W. CLARK, M.A., Fellow of Trinity College, Cambridge.
"*Mutilated and modified editions of this English classic are so much the rule, that a cheap and pretty copy of it, rigidly exact to the original, will be a prize to many book-buyers.*"—EXAMINER.

THE REPUBLIC OF PLATO. TRANSLATED into ENGLISH, with Notes by J. Ll. DAVIES, M.A. and D. J. VAUGHAN, M.A.
"*A dainty and cheap little edition.*"—EXAMINER.

THE SONG BOOK. Words and Tunes from the best Poets and Musicians. Selected and arranged by JOHN HULLAH, Professor of Vocal Music in King's College, London.
"*A choice collection of the sterling songs of England, Scotland, and Ireland, with the music of each prefixed to the words. How much true wholesome pleasure such a book can diffuse, and will diffuse, we trust, through many thousand families.*"—EXAMINER.

LA LYRE FRANCAISE. Selected and arranged, with Notes, by GUSTAVE MASSON, French Master in Harrow School.
A selection of the best French songs and lyrical pieces.

TOM BROWN'S SCHOOL DAYS. By an OLD BOY.
" A perfect gem of a book. The best and most healthy book about boys for boys that ever was written."—ILLUSTRATED TIMES.

A BOOK OF WORTHIES. Gathered from the Old Histories and written anew by the Author of "THE HEIR OF REDCLYFFE." With Vignette.
" An admirable addition to an admirable series."—WESTMINSTER REVIEW.

A BOOK OF GOLDEN THOUGHTS. By HENRY ATTWELL, Knight of the Order of the Oak Crown.
" Mr. Attwell has produced a book of rare value . . . . Happily it is small enough to be carried about in the pocket, and of such a companion it would be difficult to weary."—PALL MALL GAZETTE.

LONDON :
R. CLAY, SONS, AND TAYLOR, PRINTERS,
BREAD STREET HILL.

CPSIA information can be obtained
at www.ICGtesting.com
Printed in the USA
LVHW112315171022
730904LV00008B/344